Five O'Clock Shadow

By the same author
Flash Flood

Five O'Clock Shadow

Susan Slater

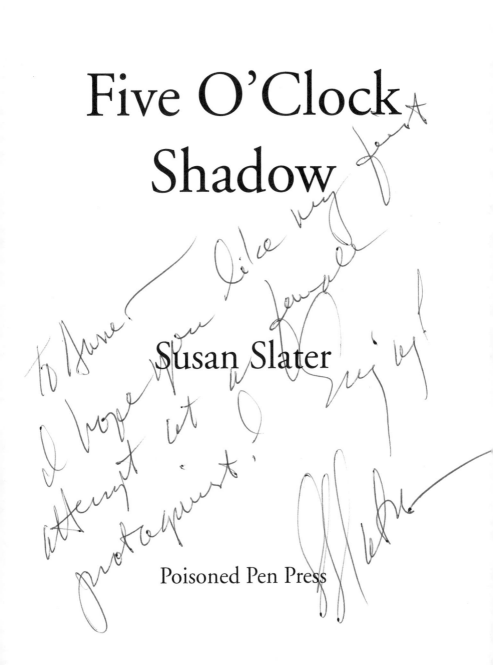

To Diane —
I hope you like my first
attempt at a
protagonist! Enjoy!

[signature]

Poisoned Pen Press

Poisoned
Pen
Press

Copyright © 2004 by Susan Slater
First Edition 2004

10 9 8 7 6 5 4 3 2 1

Library of Congress Catalog Card Number: 2003112888

ISBN: 1-59058-104-0

Poisoned Pen Press
6962 E. First Ave., Ste. 103
Scottsdale, AZ 85251
www.poisonedpenpress.com
info@poisonedpenpress.com

Printed in the United States of America

To TEE—
My thanks for your impeccable sense of the language,
your kind words and support…may ellipses and
dashes always give you pause.

Chapter One

The sharp crack of sound didn't register, hushed as it was in the whoosh of hot air being pumped into the balloon's envelope. Even when the balloon faltered some two hundred feet above the bridge and began its lopsided, rapid descent into the high-voltage wires, its importance eluded her. She didn't scream. She simply dropped the camera and clung to the bridge as the gondola burst into flames.

Then the basket broke free. Strips of flaming yellow and red nylon fluttered in the air; the embroidered logo, the Five O'Clock Shadow, flapped crazily before the gondola slipped between the wires and fell heavily the last seventy feet to thud against a sand bar in the middle of the Rio Grande.

She started running, around the edge of the concrete embankment, down the dirt road and out into the knee-high water. She scrambled across one sand bar and slipped back into the paralyzing cold of the river. She screamed for Randy, screamed his name over and over, crying, choking on the words. Then she stumbled and slipped under the surface of the freezing water, clawed her way upright, tried to stand and lean into the current, make her body move forward, make her arms and legs carry her in the stultifying numbness towards the gondola.

And that's when she saw the apparition. For lack of any better word, that's what he appeared to be. A child wearing a man's white tee shirt and Randy's jean jacket tumbled from the gondola, not fifteen feet in front of her, stood, watched as she splashed through the water towards him, and then ran. Bare-foot, bare-ass naked, small brown limbs seemingly oblivious to the temperature as he entered the water, floundered, drifted a moment then got his footing. Without looking back he reached the opposite bank and disappeared into the thick brush that even in November instantly swallowed him up.

But she had no time to wonder how he had gotten there; he hadn't been at the launching some forty-five minutes earlier. She pushed the image from her consciousness and stepped over the body of the pilot, his eyes open, but unseeing, a round almost bloodless hole opened in the middle of his forehead and the back of his head obliterated. She swallowed and tried not to step on the bits of pulp that had ten minutes ago made up a reasoning human being. No, she had to stop. She couldn't allow herself to think, not yet, not until she knew. Knew for a fact. She took a deep breath, fell to the sand and crawled forward to look into the charred basket. Without a sound she simply rocked back on her knees.

She didn't need to prod the twisted body in the bottom of the gondola. Randy was dead. Her husband of six days, her life, her dream. And the only thought that sifted to the surface, allowed itself to break through the swirling confusion, the near massive blackout of thought, was something about hyphens. She wouldn't need to worry about hyphens. Pauly Caton hadn't been McIntyre long enough to even tack the name onto hers.

And that's the way the paramedics found her, rocking back and forth sitting in the crusty, frosty sand hugging her knees and muttering about hyphens. The paramedic who helped her up thought she had been a passenger, too, and it was a confused couple minutes before she could convince him otherwise.

"You're freezing." The man wrapped a blanket around her shoulders before adding, "You've got to get out of those wet clothes."

"I'll be fine." But her teeth were chattering so loudly she didn't think he'd understood her. The bone-chilling cold of the

New Mexico dawn had numbed her senses. She slipped off her stocking cap, shook her damp hair, tightened the rubber band around the thick wad of auburn curls and stuffed the mass back under the knit dome. She started back towards Randy but the man stopped her.

"Why don't you wait here by me."

"Broken neck," a man called out who knelt by Randy. "Impact of the fall."

She didn't comment, just sucked in her bottom lip and bit down hard. This couldn't be happening. It was a dream. Any minute now she'd awaken. She turned to the man beside her, but he was gone helping two other paramedics bring a stretcher out to the sandbar. Then the three of them lifted Randy, strapped him down and without extending the collapsible metal legs, carried him back through the water and up the sloping bank.

"I want to ride with him." She splashed behind them. "Please, I'm his wife. I have to be with him." Her voice didn't sound like hers as she frantically clutched at the blanket that had been pulled over Randy's face. Finally one attendant shrugged and motioned her forward, then helped her step into the back of the ambulance and squeeze in beside the stretcher. He gave her another blanket to wrap around her legs, then slammed the doors shut, and she had fifteen minutes to say her good-byes and make the most important decision of her brief married life.

It came to her in a rush. What she wanted, no, what she *had* to do. She knew the hopes and dreams of this man so well. This man who at forty-one felt life slipping away. Three months ago he had said, "I need to get married." And she had retorted, "I think that's my line." They laughed and he fell over himself trying to explain what he meant, but she thought she knew. She understood the loneliness, the sudden realization that life was whizzing by, and he was a non-participant when it came to feelings and sharing emotions with one special person. There was no family of his own. No little McIntyres. No feeling of belonging.

And now the least she could do would be to have his baby. She'd read about it somewhere how sperm could be harvested after death, how they stayed viable some twenty-four to forty-eight hours after the death of the host, but the sooner the better. She'd meet with the doctors when they brought him in, sign the papers, oversee the procedure. There would be a life born out of all this sadness, the sadness she couldn't allow herself to dwell on. The time for mourning would come, but not now. Now she had to remain brave, direct this one last operation, make certain Randy's wish would come true.

She gently pulled back the edge of the blanket covering his body. His face was bruised and scraped. She caught her breath but knelt and promised, whispered that a Jonathan or Zoe would carry on the McIntyre name. She would do that much for him, this man who had been her life for such a short time. But there were no tears. When the ambulance pulled up at the emergency entrance, she emerged dry-eyed and didn't flinch when the driver referred to Randy as a DOA.

She calmly walked beside the body and spoke with the nurse at the desk who said she'd get someone who could answer her questions. Another nurse offered to dry her clothes and Pauly followed her to a large room partitioned by drapes on circular metal pipes and exchanged two layers of soggy sweaters and wet jeans for a crisp hospital gown. As an afterthought she pulled off the stocking cap and tossed it on top of the pile, then absently rubbed her forehead where the wool-blend cap had raised welts. Randy had teased that she looked like a cone head but she hadn't noticed any fashion plates among the balloon crew.

She heard the attendants wheel Randy's body into an adjoining cubicle discreetly screened from view. And within minutes Dr. Marsh bounded into the room. He was sympathetic and honest and hopped up to sit on the bed beside her. They had done this particular operation just once before but with positive results, the baby had been an eight-pound boy. He understood her concerns, agreed with her that it made perfect sense. He added that he knew from talking with her that that would be exactly what Randy would have wanted. He offered to put her in touch with the appropriate medical personnel when the time came for the insemination.

Then he patted her arm, told her she could stay in the cubicle but to try and rest. He insisted she put her feet up on the bed and lean back; he would prescribe something if she wanted, a relaxant, but she declined. Then with another reassuring pat, he rose to go, saying he'd have the urologist and a lab technician down in just a few minutes and that they would have the paperwork with them. She could take care of the formalities then. He offered his condolences, again championed her decision, and left.

Pauly took a deep breath and looked at her watch. Only eight-twenty. Hadn't she just lived through a century of time?

She leaned back against the paper-covered pillow and tucked bare feet under a cotton blanket and marveled at the starched cleanliness of the bed. Her thoughts tried to stray to the bridge, the shot. Abruptly she fought to bring her mind back to what was in front of her…what she was going to do: create a living monument to the man that she loved.

Finally, she closed her eyes and pressed the heels of her hands against her temples. She applied a steady pressure and consciously made herself breathe in and out evenly. Better. She let her hands drop to her sides and tried to picture babies, some in blue, some in pink, all with curly blond hair and Randy's eyes. Then a dark-haired child in a tee shirt and jean jacket floated across her vision, naked, cold, frantic with fear as he splashed through the water running from her.

She sat up. Someone had entered the cubicle where Randy waited. She wasn't going to join them in a gaping gown, but she relaxed knowing that soon a specimen would be in the freezer and the next decision would be when to activate it. And that was a good question. Did she want to be pregnant in the summer or carry the child over the winter? Odd that it was going to be her choice, dictated by science, not chance. She heard the sound of a razor. Prepping. Of course, she hadn't thought but they would need the area to be sterile. There was the sound of something being dropped in a metal tray. There must be two people working on Randy, but hadn't Dr. Marsh mentioned a urologist and a technician?

One person was humming but not a tune she recognized. It had the disjointed atonal quality of an attempt to recreate a classical masterpiece. Still, it was comforting. Suddenly there was silence, then the clang of metal hitting metal and an exasperated, "God damn it, is this some kind of joke?"

Pauly heard the pop of latex. Was the doctor taking off his gloves? Why was he stopping?

"This cowboy's been shooting blanks for years." There was no missing the disgust in his voice.

Blanks? What was he talking about? Pauly quickly stood and wrenched the curtain aside in a clattering of C-rings against metal pipe. The two male attendants looked shocked to see her, but one managed to stammer "wife?" and point her way.

Pauly nodded but simply said, "What do you mean by blanks?"

"Vasectomy," the glove-less one offered, obviously the urologist from his authoritative stance.

"I don't believe you. That can't be true."

"Listen, I don't know what illusions you've been under but we're not talking fresh scars and the *vas deferens*.... Ed, pull one of those out again."

"Pull what out?" Pauly asked. They weren't making sense.

"Come here." The doctor stepped up beside the corpse and motioned her to join him. The technician moved to the opposite side of the table, picked up what looked like a stainless steel crochet needle, hooked at one end, and bent over the body. Pauly forced herself to watch the procedure. Randy's head was covered, green drapes reached to his waist then there was a gap and a green drape covered him from the knees down. The genital area was shaved clear and his penis had been pulled upwards and taped to the stomach. Something labeled a "hot-sac" had been pushed between his legs and propped up the scrotum. A syringe with flexible needle was in a metal tray beside the table. It would have been easy to disassociate in this brightly lighted, scrubbed-clean surreal environment, but her single-mindedness of purpose kept her focused.

The man on the right, still in rubber gloves, tore free the swath of tape across Randy's stomach, tugged the penis farther up, retaped it and stretched the mottled skin underneath to show a recent surgical cut.

"That's my original incision. Now watch. Ed will find the *vasa deferentia*—the deferent ducts of the testicles that transport sperm from the epididymis to the penis. In just a second my comment about 'blanks' will be crystal clear."

With the small hooked instrument, Ed dipped into the opening and fished for a moment before snagging what he was looking for. He brought the end of a thin stringy spaghetti-like tube through the incision, and attached a clamp to keep it from reentering the body.

"*Vas deferens*. And as my aunt would say, this guy's been snippled." Ed, whoever he was, sounded proud of himself and quickly had a matching limp duct clamped and waiting for inspection on the right side.

Pauly just stared. The end of the tiny piece of human flesh had been cut, tied-off or cauterized in some way, she wasn't certain what they did, but the urologist was rattling on about how the separation was man-made, his guess a number of years old, which meant they could test but it was almost assured that there would be a problem finding healthy, viable sperm, enough to get the job done anyway.

She didn't fight the numbness that spread over her body, kept her from forming words to comment on the urologist's findings. How could she comment? What was there to say? Randy had chosen to have a vasectomy sometime in the past, sometime before her, but had led her to believe that there would be babies, as many as they wanted. It was becoming difficult to collect her thoughts, to truly assimilate what was in front of her. This proof of deception, an ugly twisted lie that could change her feelings for him forever…and why? What did he have to gain by this colossal lie? A lie that could have torn them apart, ruined their relationship…was doing just that right now.

"This isn't my husband."

Pauly knew she sounded irrational the moment the words left her mouth in a strangled rush of sound. But she couldn't help herself. This lie was beyond comprehension. She pushed past both of them and jerked back the green tarp that covered the head of this poor unfortunate, sterile man. But it was Randy. Her husband, Randy, sallow skin pock-marked with blue bruising, mouth twisted in pain…. She clutched the edge of the table, doubled over with nausea, and sank to the floor as a blackness choked in around her and robbed her of breath.

Chapter Two

"No."

"No, you don't know? No, you don't want to help us?" The detective was leaning over her and the tone of his voice had just the edge of exasperation as it filled the sparsely furnished, stark white room. "You were in shock, could it have been possible that this strange child in white robes—"

"A man's white tee shirt." She accentuated her enunciation, punctuated each word with aspirated pauses. She wasn't crazy. She had reported what she'd seen but the sigh from her interrogator said he thought she was bonkers. And probably his pal did too—the one standing by her hospital window that looked out onto Montgomery Boulevard from Heights Psychiatric. So, maybe these guys weren't the only ones who thought she was...how did her chart read—"Possibly dangerous to self"? When instead she was simply a twenty-eight-year-old widow trying to figure out why the accident, only it wasn't an accident, had happened. One week ago.

She didn't realize she was crying until she heard one of the detectives whisper, "Should we get someone?"

"No." She willed her voice to sound strong. They were here to help, and she had to know. Some of the pain was slowly being replaced by an insatiable curiosity. And instead of killing the cat, that just might make her well, help her have a reason to get out of there.

She pulled herself up straighter and reached for a box of Kleenex on the metal nightstand. She took an elaborate minute to dab at her eyes, usually her best feature, large, warm-brown, wide-set under naturally arching brows, but now they oozed along with her nose, a roughed-up red blotch in the middle of an otherwise pale cream complexion. She had to stop crying. But as many times as she admonished herself to "get a grip," she'd slip back into a little "poor me." She took a deep breath and smoothed the light blanket over her legs and hugged a pillow to her chest before she gave him her attention again. He waited, watching her every move.

"Was the child a boy or a girl?" he asked.

"I don't know." She laughed self-consciously. "I couldn't tell....The features seemed androgynous, just those of a curly-headed kid, maybe seven or eight, nine, I don't know, probably, a boy, if I had to guess. I think I *thought* it was a boy at the time."

"But you're not sure?"

"No." She could close her eyes and see the child clearly, his or her face registering horror, then wide-eyed fear as Pauly approached.

"And you had never seen this child before? Not at the launch site?"

"No. I would swear that the child ended up in the gondola later. He wasn't there when they took off."

"Why weren't you flying with them?"

Pauly paused. What was this? Some sort of accusation? "I'm afraid of heights. My knees bang together just *thinking* about the rim of the Grand Canyon." The man just stared, then turned over a page in his notebook. Did he expect her to say more? "I was the photographer," she finished lamely.

"If you were afraid of heights, why did you arrange such a flight for your husband?"

"The flight was a gift." Pauly thought with a smile of how thrilled Randy had been. He'd been a pest, bugged the balloon crew mercilessly with a hundred questions about how things worked. But that was the engineer in him, the inquiring mind. And the crew indulged him, explained burners and ropes and flight patterns.

"Who was the gift from?"

"My grandmother. The gift was one of the reasons we honeymooned in New Mexico. Randy was starting a project the end of the month. It seemed easier to stay home."

"And this project? Do you know what it involved?"

"Randy is…Randy…was an hydrologist." She paused just a second to see if he would ask her what that was. He had seemed to hesitate over the spelling. "The contract was funded by the Federal government. There's been a lot of talk about New Mexico selling water to neighboring states in the future. Randy was to have assessed the Rio Grande and its tributaries to see if, combined with the aquifers around Albuquerque, that would be possible."

"In this state that could get a little dicey." The cop by the window threw in. Pauly glanced over her shoulder. God, he was cute. But that didn't seem an appropriate thought for a widow. She cleared her throat.

"It's controversial, of course. Randy called it a 'political hot potato.' He would have checked on toxic waste, equal distribution of resources, things like that. Toes would have gotten stepped on."

"Were you familiar with the flight plan?"

"What?" The abrupt change of subject caught her off guard.

"Did you know the route that the balloon would take?"

"Only that they would fly from the West Mesa, along the Rio Grande river, and touch down somewhere three or four miles south. Buffalo Corner, I think. The pilot had promised Randy a little splash and dash. That's where they go up and down quickly, skimming the gondola across the water."

"Yes, I know. Did you have an unobstructed view of the balloon from point of ascent to when they reached the Alameda bridge?"

"No, of course not." Pauly paused; she couldn't keep the exasperation out of her voice; it was like explaining something to children. "I got into my car and went directly to the Alameda bridge to set up for pictures. I stopped by Grams—my grandmother lives just a mile from the bridge, to see if she'd like to watch. That took approximately twenty minutes, then it took another twenty or so before the balloon came back into view as it followed the river and floated towards the bridge." She paused to take a breath: "Have you asked the crew these questions? The company's name is Mesa Landings. I'd think they would be the ones who could help you."

"We've questioned the crew. No one saw a child."

"That doesn't mean a child didn't exist. He could have jumped into the gondola while they were playing splash and dash. The pilot had been skipping along the sandbars for a good fifteen minutes before I started taking pictures. Maybe, the child had been stranded in the middle of the river on a sand bar and when they ducked down, he jumped in."

The detective looked at her. "Not wearing any clothing at six o'clock on a Sunday morning?"

She had to admit it didn't make sense, but she didn't have another explanation.

"Do you feel up to going over your pictures?"

She hadn't noticed the stacks of eight and a half by eleven glossy photos on the table in the corner. They had been enlarged, probably to show detail, which meant they might have found something. She slid out of bed glad that there wasn't a mirror to show her the tangled, clumped mess of her hair that she could feel clinging to her head. She pulled the night-shirt below her knees but not before she saw the detective by the window give her legs an appreciative once-over.

"You're on duty, and they're off limits." She lowered her voice just above a whisper and smiled sweetly then watched the red creep up his neck before she pulled a chair out from the table and sat down. The first hint of the old Pauly. Maybe she was going to be all right.

And then she heard her breath coming in thick, short gasps. There in front of her was a pictorial reenactment of the murder, murder and death by coincidence…frame by frame. The brutal death of her husband because Randy had been in the wrong place at the wrong time…but, maybe, so was the pilot.

"I don't think I can do this. I don't think I'm ready."

She had pushed back from the table but was clutching the edge, steadying herself, staring at the glossy muddy brown river in sharp contrast to the glossy yellow and red balloon and the glossy brittle trees. The starkness drew her back and something else. Death was hidden somewhere in those trees. What if someone had been stalking them? Hidden from view at the launch site, tailing her in a car, adjusting the sights of a long-range weapon, aiming it at—

"There. What do you see?" The detective leaned close as he separated one photo from the rest. Clean-shaven, Aqua Velva fresh, fortyish, intent on noting her reaction, his gray eyes swept her face.

The man at the window had moved to stand behind her. He was younger, still in his twenties somewhere, with a hard muscled physique and trim-fitting uniform. Maybe he was still in training; he hadn't added much to the discussion so far. The detective in front of her was pointing to something, a blur of black roundness, just a knobby protrusion high up in an ancient cottonwood at the river's edge, the tree's sparse fall foliage not quite concealing him.

"Try this shot." He rummaged through the stack before finding just the one he wanted.

Pauly gasped. In the enlarged photo she was staring into the round eye holes of a dark ski mask and could see the outline of a long-barreled weapon.

"Sort of rules out kids trying to scare up a rabbit with a .22, doesn't it?" she said.

The detective looked at her, tight-lipped, no hint of a smile. She wanted to scream, "it's a joke," but she didn't. She just sat there waiting for someone to say something. The man in back of her shifted his weight from one foot to the other.

"We're talking SWAT team accuracy. Must have shot the pilot just as he was ascending full throttle. Here at the corner of this photo is a flash. Then you're concentrating on the balloon, and I think that's the last picture we have of the perp." He quickly looked through the stack in front of her. "Yeah, that's it."

"But no kid?" The question came from the man standing behind her. At least he was allowed to speak once in awhile. Pauly didn't turn to look at him.

"*Nada*," his pal answered.

At any other time, she would have been impressed with her photography. The shots were good—good light, good framing. Pauly picked out five enlarged photos of the gondola when it was twenty, then thirty feet above her and scrutinized each. The detectives were right. There was no hint of a child. The pilot was obscured from view, but Randy was leaning over the side, waving at her, something in his hand, possibly a helmet? Yes, he was holding a helmet. Would it have helped if it had been on his head? She didn't think so because the next series of photos showed the explosion. She couldn't even remember taking those pictures. A knot of pain constricted her chest. She shuffled the pictures together and placed them back on the table, then, on impulse, pulled out the shot of the murderer again.

"I'm sure you're investigating the pilot, and this company, Mesa Landings. Maybe there was some reason, some *one* who might have wanted the pilot dead." She looked from one to the other. "Bad business dealings, that sort of thing."

"Right." The detective swung a leg over a chair opposite her and leaned against its back. "Unless the pilot wasn't the primary target."

She jerked her head up to stare at him as he stared back. *Not the target?* That left Randy. "That's absurd." She turned to look at the man behind her. "In fact, that really pisses me off. That you two could come in here and suspect, and accuse." Nothing. Both men were biding their time. Watching her, waiting for her to do what? Most likely, they didn't know. She took a deep breath.

"Is there something you're not telling me?" She was feeling stronger.

"Not necessarily. Is there something you're not telling us?"

Cute. They probably rehearsed this. Just dicking around.

"Such as?"

"Were you getting along with your husband?"

"Getting along? We had been married one week, for Christ's sake." She wanted to throttle them. But she had to admit the anger felt good, washed away any 'poor me' feelings in two seconds.

"Was there a reason you got married after what...a whirlwind courtship?"

"You mean, like I could be pregnant?" It was painful to even say the word.

"Are you?"

"No." She didn't try to keep the sarcasm out of her voice. It was obvious that they didn't know about the little debacle at the hospital, the discovery of the *vas deferens* in two pieces. Abruptly she asked, "Where is this leading?" And with a look, she dared him to get cute again, say something like "where do you want it to lead?" But he didn't. He leaned back against the wall, tipping the chair off of two of its legs, and looked relaxed and in control.

"Tell me about your husband. His business, how you met, that sort of thing." From somewhere under the pictures, he produced a tape recorder, small, not much bigger than a pack of cigarettes.

She wasn't thrilled, but this was probably inevitable, might as well get it over with.

"I met Randy—"

"Full name of victim?"

They both laughed—a spontaneous burst of sound. Victim of her meeting him and marrying him? Macabre humor. It broke the tension for a moment.

"Randall Vincent McIntyre. I met Randy when I interviewed for a technical writer's position with his company in April."

"April of this year?"

"Yes. I started immediately and was promoted to supervisor of technical editing and writing within two months. I began dating Randy sometime later, in the summer."

"Name of the firm?" The man sitting opposite her still asked all the questions, but the presence of the other detective behind her, the pressure of his hand weighing against the back of her chair made her feel cornered. Every once in a while, she knew their eyes met above her head. Silent messages? A strength in numbers thing? She just wished they would get this over with and leave.

"There were three founders, Randy, Tom Dougal, and Archer Brandon. MDB, Inc."

"And to the best of your knowledge, the firm is solvent?"

"Yes. They've grown from the three of them to over one hundred and twenty employees in a little over three years."

"Any idea of the company's worth? Maybe, I should ask, do you have any idea what your cut will be?"

"My cut?" No, she hadn't thought of that. Would she be rich? She guessed she would be. In the last two weeks money wasn't very high on her list of concerns. But, it was obviously one more thing she needed to consider. "I haven't looked into insurance, or a will, that sort of thing yet if that's what you mean."

"Let me help you." The man in the chair leaned across her to take an envelope from his pal. "Randy's lawyer provided us with a will that was drawn up two days before the wedding, let's see, that would be three weeks ago."

He seemed to be waiting for her comment. But what was there to say? She had no idea that a will even existed, but that was like Randy to take care of details. She wasn't surprised.

"This leaves everything to you. His share of the business valued at two million, any 'holdings,' investments, bank accounts which in this case add up to another tidy *one million*." He was staring at her now, holding eye contact. "Makes the paltry hundred thousand in insurance look like chicken feed."

She was flabbergasted. Did it show? Her chin had to be on the table. One million above and beyond the business? She never thought of Randy as having big bucks, unlimited discretionary spending money, what she would consider substantial wealth. Wouldn't he have told her? His apartment was spartan. When they had started looking at houses before the wedding, they had looked at reasonably priced, nice neighborhood ones in good school districts, but nothing exorbitant. Yes, she knew that his third of the business had quickly grown, but it was money invested, working capital that he had struggled to pour back into an expanding company. Things had been tight. None of the partners breathed easily unless there was a backlog of contracts. And that had taken awhile. The loss of one large contract, even now, could make things shaky again. So, how had he amassed the other million? His parents hadn't been wealthy.

"I find it hard to believe, the part about the investments, I mean." There had to be some mistake. One million gathering interest, and he had never mentioned it?

"That's not even the interesting part. Your husband might not have known how rich he was. The bulk of the one million, some eight hundred thousand plus, was dumped into his account, listing you as beneficiary, two days before he died."

Now she was stunned. She felt both men suck in their collective breath waiting for her answer. Finally, she managed to shrug her shoulders.

"Not good enough." The silence was broken by the man opposite her standing to lean over the table. She could smell the sharp mint scent of his gum. He scrutinized her features.

"We think you have an idea of where this money might have come from." This from the man with his hand on her chair. She felt his shirt brush her hair. She pulled back and shaking her head looked from one to the other. How could she know? What did they know that they weren't telling her?

"You have to admit that three million would seem to be a pretty good motive for killing someone." Back to the detective leaning over the table.

"The pilot was shot, not Randy." Just an edge of anger crept into her voice.

"Same difference. The one who pulled the trigger must have known the flight plan. Waited in advance, got his equipment together, chose the perfect spot, timed it so that the balloon was directly over the wires, planned it so that there would be no survivors."

She couldn't control a shudder. She'd tried not to think of it that way…hadn't allowed herself to dwell on the obvious premeditation.

"What does this have to do with me?"

"Is this familiar?" The man across from her sat down and rummaging in the stack of photos pulled an eight by ten from a manila envelope, and tossed it toward her. It looked like an ad for some kind of breakdown assault weapon, showing the gun in pieces at the top of the picture and then together at the bottom.

"It's a gun. Do I get any points?"

"I'll tell you what you don't get points for and that's being a smart ass." His chair had clattered to the floor in his lunge to lean across the table into her face. "You think long and hard, Missy, before you blow this off. You wouldn't want me to have to get a warrant for your arrest, now would you?"

Pauly stood and faced the two of them, surprised by the hardness in her voice, "I don't have anything to tell you. I don't know where the money came from. I don't know who shot the pilot—"

"And I suppose you don't know how the gun got into the backseat of your car?"

She sat down heavily as her knees turned to mush, only there wasn't a chair. Both men rushed to help her up.

"Are you all right?" She thought she heard real concern in the voice of the man who had stood behind her. Or did she just want to hear it? He held out his hand, strong, warm, steadying. She let him pull her upright.

"Yes." But she knew her face was blanched and every freckle must look like a crater. "I need to sit down."

"Sure. Here." The younger man pulled out a chair, and the other one found a glass of water.

"Look, I don't want to get off on the wrong foot. If it's any consolation, I'm just doing my job. It's been suggested that we check out any connection that there might have been between you and the sniper." Something in her expression must have said 'big fucking deal' because he covered with, "Hey, I feel badly about coming here to the hospital. It's just that—"

"It's your job. You said that." She wasn't going to cut them any slack.

His sigh was audible, and he sat back down in the chair across the table. "Are you going to help us?" He made eye contact but didn't wait for an answer. "Let's say you're telling the truth. You don't know anything about the money, or the murderer. But somebody who knows you does. My suspicion is that the two are connected. You could be in danger. There's no proof that the murderer didn't think you'd be up there in the balloon, too."

She hadn't thought of that, and she knew the surprise showed on her face. Could she be in danger? She seemed to be moving from bereavement to scared shitless in under sixty seconds.

"What do you suggest that I do?" There was no animosity in her voice and more than a little fright—would he pick up on that?

"Keep in touch. Lie low, but don't run away. Shut down your apartment and move in with someone; don't live by yourself. You have family here in Albuquerque, don't you?"

"Grandmother."

"Stay with her. No one can put a lock on the money, but if I were you, I'd treat it like a landmine."

She nodded. She had no intentions of touching a penny of it. She could put school on hold now that there wasn't going to be a pregnancy. Maybe she should just kick back for six months, not worry, not force herself to pick up the pieces too soon. Hope that in the meantime someone would come up with answers.

"Out of my way."

Pauly saw the door to her room burst open—no mean feat since it was on hydraulic hinges—and a willowy woman with bushels of lightning-white hair cascading down her back swept into the room with a nervous nurse two steps behind.

"Here. Just toss it on the bed." In one practiced move the woman slipped out of her Black Diamond mink cape and handed it to the nurse.

"Grams."

Pauly threw her arms around her grandmother and tried not to think that Grams wasn't wearing a bra and her two grapefruit-perfect enhanced breasts strained against a flimsy silk tee.

"Oh, child, look at your hair."

"This is my grandmother." Pauly hoped she didn't sound apologetic. She had discussed wearing underwear with her grand-mother on numerous occasions but the answer was always the same—"no one wore bras when I was your age, we burned the things." Of course, when Grams referred to being Pauly's age in the sixties, it put her in her fifties today, making her about the same age as Paul, Pauly's father, Grams' son. It was no use. She was incorrigible.

"I hope you've told her to stay put. You are detectives, aren't you? And you've warned her not to leave town? Because I plan on taking this adorable child home with me. She's been released to my custody. Oops." Grams looked from one to the other of the two detectives. "Not the best word, right? But she's not being detained, is she?"

Pauly saw both men shake their heads. They seemed mesmer-ized, staring at her grandmother, their eyes locked not at the too-perfect boobs but at her face.

"Oh, Grams," Pauly pointed to her mouth, "you missed removing some makeup."

"What? Oh, drat. Is there a mirror in here?" But she had already pulled a large round compact from her purse. "I'm in entertainment, this is just part of the show. Pauly, honey, hand me a tissue."

No one seemed to have anything to say as her grandmother worked at removing the red circle around her mouth, enlarged lips bordered in white and lined with black. In addition to operating a bed and breakfast, Grams hired out as a clown, sometimes traveling with one of the half dozen carnivals that she owned. Pauly had considered herself to be the luckiest child in the world. She spent every summer after her parents' divorce on Ferris wheels, pony rides, in haunted houses.

"This is on for life without a little cold cream."

Still no one found an appropriate comment, but it seemed Grams was telling the truth; five tissues had only made a dent in the brightness of the red.

"Oh well, I was just waiting for the hospital to let me know when I could pick you up. I didn't expect a call so soon, sweetheart. You must be all well now." Grams was fussing with Pauly's hair, pulling what she called "wisps" forward and trying to smooth other naturally curly strands, pat them in place across the crown. It was a losing battle. Pauly could have told her that, but didn't say anything about her hair or the "all well" part. How could she get well from the death of her husband, murder of her husband, and his deceit? She made eye contact with the detective who had questioned her. Was there a hint of sympathy?

"I'll give you a call in a week or so. Let you know how the investigation's going. You'll be staying with your grandmother?" The younger man made it a question more than a statement, and looked from one to the other.

"Oh dear, here, let me give you one of my cards." Grams dug to the bottom of her bag and produced a fluorescent pink card shaped like the head of a clown with *Lulu's Live Entertainment* printed across the bottom next to a phone number.

"Home entertainment, the works for little people. Clowns, magicians, live animal acts, no party too big or too small. Oh mercy, I am forgetting my manners. Lucille—I prefer Lulu—Caton." She held out her hand. The one with the three-carat diamond in platinum. One of her nicer engagement rings, Grams always said. Worth more than the giver, which was why he was no longer around.

Pauly sighed. It was a barely concealed family secret that Grams had performed more acts behind the footlights than those aimed to entertain children. More along the line of shedding clothing to music. Oh well, at least Grams was using her first married name. Pauly's grandfather had been husband number one, or so Grams had led them to believe. If the new boyfriend got her to the altar, that might be number five. Or was it six? Pauly thought six.

"Now, unless there's something else, I must get this poor child home." Grams looked brightly from one detective to the other. "No? Well, then, I suggest you just shoo on out of here. Our little girl needs to make herself presentable."

Amazingly, the men followed her directions; one shuffled the pictures together, stuffed them into a manila envelope and picked up the recorder while the nicer, cuter one offered the customary "call us if you need anything—we'll be in touch" before both disappeared into the hall.

"I just bet you will." Grams muttered under her breath. "Were they hard on you?" She didn't wait for Pauly to answer but continued, "I told the hospital not to allow visitors unless I could be here. And definitely not the police. Not alone. But do you think they listened? No. You'd think in this kind of hospital, they'd know better."

"Grams, please. I'm doing fine." A lie, but maybe if she left this place, got out into the sunshine and fresh air, away from the blank walls, she would be.

◇◇◇

"I took the liberty of moving you out of your apartment."

Pauly started. She had been staring out the car window at the winter-bleak landscape. No more vestiges of fall after a rain had beaten the last of the foliage from the trees.

"You broke my lease?"

"It was easy, uh, under the circumstances. And I might have thrown in a couple free performances for the owner's grand-kids."

"Thanks."

"Well, that doesn't sound very convincing. I honestly thought it would be too painful to go back to a place that had memories of what's-his-name."

"Randy, Grams. Saying his name doesn't hurt."

Grams had been against her marriage and had wanted to know why Pauly couldn't have found someone 'already broken in,' whatever that meant. But if she knew Grams, there was a sexual innuendo. So a man waited until he was forty-one to marry, so what? It didn't mean something was wrong with him. Their sex had been adult. A coupling that quickly became comfortable and secure, maybe not as romantic, or not as frequent as she had hoped for, but adequate.

Contrary to what his name implied, Randy never thought with his penis. And hadn't that been one of the welcome changes? One of the things that had attracted her to him? She'd had enough of great sex and no substance. Randy had been successful, wealthy if she could believe the cops, and "together" in every sense of the word. The worst thing she could have said about her boyishly handsome husband was that he had been a nerd. Pauly sighed.

"Oh, baby, I know this is so hard. But you'll feel better with your own things around you." Grams patted her knee.

"Where am I staying?"

"East wing. Private bath, view of the Sandias. Sitting room/bedroom combination. A little over seven hundred square feet with private entrance." Grams didn't miss a beat as she maneuvered the Lincoln through heavy end-of-the-day traffic.

Pauly thought of reminding her grandmother that she wasn't a potential bed and breakfast customer; she knew the rooms. But she realized with a jolt that her grandmother was thoughtfully taking Paseo del Norte and not driving her over the Alameda bridge. Pauly wasn't quite ready for that reminder, and for all Grams' strangeness she must have realized it.

"Hofer's fixed up a real nice work area for you downstairs, off the kitchen. Set up your computer, moved in some bookcases."

"Sounds great."

"You don't need to pretend with me. I detect a genuine lack of enthusiasm. Honey, you just have to give life a chance. Time alone is a powerful healer. Just don't fight it. Get involved. Take your mind off of what happened. You can't dwell on water that's already passed under the bridge. Oops, not a very good choice of words."

Pauly smiled reassuringly. Then she pressed her cheek against the coldness of the car window and closed her eyes. Nobody had promised rehabilitation would be easy. And she knew her grandmother meant well. But Pauly's life wasn't going anywhere at the moment. Actually, for the time being it seemed stymied. She felt like she was treading water.

"Here we are, sugar." Grams turned off Coors Boulevard and nosed the Lincoln down a dirt lane that wound back towards the river. They were just passing the huge windmill that marked the beginning of Grams' property when she slammed on the brakes and skidded to a stop.

"Damn. I've told him to keep those things corralled."

"What things? What did you see?" But Pauly, who had hit her head on the visor, was talking to empty space since her grandmother had hopped out and was bent over something by the side of the road.

"Big one for its type. I think this is an Egyptian albino something or other." Her grandmother held a three foot, almost transparent, and completely lethargic snake away from her fur jacket as she climbed behind the wheel.

"Here, you hold him." Grams gripped him behind his head with a tight-fist.

"Can't you put him in the backseat?" Pauly squirmed away.

"Oh, for pity's sake, he won't bite." But Grams hopped out again, opened the rear door and tossed the snake across the dove-gray leather cushions behind the driver's seat.

"He looks dead." Pauly leaned over the back of her seat to keep an eye on the snake, make certain that it didn't slither off its perch.

"Just cold-stunned. Sometimes they wander out of the garage."

"You mean there's more?" She hated snakes but tried not to let her grandmother see how upset she was.

"Maybe a half-dozen. Snake acts are a big draw. Bigger the snake, bigger the audience. We own the world's record reticulated python. Eighteen feet. Can you believe that? Actually, there are a couple real doozys out there."

"Out there" must mean the garage. One place that Pauly would make off-limits. But her wondering was interrupted when Grams jolted to a stop in front of the house and stepped out to yell at a tall, lanky, not-so-young kid who was loping across the yard.

"Harry, put this snake back where it belongs. This poor critter was almost road-kill. I've told you to keep an eye out." The young man walked towards them, followed the wave of Grams' hand and opened the back car door, nodded at Pauly but didn't say anything, just scooped up the snake, tucked it inside his shirt, and headed towards the garage.

"Do you understand what I'm telling you?" Grams yelled after the disappearing man. "I told you to watch them. Keep those cage-lids tight." There was no response and the nearest garage door thudded shut.

"Come on, let's get you into the house. The quicker we get you settled in, the better you'll feel."

Pauly acknowledged that that was probably true, and she was ready for any change of scenery after a week of white walls. And she had to admit it was comforting to see her own bed, loveseat, TV, end tables.... She gave her grandmother a hug. It had been a thoughtful thing to do.

"Now, enough of this mush. Dinner in half an hour." Grams walked to the door then turned. "Sweety, it'll be just great having you here," and with a little wave was gone.

◇◇◇

Dinner was strained. No, strange, Pauly thought. The big oak island in the center of the cobalt and yellow tiled kitchen overflowed with the fixings for tacos. It was a do-it-yourself meal. Go around the table single-file, fill your plate, then adjourn to the plank tables in the dining room. Buffet-style was probably the best way to feed the crowd gathered in the large kitchen. Sometimes the personnel from one of Grams' carnivals stayed for a month or so before traveling on, and Pauly couldn't keep her eyes off of the man beside her. Definitely carny material.

Every inch of his body, at least what was exposed, was covered with tattoos. The bicep on the arm next to her was large enough to show a complete sketch of the rape of Europa, bull and maiden frolicking among clouds, then the bull mounting.... She bent down slightly to see the completion of the coupling which curved under the elbow. Suddenly the arm flexed to give her a better view. She sprang upright realizing that her face was probably flame-orange and managed to stammer, "J-just curious. Actually, they're really well done." And willed herself to try to regain lost ground by referring to it as body-art and appear to be a connoisseur and not a lech.

"Glad you like it."

Looking upward, she paused at the sight of inked tendrils that licked up his neck.

"Nice stuff on the neck." She waved her fork in the general direction of the tendrils. Art, she admonished herself, refer to it as art.

"Guaranteed camouflage for hickeys. Every teenager's dream."

Shit. She'd left herself wide open for that. But she realized his eyes were teasing; this wasn't some kind of pick-up line and she relaxed, even managed a little smile as she distributed the lettuce across the top of the taco shell. She had moved on to the grated cheese before she realized that she was staring at the man again, watching as he filled a bowl with green chili stew.

The man was startlingly handsome. Once you got past Europa and the other doo-dads. Bodybuilder's physique, dark hair combed straight back, high cheekbones, dusty gray eyes, long lashes, permanent tan, could be her age or maybe early thirties. He was probably part of a strong-man exhibition.

"Snakes."

"I beg your pardon?"

"Thought you might be wondering what I do. I work with the pythons."

And read minds. She couldn't think of another thing to say, so she just nodded and prayed that she'd find a table to herself in the dining hall. The thought of sitting next to him was somehow unsettling. It would mean that she'd have to carry on a conversation, be amiable, and admit that her interest was piqued. And that didn't seem exactly proper for a widow. A new one, at that. She set her plate down at a table just inside the dining room door and hoped that he'd sit with friends.

"Mind if I join you?" Snake-man scooted onto the bench beside her. So much for wishing he'd go away.

As the other tables began to fill, she realized that the group was large, maybe thirty people, and would stretch the room's seating to capacity. Grams had knocked out a wall to the living room in order to expand her dining facilities; then pushed the opposite living room wall a good twenty feet to the south, added a stone fireplace, brick flooring and vigas to support the ceiling and finished the two-foot-thick adobe walls in white plaster. Great room was not a misnomer.

"Lulu's really outdone herself—all the right Southwestern touches." Snake-man's gaze seemed to be following hers around the room.

She blushed. This man could make her uncomfortable. "I'm probably not going to be very good company. I wouldn't know a python from a boa if it bit me on the elbow." She said it sweetly but felt he couldn't help but catch the tone of dismissal. She wasn't going to let herself get dragged into polite chit-chat or anything else for that matter.

"I can tell. Neither one is likely to bite you. At least that's not their initial approach." He was grinning. And other than being put off by the one tendril that had escaped to caress his ear, Pauly found herself smiling back. If the truth were known, she probably didn't want him to sit anywhere else and was honestly glad that he'd followed her with his loaded plate of six tacos, refritos, and salad. Grams might as well be feeding harvest hands. And if she offered three meals a day, this was a costly operation. Pauly hoped that the carnival business was booming.

"If you ever find yourself overcome with curiosity, I'd be glad to give you a tour of the garage. Snakes are an interesting sort."

Was he serious?

"I may be able to restrain myself." But she grinned. "You might say I'm the Pandora type, but smart enough not to start anything—most of the time."

"Actually, I was hoping you didn't put too much stock in Freud. Snakes and—"

"I think I'm following." She interrupted and knew she was blushing. And then found herself thinking how glad she was that he didn't seem to be an idiot. One of the nice body but nothing between the ears types that proliferated the midway. And, she realized with a start, he was keeping her mind off of things. She hadn't thought of Randy once in twenty-five minutes.

"Are we all here?" Grams' voice sang out from the front of the room. "Hofer will bless our food now. Let's bow our heads and give thanks."

A tall white-haired man unfolded from a bench and cleared his throat as he gazed around the room. The benediction was short, made singularly interesting by the man's resonant voice. It had the quality of bells. Deep bass tones that reverberated around the room. Grams had hinted at a boyfriend sometime back, someone serious. "Altar material" was the term Pauly remembered. She could see why this man might be lined up as number six. He was striking, even with silver-white craggy eyebrows knit together for God. But a Bible-thumper? Hadn't there been that nasty incident with the Gideon people when her grandmother boycotted Motel Sixes? All things change in the name of love, Pauly guessed.

"…and we ask that you welcome our sister, Pauly Caton, into your warm and loving arms.…"

Pauly tuned out. Hadn't she been married even long enough to use McIntyre? She would have bolted from the table if the snake-man hadn't put a hand on her arm and mouthed, "He means well." Then whispered, "You'll get used to him. Real Elmer Gantry without the deviousness." And then he'd winked and sort of squeezed her hand and Pauly felt an electric surge, a tingling warning that told her to beware an attraction that she already knew pulsed between them. And then there was another little voice that said Randy had never made her feel that way. And she recoiled in shock, pulling away. But it was true.

"Are you okay?" He still whispered even though Hofer had sat down. And he looked genuinely concerned.

"I'm fine," she whispered back. One of her bolder lies but she smiled broadly and kept her hands in her lap. "I can't refer to you as snake-man forever. Is there a name?" And please God, don't let it be Boa-Bob or Python-Pete, Pauly prayed to herself.

"Sorry. Stephen Burke. Steve, actually." He held out his hand and Pauly took a breath before clasping it firmly.

◇◇◇

"I think the sooner, the better." Grams was busily buttering an Eggo before passing the toaster-waffle across the counter to Pauly. It was after ten. Pauly had missed the crowd that must have feasted on breakfast burritos from the looks of the pans in the stainless steel double sink behind her and the smell of green chili that hung pungently in the air.

"I'm not saying that they won't be fair, but you've got to have your wits about you. You need to tell them what you'll accept. And I don't want you dropping everything and running."

"What constitutes 'dropping and running'?" Pauly pulled the cork out of the jug of maple syrup. Real maple syrup. One of her favorites.

"Accepting their first offer. It'll be low. They're businessmen, and won't give anything away. But you own one third. We're not talking peanuts here." Gram paused to lean towards her. "Their stock recently split and is going through the roof. That water project alone will keep them going another five years. Listen, sugar, this is your life now, your livelihood. You've got to make the most of it."

"So, what are you saying? Not sell?"

"Exactly. My broker says to give it a year. Hang on. Get active in the business yourself. I have a feeling they'll welcome you once they realize they can't short-change you. Too many contracts give women-owned firms priority. I think you're going to get the old red-carpet treatment."

Stock market. Money. Pauly would just as soon someone else handled those things—thought about them, for that matter, for her. It wasn't how she saw her life right now. Board rooms, tailored suits, a briefcase…and wasn't it money, a huge unexplained lump that had been found in Randy's possession, *their* bank account, that tipped the cops to suspect wrongdoing on Randy's part? The unexplained lump that she wouldn't touch, didn't want to think about because it might have caused his death.

But the business, Randy had left his share to her. And that one third was hers, legally, free of strings, and the only money, aside from insurance, that she could call her own. Roughly two million dollars. Not that she was in need, she wasn't. She could stay put for awhile. But maybe working wasn't such a bad idea…maybe taking part in Randy's life would make her feel better, hasten the healing….

"You need to protect your share."

"What?" Pauly realized she hadn't been listening.

"It should double if Caton, Dougal, Brandon"—Grams looked at Pauly; yes, Pauly had caught the emphasis on "Caton." Grams waited a split second before adding, "continues to grow in the private sector. One of the smartest things they did was shed the weaponry image when they had to."

"I'm not a behind-the-desk type." Pauly was resisting running her index finger around the rim of her empty plate to get the last of the syrup. Two million. Rich. Could she call herself rich? Maybe she should sell. Invest. Live off the interest. Somewhere interesting. An island in the Caribbean. She gave in and drew a cross-hatch pattern in the syrup before sucking the sweetness from her finger and could almost hear the waves crash against the shore.

"Are you listening to me?"

Pauly bounded back from St. Croix and gave her grand-mother an apologetic smile.

"I don't think you have to be a certain type to appreciate money—to want to make the most of your investment. You were slated to work on that water project. Well, do it. Work in the field. Get to know what the company's about. And don't make a decision to sell for one year. That's all I'm asking."

The suggestion seemed reasonable. But did she have to make up her mind so soon? Couldn't there be a period of grace? Mourning in her case. A time to collect herself? It had been three and a half weeks since…. She still had nightmares of hooded men shrouded by trees aiming high-powered rifles at her. Men with bags of money strapped to their backs. And children tum-bling from baskets in the sky. Small brown children in white tee shirts who pointed at her, seemed to blame her for something…. She'd reach out in her queen-sized bed and realize that she was alone. Not Mrs. Randall McIntyre but Pauly Caton, alone in a cold sweat, frightened more than she would ever admit and rich beyond her wildest dreams.

But all the tears in the world didn't seem to change anything. There was no sperm tucked away in a lab freezer waiting for her, no hope of children from the husband she'd trusted, and no way of finding out why he'd lied to her.

◇◇◇

"Pauly, Pauly, Pauly."

One iteration of her name would have been enough, but Pauly left her hands buried in the beefy, slightly moist, manicured ones and tried to resist wallowing in the 'Oh, I'm so sorry' sentiment that washed over her.

"Archer." Gently, she extricated her hands and fought the urge to wipe them on the sides of her navy serge skirt. Instead, she kissed him lightly on the cheek. "I've appreciated your support. It's meant so much to me."

There had been flowers. A horseshoe wreath of mums on a stand at graveside, bigger than anyone else's contribution, then roses for the house. And calls. The solicitous inquiries that would make Miss Manners proud. It had taken three boxes of Thank You notes on Pauly's part to make a dent in the avalanche of condolences. But murmuring niceties had become second nature to her in a very short time, and she took Archer's arm as they turned towards the building. Hopefully, it wouldn't be a difficult habit to break. The cloying attention was suffocating her.

"Tom's waiting for us in his conference room." Archer pulled ahead to open the heavy plate-glass door. He had rushed out to meet her on the front steps. She had called, deciding that impromptu might not be appropriate. The basis for the visit was business. They would want some warning. Give Barbara, the ever-present administrative assistant, time to make coffee, fresh, something from the private imported stock, fill the heat-retaining bronze canisters and run next door for some kind of sugary pastry.

She'd given them forty-five minutes. Make Babs hustle a little. The barely glorified secretary had never been on Pauly's list of favorites. Anyone who got pedicures on company time was suspect. And on Babs' part, it was probably jealousy, a younger woman with a couple degrees who had the audacity to run off with the boss.... There had never been any love lost between them.

But Tom, that was a different story. She allowed herself to be embraced warmly. And believed that he meant it as he had quickly come around the end of the conference table and simply held her. No mumbling of something supposedly appropriate. Just a hug and a squeeze before he pulled a chair out for her.

"Glad you called. It's crazy trying to do the right thing. Allow the right amount of time before talking about what we have to talk about sooner or later anyway."

He smiled ruefully and thrust his hands into his jacket pockets. He always looked like he was posing. Man with steel-grey hair, naturally curly, cut short but with just enough left to twist over a tanned brow. He could probably do "sophisticated slouch" better than any man she'd ever met. He had been a knock-out at the wedding in his tux with the latest date-of-the-month on his arm.

He never let the philandering get in the way of business; he was always the jump right in, get things going type. She didn't mind that. She liked his honesty, nothing wishy-washy…and nothing pushed under the rug, either.

"It's okay, really it is." Pauly accepted a cup of coffee from Babs. "I've made up my mind to get involved. Stick around for a year or so. Become an active partner." Might as well just come out with it. She had never been one to wait for the right moment. All too often she only realized them in retrospect, anyway.

"Not sell?"

Archer covered what might have been misread as a mixture of anger and shock by quickly changing his tone and adding, "No one's pushing you into something that you don't want to do. But look at our offer. It's generous. Tom, help me out here. Wouldn't you advise Pauly to at least take a look?" Archer inched a folder of papers across the table in her direction.

"Let's hear what Pauly has to say, first." Tom looked amused, a little Cheshire-cat smile played around his eyes.

"It's simple, really." Pauly gave him a grateful smile. "I was going to be involved in the Rio Grande River project anyway. Why shouldn't I stay on? At this point I see myself more in the field than here." She indicated the boardroom with a wave of her hand. "I could act as project manager—"

"That's a multi-million dollar project, not one to be trusted to—"

"What Archer means to say is that your inexperience could get in the way of things working smoothly. We don't mean to imply that we don't believe in you, in your ability to learn. I believe in time you could hold your own in any project you choose, but for now this one might be a little out of your league." His smile seemed forced.

The tiger's stripes were showing. Wasn't that what Grams used to say when Pauly's docile kitten would suddenly arch its back, spit, and strike out? So much for Grams' thinking they'd roll out the proverbial red carpet. But Pauly's expression didn't change. She masked the beginnings of anger, an anger that started from it being assumed she was incompetent. This was a female thing and the ugly scent of male chauvinism only made her more determined. She owned one-third of this company and that gave her a pretty hefty voice in what went on.

She looked from one to the other and then said calmly, "I've shared my intentions with my lawyer. He's anticipated a, what would you say, lack of cooperation? We've put everything in writing, too. I'll have our prospectus in front of you by Monday."

Why was she lying like this? She probably needed to contact a lawyer, but she hadn't. But something was telling her that playing hardball required more than just her on the team. She picked up the folder that Archer had been so anxious for her to read. "I will give your offer the courtesy of my consideration. No promises, though. I suggest that we give ourselves a few days. May I suggest that we meet a week from Friday at one?"

Aloof? A hint of frostiness? She was pleased with her performance and wished she could laugh out loud. The look on Babs' pinched face was shock, made the lines darting outward and upward from her pursed lips look like tiny stakes, red stakes where her lipstick leaked into the crevices. But her expression said it all. How dare Pauly go against the icons of industry, propose that she join them? A partner. A woman. A *young* woman. Take over one of the bigger accounts?

"I think all this can be worked out." Smoothly Tom rose to walk her to the door, his voice not offering a hint of what he was feeling. Archer's jaw seemed locked in a permanent grimace as he stayed seated.

"I believe you know why I need to do this. Carry on something of Randy's. It keeps his memory alive for me." More niceties and a teeny white lie. She stood on tiptoe in the doorway to kiss Tom's cheek.

"It'll take getting used to. Maybe, we just need some time." That smile again, slow to spread past the corners of his mouth. "See you in a week." He squeezed her arm.

She turned to walk back down the hall, around the receptionist's desk, past the restrooms and out the front door. For the first time in two weeks, she felt she had made the right decision. But what she had decided and why would surprise even Grams. Pauly Caton, sort of McIntyre, was going to put herself in Randy's place. She was going to recreate his world, become a part of where he worked, whom he worked with because Pauly Caton, barely McIntyre, was going to find out who her husband really was, why he had felt he had to lie about the money, about the vasectomy. More importantly, Pauly Caton McIntyre was going to find his killer.

Chapter Three

"So, everyone needs a reason for living. What's new? But getting involved in something so big, so ugly as premeditated murder and trying to find a murderer...." Grams seemed at a loss for words and finally stopped pacing to sink onto Pauly's loveseat. "You are the only child of my only child. You are my namesake, Pauline Lucille. How can I be plainer? You are all I have. I'm asking you—no, begging you—don't try to figure things out."

"Grams, I don't want to upset you but this is something I have to do. I have to know why. I have to know that it wasn't Randy they were after. That he just got in the way. You know, maybe wrong place, wrong time." She sat beside her grandmother. "Don't you see, I'd never rest if it had been me and my husband weren't doing everything within his power to find my killer."

"That's ridiculous."

"Are you saying that Randy wouldn't try to help if the shoe were on the other foot?" Grams didn't have to like Randy, but to imply that he wouldn't have cared enough to find her killer....

"Ignore me. I'm just upset, sweetie. I don't know what he would have done. I didn't even know him well enough to guess." Grams tipped Pauly's chin back. "But you, sweet thing, I know. And I know that you don't have the moxie, the stomach for ugliness. A professional killer. Isn't that what the police said? Some crack shot who did that sort of thing for a living? Randy or no Randy, why would you even think that you could get to the bottom of it?" She reached out to stroke Pauly's cheek. "Make your grandmother happy. Leave everything to the police. It's just too risky."

This was the second time in one day that someone thought she wasn't competent. Two different subjects. But the same conclusion. And it pissed her royally. And again the anger felt good.

"This entire conversation started by my asking you for the name of a good lawyer." Pauly smiled. Could she sidetrack her grandmother? Get her back to business at hand? She needed to see a lawyer and soon in order to deliver the promised prospectus.

"Give Steve a chance." Grams suddenly leaned forward, ignoring the lawyer ploy but at least changing the subject, Pauly noted. "I know you're put off by the artwork, but he's great. A truly caring person. If you give him half a chance, perhaps, he could be instrumental in getting you through these difficult times."

Had her grandmother just winked? What was worse, had her grandmother set her up? Meet the hunk and forget what's-his-name. Wasn't this the way someone with almost six husbands would think? Hop out of one bed into another? And let great sex or even mediocre sex block out the past?

"I'm going to pretend that you didn't say that. And I'm going to warn you to keep him and any other Lotharios that you might have waiting in the wings AWAY FROM ME."

"Don't yell. You have a temper like your father." Grams held her hands over her ears, but only after carefully fluffing the white-blond ringlets that hung below her shoulders. "I'm only trying to make you happy. I can't stand to see you so upset and not be able to help. Sugar, you've got to believe that. Love is medicine. A cure for whatever ails you. Don't close out the world, the possibilities for another relationship."

"Finding Randy's murderer is the only kind of medicine that I need. I don't think my schedule will allow any play time."

And doesn't anyone care that it's only been three and half lousy weeks? What was she supposed to do? But Pauly felt calmer. She couldn't blame her grandmother for providing a diversion. It was just her way.

"I applaud your getting involved in McIntyre, Dougal, and Brandon. But if they're going to try to squeeze you out, you do need a lawyer. Call Sam Mathers. You met him at the funeral. I've used Sam a number of times on contract matters with the carnival. I believe he's also the McIntyre family lawyer. It's time you two met. Give me a minute, I have his card downstairs."

"The name sounds familiar."

"And promise me one thing, that you don't do anything foolish." Her grandmother caught her hand. "Now is that too much for an old woman to ask?" She lifted Pauly's hand to her lips and brushed the top of her fingers.

Old woman? Grams had never called herself that. Impulsively, Pauly put her arms around Grams' shoulders and buried her nose in the poofed mound of hair above her ear. Tea Roses. Her grandmother's scent. Always had been as long as Pauly could remember. When she was little Pauly had told her grandmother that if she closed her eyes, it was forever summer and they were standing in a garden even if it was really Christmas. Pauly suddenly choked up. What would she ever do without this woman? With all Grams' eccentricities, she couldn't bear to lose her, too.

◇◇◇

"I just got the file out yesterday. Thought I might give it a day or two more, then call." Sam Mathers was somewhere in his late sixties and looked like a lawyer, a successful one. But Pauly wasn't sure what made her think that. The little round tortoise-shell glasses rimmed in gold? The heavy twisted gold rope bracelet peeking out from a perfectly pressed French cuff with gold nugget cufflink? Or just his office in thick cherry wood panels that gleamed from multiple waxings. If they waxed walls, that is. Pauly didn't know. But something had given the wood a patina that added richness, an old world flavor. She expected to see a globe, something from Columbus' day in decoupage, tilted on a wooden axis displayed in the corner.

The man himself was decorum personified. Sympathetic without seeming solicitous, just the right amount of eye contact, slight frown, no undue levity; yet, she liked him, believed him right from the start. He oozed expensive good taste—the silver hair neatly trimmed, parted on the side but abundant enough to cover the crown in soft waves. A hundred dollar haircut? Probably. And the tan, beach-natural or lighted booth? She couldn't tell, but sank into the proffered forest-green suede armchair that perfectly matched the border of the Persian rug.

"I suppose you know that Randy's last will was drawn up by the corporate lawyers." He must have caught her puzzled look because he hastened to add, "Not unusual. They pay those guys handsomely to catch loose ends. And the marriage of an owner changed a lot of things. I simply want to assure you that it was done correctly. Supersedes the one we had on file here. I've already attended to the filing on your behalf. Everything's in order." He beamed at her from across the expanse of mahogany. "I think before we get to any questions, I'd like to address the matter of *your* will. We, ah, obviously need to make some changes...."

He wasn't looking at her as he rummaged through the two-inch-thick folder in front of him so missed her startled reaction. She didn't have a will. Never had had one. The thought of it didn't bother her. It was a necessity of life. But one didn't exist, so what was he talking about?

"Ah, here it is. Drawn up..." He paused and flipped through the pages. "Oh dear, just four weeks ago." He looked at her. "I'm sorry that we need to attend to business so soon."

"Life must go on. I'm finding there's no escaping it." How trite. But her life was trite. "Let me just refresh my memory." She held out a hand to take the document that he passed to her.

"I remember Randy saying that you had enough on your mind with the wedding and wanted to know if you outlined what you wanted it to say and he brought it in, could we type it up and get it back before the big day. Looks like you signed it with his business partners as witnesses."

Pauly willed her hands not to shake. She had never seen this collection of papers before. Never. Yet it was her will. A will giving everything to Randy or to her grandmother if he preceded Grams in death. It would have been what she had wished. How ironic that that's the way it happened, a seventyish woman outliving a forty-one-year-old man.

In the two spaces for witnesses, there were the names of Archer Brandon and Thomas Dougal. They were witnesses to how she wanted her property bequeathed, the shares of the business, their house when there was one, cars, insurance, a policy in the amount of—was she reading this correctly? One million? This will was written as if she were the one about to die. She swallowed hard. It was difficult to stay calm. Three days after the document had been witnessed, Randy had died. Could she have been the real target? Could someone have thought she would be in the balloon, too?

"Here. Just take a sip." Sam Mathers leaned over her with a glass of water. She hadn't seen him come around the desk. She must look shocked. She looked down at her hands. They had lost all color. Then it dawned on her, a tiny spark of curiosity.… If there was a will she hadn't known about could there have been…?

"Do you have a copy of the prenuptial agreement?" Her hands shook as she sipped the water.

"Right here."

"May I see it?"

"I assumed you had a copy." He looked undecided but handed her the sheaf of papers.

"Please, could you give me a moment." Pauly swallowed hard; the tears were difficult to hold back. But tears of what?

Shock? Anger? No longer sorrow, that was for certain. She had in her hands two documents, legal instruments, binding any decisions that might be made by her or for her and she'd never seen either one of them before now. Randy's deceit seemed to know no bounds. "Should I ask my secretary to step in?"

Pauly took a breath and attempted to collect herself. "No. It's just that I think I'm fine one minute and then the memories flood in.... It's only been—"

"I know. I should have realized. Please forgive my crassness. It wasn't a good idea to discuss this today. We can go over everything another time when you feel ready."

"Today's fine." Pauly smiled up at him. "Really. Just give me a moment to look through these. I can't seem to remember all the details.... I know a month isn't a long time, but in this case it seems like years." The smile was wan. She tried to put more effort into it but her lips stuck to her teeth. She glanced down at the documents in her lap and picked up the prenuptial agreement.

In perfect legalese one Pauline Lucille Caton forfeited all rights to any monies or properties or holdings in the event of a separation or divorce sought by her and contrary to the wishes of her husband, Randall Vincent McIntyre. She felt a tremor in her hands and tried to control their shaking. Zero. She would have gotten nothing if she had decided that she wanted out. And maybe she would have once the deception was uncovered—the vasectomy would have been a pretty good incentive.

She picked up the will. It seemed in perfect order. Even her signature. Fake, of course, on both documents, but good ones. Possibly traced, then copied here. She idly trailed the tip of her index finger over the big P and the big C. It was good. And the witnesses. Had their signatures been traced and added later? She'd find out. She wasn't sure how, but she would. How could she have married this man? This malicious liar?

"Do you have any questions?" He was still standing in front of her but had leaned back against the front of his desk.

"Mr. Mathers—"

"Please, call me Sam. I've handled the estates of the McIntyres for the last thirty years. I can't imagine the newest member calling me Mr. Mathers."

He smiled reassuringly.

She held up the will. "I don't see any provision for children, possible children that we might have had." She pretended to scan the pages. She might as well find out how much information he was privy to. But the will struck her as very short term, just a little something for the present, maybe the first six months. This was not a document that had a lasting feel to it.

"Children?" Sam was looking odd, frowning, like she had just said the strangest thing. Wouldn't Randy have told the family lawyer about wanting children to keep the sham going?

Afraid that she might find out otherwise before they'd have time to try and try and then just have to give up? Maybe do something artificial when it was proved that infertility wasn't her problem? They had even set a time frame. She would be pregnant within two to three years because of Randy's age. He used to joke that he didn't want to be eighty and have to worry about a teenager borrowing his car, which in a very short time was going to be a Ferrari if business continued to boom. She almost grimaced when she thought of how he'd rub her stomach and smile in that secret, dreamy way. No hint of that little *vas deferens* snipped, floating loose never to carry anything, certainly not sperm from one place to the next.

"I know there was some talk a few years back about reversing the vasectomy, but the operation's not without risk. And I probably don't have to tell you its success rate. Hadn't you spoken of adopting? Randy had looked into the legal implications just recently."

Ah, he had known—maybe everyone had known but her, the bride. Pauly felt her head move up and down. Yes. It was safer to just agree. Adoption? Where had that come from? She couldn't trust herself to say anything, not until the numb, tingly feeling had passed. Who else knew about the vasectomy? It certainly had been no secret from Sam Mathers. But adoption? Never, never had Randy suggested they do that. Randy had insisted that she stay on the pill for one more year. The timing of "the children" was all important. Bear with him and the business and in a couple years all would be well. What a farce, what duplicity. Would she ever be able to bury her anger? Suddenly she felt lightheaded. Her breathing was shallow and she knew she couldn't stand even if she tried.

"You're as cold as ice." Sam knelt beside her holding a box of Kleenex. She saw the splashes of tears on the will before she felt them rolling down her cheeks and gratefully took a tissue and dabbed at her eyes. "I'm going to give you a few minutes alone. Just take your time. Collect yourself. Here's a glass of water. Tissue." He was pointing to each item on the edge of his desk. Like she might be unable to understand even the simplest of instructions. "I'll be right outside. Just holler and I'll be back in a flash." A friendly pat on the shoulder and he walked to the door. There was a muffled thud, then the snap of a latch catching and Pauly was alone.

It was thoughtful of him to leave. She really did need to compose herself, disperse the wad of anger that constricted her chest and threatened to explode. She needed to think. How could this be happening? How could any of this be true? Wasn't she dreaming? But no, there were the wills. Hers and His, not to mention the prenup. Truly incriminating documents. And nothing about children. But, of course, there never were going to be children. Any produced by the two of them. All the talk. Some kind of game—a game turned deadly. Yet the family lawyer knew about the vasectomy and had assumed *because Randy had looked into it* that they were going to adopt.

She grasped the arms of the chair and pushed, steadied herself, and after a deep breath, stood and walked to a window facing Indian School Boulevard. She adjusted the forest green designer blinds and gazed out at traffic. Life was continuing. Cars stopped, started, as lights turned green. A feathery dusting of snow was sticking to the sides of the street. The world was in order. It was just her life that was chaos. She placed her hands flat against the cold pane of glass and felt the chill travel up her arms. Better. It seemed to remind her that she was alive. She turned when she heard the door.

"You look much better." Sam sounded relieved. "If you're up to it, let's put the will aside and talk a bit about the prospectus you mentioned on the phone. How does that sound?" He stood beside her now, and reached out to put his arm around her shoulders. Fatherly. Not insistent, just supportive. Men always assumed that she needed them. Needed to lean on them. And didn't she? The answer surprised her, almost brought a smile to her lips—because maybe, just maybe, she *didn't* need them anymore. Maybe she'd found some reserve, some stockpile of strength that was beginning to obliterate those old feelings of dependency.

◇◇◇

"I thought it was important that you knew that we believed you." The detective had stood in line for two coffees, one cream, and now put a steaming, multi-hued mug in front of her. He was the young one, the one who had eyed her legs and seemed sympathetic, the cute one. She'd only known him by his first name, Antonio, which he quickly insisted be Tony when he'd called to suggest coffee and then added that his last name was Ramiriz.

She'd suggested the Park Square coffee shop since she'd be coming from Mather's law firm across the street. And the place always lifted her spirits, Santa Fe style sporting handcarved wooden tables and chairs and giant stuffed green cloth cacti with plastic spines. A tube of fuchsia neon light outlined the cash register. The place was bright and cheerful and warm, just what she needed. It had been a good choice.

She had nabbed a table by the window and watched people turn up their coat collars or adjust scarves as they met an icy blast after coming out of the warm shops that ringed Park Square Plaza. Christmas shopping? Could that be? It wasn't quite Thanksgiving. But all those packages could only mean….

"I went back to the area off the Alameda bridge, where it happened." He sank into a chair opposite and emptied three packets of Equal into his cup before continuing. "I really think you saw a kid." His spoon clinked against the mug's sides.

"The child in the white tee shirt," Pauly said. He had all of her attention now. "Why the change of heart?"

Tony looked a little sheepish. "It wasn't that we…uh, I… didn't believe you at first, but it's a piece that doesn't make sense. So I went back and found drag marks on a sandbar about a hundred and fifty feet to the west, but out of your view. And I found this. There's no way of knowing, but it's possible that it belonged to this child."

He reached into a sack beside his chair and brought out a much bedraggled, small teddy bear. Quite fine in its day but now ragged, missing an eye, fur clumped with mud. Forever frozen in a sitting position, it measured no more than five inches high.

"And we found a jacket. I need you to identify it as your husband's. I believe you said the child was wearing his jean jacket?" He paused at Pauly's nod. "This was found across from where the gondola went down on the opposite side of the river and back a ways in the trees."

He moved his coffee mug to one side and spread a jean jacket across the table. It was Randy's, with two shiny balloon pins still stuck in the collar. Pauly reached out to touch it and blinked back the tears that felt warm at the corners of her eyes.

"It's his." She couldn't say any more in the midst of the rush of memories, happy memories before she knew any better about her marriage. But Tony didn't seem to expect anything. Just jotted down something on his notepad and put the jacket back in the bag under the table.

"This little guy has been through the wars." Pauly picked up the bear. Anything to change the subject. Stop thinking about the jacket and the day it was lost. She turned the bear over and over in her hands and noticed that the fur on one paw looked plucked. The felt backing was smooth and hairless. It had probably found its way into a child's mouth at nap time on more than one occasion.

"The pilot definitely set that balloon down," the detective continued. "And could have taken on a passenger. There was enough disturbance in the sand to indicate a scuffle or maybe someone stepping out…hard to say. And no indication that it was a forced landing. You didn't report that the pilot appeared to be having any trouble." He paused to look at her.

She shook her head. Weren't there pictures to show an exuberant Randy leaning over the basket while the balloon drifted slowly towards her? No, everything seemed normal until the shot.

"I'm not accusing. I don't believe that they were having difficulties. Just—"

"Your training. Part of the job. I remember." But she smiled. She was pleased that the detective, that Tony had called. She found herself enjoying being with him. He was attentive and eager to reassure her, prove that he believed her. And the teddy bear was sweet. It kept her from thinking she'd lost her mind, fabricated the child in some shock-induced stupor.

"Do you have any idea why they would have picked up a child?"

"None. It's a puzzle. Could be, the kid was stranded or running from something, in some kind of trouble. They swooped down out of the sky and saved him." Was he making fun? Sort of, Pauly decided, and grinned back.

"Something for the caped avengers?" It felt good to joke, then, serious again, she added, "Tell me about Mesa Landings. I'm sure you've talked to the owner of the balloon and the people who crewed that morning."

"They're as baffled as we are. The pilot was new, hadn't worked with them long, a month, I think. But he was qualified. Member of the family with no history of problems. Left a wife and two children."

Pauly started. She'd been so wrapped up in her own problems that she hadn't thought to inquire. The pilot. Hers hadn't been the only loss. She suddenly felt terribly guilty. Terribly self-centered. Maybe she could find out if the children would be taken care of. Their education. Shouldn't she be doing something good with her money?

"And there's another thing." The detective seemed to be stirring his coffee overly long, Pauly thought. "When things like this happen, we put feelers out, try to scare up someone who might know something. Street-news, so to speak." The coffee was swirling around and around even with the spoon out. He looked up to make eye contact. "The firm where your husband worked has hired a PI. Word has it that they're investigating you."

"Me?" Had she heard correctly? Archer and Tom were investigating her? "Do you know that for sure?"

"Fairly reliable source. Of course, it could just be routine. Unusual circumstances. New partner."

How did he know that? Was he fishing? Or did the informant also know that she had decided to join the firm? Had just picked up the prospectus, would hand-deliver it later that morning?

"What do you think all this means?" She was interested in the answer. Would he be truthful with her? Better yet, would she be able to tell?

Tony shrugged. "Hard to say. Could be routine, like I said, or could be they have reason to suspect something."

"What?" She was on guard but held eye contact.

"Believe me, I wish I knew." He looked down at the table and fiddled with a paper napkin. "I shouldn't be telling you this. I think you know that."

"I appreciate the warning. Do you have any idea who this PI is? What he looks like?"

"Not from around here. He's an import, supposed to be the type that only big bucks can buy you. Whatever that means."

"But no name or face?"

"I'll try to come up with one."

"But for now there's nothing to give me a clue as to who might be following me." She heard the irritation in her voice.

"Has someone been following you?" He looked up quickly.

"Not that I know of," she admitted sheepishly. "I haven't really been paying attention."

"Want some free advice? Pay attention. There's a lot of money involved. Someone's going to want to protect their investment. Am I making myself clear?"

She nodded. Too clear. In addition to false wills, and lies from the man she had married, she now had to look over her shoulder. For a moment she hated her life. Hated what it had become, some travesty of deceit.

"I hope I don't have to tell you to call me if anything happens. Anything at all that you think is unusual."

She looked at him. "I don't know if I could tell anymore. The unusual has become the usual, it seems." And wondered to herself if she should share the contents of the will? Randy's deceit about the vasectomy. The appearance of *her* will, one she'd never signed, not to mention the prenuptial agreement. But that pointed a finger at Randy and she realized with a start that she couldn't bear to think she'd been duped, married to someone who wasn't quite what he pretended. Could she have been that stupid? Hadn't finding his killer really become finding out that she hadn't been taken? That somehow all of this was just a colossal mistake?

"Well, let's stay in touch." Tony handed her one of his cards, then rose to go. "I'll give you a call later in the week, maybe we can get together." He stood there expectantly, all boyish anticipation. She didn't want to encourage him, but then again, it wouldn't hurt to have an ally, a really cute one.

"I'd like that." Her smile was sincere.

He paused by her chair long enough to say, "hang in there" and add that he was sorry but he had to take the jacket with him. She nodded and felt relieved. She wasn't up to worrying about what to do with articles of clothing. There was a storage bin filled with personal effects that needed her attention, someday, not now.

Tony pushed a dark blue cap over his thick almost-black curly hair. APD stood out in yellow embroidery on a crest above the bill. Tony Ramiriz was one of those young hunks who looked good in uniform and took his work seriously, she decided, and that was comforting. Maybe she should stay in touch. He waved from the door, and she watched him drive away, then propped the teddy bear against his empty coffee cup and wished with all her heart that it could talk.

But since the bear couldn't give any answers, maybe she could go scare some up. She borrowed a phone book from alongside the cash register and searched for an address for Mesa Landings. It couldn't hurt to visit. She felt a need to offer her condolences, see if there was anything she could do for the children.

◇◇◇

There were two pickups parked in front of the quonset-hut shaped metal building on Jefferson Street. One was the three-quarter-ton, extended cab, tan Ford that had been on the mesa that morning. Pauly pushed open the front door and stepped into a twelve-by-twenty room that had been partitioned off from at least eight hundred square feet of work area in back. It was obvious that they repaired balloons and gondolas, as well as selling new ones.

"Be with you in a minute."

A man poked his head through the double entry-way leading to the shop. Welder's goggles distorted his features, but Pauly thought it was the owner. The one she'd met the day of the flight.

She walked over to look at the fifty-odd photos of hot-air balloon flights and landings that covered the front wall. She wasn't prepared to see the Five O'Clock Shadow, but there it was, the hands on the eight-foot appliquéd clock straight up five with shadows pooling out behind. Most of the pictures had been taken during the Balloon Fiesta, one of Albuquerque's claims to international fame. She quickly turned back to the counter.

"Now, how can I help you?" The man walked through the doorway, wiping his hands on a paper towel, the goggles around his neck. "Say, haven't we met? You sure do look familiar."

"Pauly Caton. We met at the launch of the Five O'Clock Shadow. Randy McIntyre was my husband."

"Of course." He frowned. "Look, I don't know why you're here. We've gone over everything with the cops." His voice suddenly had an edge. "Isn't it about time we all try to get over this...past it, anyway."

"I was wondering about the pilot...and his family?"

"My wife's brother. Ten years experience and he takes up some ass-hole that's marked for elimination. No offense to you, Miss."

"Wait a minute. Who's said that the pilot was above suspicion?" She felt the anger flood her voice.

"Retired Air Force. Decorated. You figure it out." Then his eyes narrowed as he leaned towards her. "You going to stand there and tell me your husband was squeaky clean? That there wasn't someone out there who just might have wanted him dead?"

She looked down. Had he seen the flicker of doubt? He was right. She couldn't say...swear...to Randy's being anything, not even honest.

"Listen." The owner hesitated, but his voice had lost its edge. "I'm just upset. No reason to take it out on you. Your lawyer has been generous. Bob's family won't be hurting."

"My lawyer?"

"That Mathers guy. We were covered, had pretty good insurance, but he sweetened the pot for all of us. And I don't want to sound unappreciative."

Sam, of course. He would have taken care of things. She vaguely wondered where he'd gotten the money, what account was it that hadn't required her signature for withdrawals. There was every indication that the sum was sizeable. She was tempted to ask how much, but it would seem a little gauche and too much like equating exchanging lives for payoffs. Maybe Randy had left some fund to be administered by his lawyer.... She really needed to take a more active part in managing her affairs.

"Well, I'm glad the money end worked out." She cleared her throat. "And please offer my condolences to your sister-in-law," she offered lamely. There didn't seem to be anything else to say. She backed a couple steps towards the door. The owner nodded, then abruptly turned on his heel and walked back to the work area. She felt dismissed…somehow she seemed to be part of the problem, at least to the dead man's brother-in-law, and certainly less than popular with him.

She stepped out into the sunshine but couldn't shake the depression that settled around her. The wind had died down and the air was crisp but not bone-chilling. Still, she felt cold. She sat for a moment before starting her car and tried to gather her confidence.

Chapter Four

Archer and Tom hadn't exactly welcomed her back with open arms, but after reviewing the prospectus, they'd backed off, decided that she meant to join them, become an active partner no matter what they threatened. So they'd conceded, at least for now. And it felt good to be doing something, giving her attention to something other than herself.

Her office had been nicely equipped. Someone had been thoughtful enough to remove Randy's furniture, desk, credenza, book cases, but it had his feel to it. She'd have to work at getting used to it. Maybe not get used to, but practice ignoring, that would be more like it. She had a private bathroom. And a cloak closet. Which struck her as archaic. Cloaks? But that's what her secretary insisted on calling it.

The fortyish woman seemed nervous as she pointed out the new desk, a little number in walnut with delicately carved legs. Apologetic for her choices, afraid that Pauly might not like her decisions in office trappings. But Noralee's taste was perfect in furnishings, just markedly floozy in dress. Her blouses always dipped a little too low and looked out of place with her usual choices of straight-cut navy or black suits with short skirts. And the jewelry always jangled.

Noralee was a fixture, and Pauly trusted she had stock in a company that specialized in pancake cover-up. The receiver of the white phone at her desk was permanently dyed orange from being nestled against a thickly layered cheek. By Noralee's own admission "she had had everything tucked that could be." And looked pretty good, Pauly admitted, tucks and makeup included, faintly reminiscent of a starlet of some sort. But it wasn't an image that would wear well.

"The print is great." Pauly indicated the three by four foot framed poster of the Bernalillo Wine Festival hanging behind the desk, a Betty Sabo with adobe church and gnarled grape vines in varying shades of fall brown.

"Mr. Dougal chose that. It's just right for this room, don't you think?"

Pauly agreed and thought of how helpful Tom had been. Apologized for his hastiness in thinking she might not be right for the Water Conservancy project. Said that it was hers if she still wanted it, that he'd help fill in the gaps, sort of tutor her if she thought she needed it. Then he'd suggested dinner.

On Friday. If she didn't think it was too soon. And that was his way of letting her know that he considered it a date, *wanted* it to be a date, had even sent a dozen yellow roses to confirm it.

"Will there be anything else? You can buzz me on the intercom."

"That's fine, Noralee. Thank you." Pauly waited for the door that connected her large office with the secretary's alcove to click shut. Then she sank into the high-backed leather executive chair and half-heartedly wished that sitting in such a chair could turn her into one—an executive, savvy and slick and self-reliant.

If the truth were known, her bluff was wearing thin. All those reserves of self-reliance didn't seem to remain so readily available. Did she really want to do this? Take over a project on which no one wanted her? How far would she go out of spite? Just to prove that she could? But then again, what else did she have to do? And wasn't she committed to finding a killer? That part of her resolve hadn't wavered. She would devote her life to finding that answer.

On impulse, she rose and walked to a file cabinet, pulling the top drawer open. Empty. The second, the third, the fourth drawer—all empty. Just more proof that they thought her incompetent. Empty head, empty files. She hit the intercom button with her fist. Noralee answered the buzzer immediately.

"I need the files on the Rio Grande River project, especially the University study, the one completed last summer."

"Mr. Brandon and Mr. Dougal thought that it would be better if—"

"Noralee, please step in here." Pauly wasn't going to discuss Brandon/Dougal issues over the intercom. The door opened and Noralee fairly slunk into the room as she avoided eye contact.

"Get comfortable. We have some things we need to discuss." Pauly waited for Noralee to pull up a chair upholstered in wine-red leather, its rounded arms defined by brass studs. More furniture of Noralee's choosing; she must find the place quite comfy. Pauly gave it another minute, a little squirm-time, before she began.

"The files are empty. I have no supplies, no computer. There is furniture in this room but little more. I am not a figurehead. I'm here to work. And that means tools and materials. I believe that you can make arrangements to supply those?"

"It's just that Mr. Brandon and—"

"Noralee, I will say this just once. I don't give a large rat's behind what either of the two *other* principals think, do, et cetera—you work for me. If that's going to be a problem, let's give your replacement some thought right now."

"No." Noralee looked startled. "I mean I really want to work for you. I worked for Mr. McIntyre." A nervous laugh while she checked the heel of her shoe. "But, of course, you know that. It's just that it will take some getting used to, that's all." The woman was obviously uncomfortable.

"How 'bout I allow you the next two seconds to do just that?" Pauly could feel the anger. How dare they set her up to be ineffective. To fail or just not work at all. Give her the office, the title, and nothing more. Take for granted that she couldn't handle the workload without giving her a chance to prove herself.

"Anything I can help with?" Tom had pushed open the office door.

"Mr. Dougal, I was—" Noralee had jumped up.

"Noralee, sit down. I don't think we've finished here." Pauly's voice was firm and she waited until the flustered woman sank back into the chair, nervously and hopelessly pulling her skirt towards her knees.

"Actually, Tom, maybe you can help. I seem to be missing the files on the Rio Grande project. I'd like to keep at least a copy in my office. Recent decisions by legislators, reports by special action groups, U.S. Fish and Wildlife Service concerns, that sort of thing. All the data that Randy had collected."

"Sure. That can be arranged. We've set up an archive down the hall but if you'd rather work here, that's fine. The decision to move everything out was mine. Thought I'd let you tell us what you wanted to keep close by. Have Noralee help you get set up." He smiled broadly at the nervous secretary. "Is it any secret that Randy wasn't exactly the neatest person? I've left everything from the files in boxes, pretty much in the order they came out of the drawers or off the tables. I can have the stuff brought back. But you should have seen this place. Had to get rid of the clutter just to decorate."

Pauly had to laugh. Randy was a slob when it came to surrounding himself with a project. Literally. Stacks of papers, manuals, everything within reach in case it might be needed. She had helped to refile after more than one project. "I won't promise to be any neater. Noralee, get a couple guys from the mail room to help cart the stuff up here. Just leave the boxes beside the cabinets. I'd like to pick through and decide what I need, at my leisure." Noralee nodded and left the room. A little too hurriedly, Pauly decided. She was going to have trouble with that woman. Loyalty problems. It was going to be "Mr. McIntyre this, Mr. McIntyre that." Would she be able to handle it?

"I'm looking forward to Friday."

She'd almost forgotten Tom. "Me, too." And that wasn't exactly a lie. It would be good to go out.

He moved to stand beside her and take her hand. "I hope any misunderstandings are forgiven. I want you to be comfortable here. I want you to be successful. Can you believe that?"

"I want to believe it." Almost desperately, Pauly thought. She needed to trust both Tom and Archer. Needed to be able to go to them with problems. But what had Tony said? The firm had hired a private detective? This might be as good a time as any to let him know that she knew.

"Tom, why are you having me investigated?"

"I'm not sure I'm following you." He looked perplexed but let her hand drop.

"I believe the firm has hired a PI, and I seem to be his target." Her voice was low, matter-of-fact.

"That's simply not true." Tom's hands were on her shoulders, turning her to face him, and his eye contact was steady. "We wouldn't do such a thing. But more importantly, there would be no reason to do something like that. Do you know the supposed reasoning behind it?"

"I hoped you could tell me." Pauly wanted to squirm away but she didn't. She was as direct as he was and as deliberate; her eyes never wavered.

"I can't help. It just isn't something we'd do." She thought he looked a little apprehensive. "Who told you this?"

His hands tightened on her shoulders, and he didn't wait for her answer before going on. "Is someone trying to scare you?"

"No. But I believe my source, who shall remain nameless for now." She gently pushed Tom's hands away. "I want this partnership to be successful. I'll do everything I can to make it so."

"No one thinks otherwise." Tom had stepped back but was watching her. Like he was seeing her for the first time? Trying to size up her independence? "Do you feel comfortable having Noralee as your secretary?" The question seemed sincere. Was there some reason she shouldn't? God, Pauly chided herself, she was beginning to suspect everything.

"You think there might be problems because she was close to Randy?" she asked. Everyone knew how loyal Noralee had been.

"Their affair was history. I hope you know that. I just may not be aware of any hard feelings on her part. Some residual anger at not remaining the favorite. I'm not saying this very well. I just want you to know that you can hire someone else, someone outside the company, if you want."

Mistress? Pauly hoped she hadn't noticeably winced. But did this revelation really matter? Personally, that is? She could have guessed. And wasn't it big of the firm to offer to let her hire a new, unblemished replacement? Damn, it was not something she'd seek permission to do if she chose to go that way. She was getting very tired, very quickly at being "allowed" things. The newly dead, lying husband's old mistress was now her secretary. She wasn't even jolted. It was just one more unknown to face…not really another fib, just something that had gone unmentioned.

"I'd like to give Noralee a chance, be fair, try to appreciate how she must feel." Not to mention me, Pauly thought.

"You're a trooper. Could I interest you in lunch later?"

"I have some errands. How 'bout a rain check?" She smiled sweetly, didn't want to disappoint her only ally, but she also wanted to be alone. She was a little bothered that she hadn't known about the affair. The only thing she'd known about Randy's relationship with his secretary was that he had had to reprimand her for wearing patterned stockings with rhinestones and had struggled with whether or not he should put it in her personnel file. She felt like laughing, but thought that maybe once she'd started, she wouldn't be able to stop.

"Fair enough. I can wait until Friday." Tom turned at the door. "You know, you're going to do all right. Just give it some time." A mock salute and he was gone. She swallowed hard and felt the urge to laugh melt away.

By lunch some thirty boxes had been deposited around the office—some stacked next to the filing cabinets, others on the conference table, still more on the floor along the wall. And she felt overwhelmed. For the first time in almost a month, she would be going through his things. She thought of the storage bin. Grams had thoughtfully boxed and stored Randy's belongings from the apartment. Pauly could take her time looking through the odds and ends of clothing, toiletries, whatever else had been collected over his lifetime...but this, this couldn't wait.

She pulled open the box nearest the desk. Folders were crammed to its limit. She lifted a handful out and saw his handwriting—notes, telephone numbers, doodling—and it was too painful. She closed the box and pushed it aside. Maybe she wasn't ready. She glanced at her watch. What she was ready for was lunch. Fortify herself with something from Cristy's, then come back and tackle this mess. She complimented herself on a good plan, grabbed her purse and coat, and locked the door behind her.

The man looked familiar leaning against her car in the parking lot. But it wasn't until she got closer that she realized the mouton collar of the leather bomber jacket had been pulled up to hide the inked tendrils running up his neck and what the collar didn't cover, the black wool turtleneck did. And the result was an absence of carny flavor, leaving a starkly handsome man who left her a little breathless, and irked with herself at the attraction.

"I'd just about given up hope. Thought the first day on the job was going to mean working through lunch."

"Almost did. What are you doing here? You didn't just drop by some twenty miles out of your way."

"I cannot tell a lie. Your grandmother was worried about you and I volunteered to check out the situation and give her a full report." His grin only made him more irresistible, and she felt herself relaxing.

"So? What do you think? Am I okay?" She pirouetted and was instantly sorry she had when she heard his appreciative whistle and felt the red creep up her neck.

"More than okay, Grams will be happy to know. So, your wheels or mine?"

"For?"

"Lunch."

Had she thought there was a chance that the Harley wasn't his? Probably not. The gleaming black machine parked beside her car went with the bomber jacket. Finished the "look" as it were. And why not go to lunch on the back of a Harley? Maybe this was the diversion she needed. She was feeling a real need to do something she wanted and not something that was expected of her. He certainly came with Grams' endorsement. And she could use a friend she could trust.

"Yours." She pointed at the bike and thought he looked surprised, then pleased.

"Give me a minute." She slipped off her heels and rummaged in the trunk for a pair of running shoes, hiked up her suit skirt to Noralee heights, and climbed behind him as he steadied the machine. Even in late November, New Mexico sunshine had warmed the day to the low sixties. Snow one week, spring-like weather the next. Probably what drew people to the Southwest. She wound a scarf around her head and adjusted her sunglasses. She'd be comfortable *and* difficult to recognize, she hoped. She was glad she'd parked so far from the front entrance, but glanced back to see if anyone was watching just the same. All clear.

"I know just the place," he said, before the roar of the bike put an end to conversation. She bent her head against his shoulder and leaned forward, arms hugging his waist. It felt good. Better than she wanted it to. She liked the leather smell of his jacket, the wind as it caught the scarf, swirling it around her face, and the feel of another human being, close, molded to her body, moving to balance, in unison, leaning into a corner, righting, then leaning again as he expertly moved through traffic.

The restaurant was on South Broadway. A Mexican bar and grill known for its posole. He helped her off and then said, "You're good." She knew what he meant but fought back a cute remark with a sexual innuendo and simply said, "Thanks."

They took a booth in the back. One of those cozy, orange naugahyde-slick padded back and bench arrangements with a

Formica tabletop between that shouted intimacy even during the crowded lunch hour. Pauly found herself unwinding. Leaning back she tucked a leg underneath her, slowly sipped an ice-cold Negra Modelo, and munched tortilla chips with the realization that, just maybe, she didn't want to go back to Noralee, the former mistress, the hellish stack of boxes and a firm that felt it had to investigate her. Not for awhile anyway. She needed this. Someone paying attention, not gushing condolences. Someone who thought of her as Pauly Caton, not Act Three of a Greek tragedy. Maybe she was beginning to distance herself from Randy and the lies.

Steve insisted they have the posole and the choice was a good one. Homemade. Red-chili hot. She ordered another beer.

"Tell me about Randy," he said.

The request didn't surprise her. And maybe it was the second beer, or the lulling cocoon-warmth of the restaurant, or the exhilaration of being with someone who made her feel so alive… valued…yes, and wanted. It wasn't just Grams' encouragement; it was his sincerity. And she was going to grab it. Grab it before he could take it back. She needed a friend. And with the first outpouring of words, she realized just how much.

She paused long enough to sample the steaming bowl of posole when it was set in front of her and then continued to describe Randy's death, the sharpshooter killing the pilot, the horrible descent of the balloon, the gondola crashing against the sandbar.

"This is terrible luncheon conversation."

"I asked for it." He smiled, giving her his attention as he buttered, then folded a tortilla and dunked it in his stew.

"The sadness of all this is how little time we had together. I met him, we married, he died. I never got to know him. Not really."

"I'd think the knowing part would be a prerequisite for marriage."

The comment didn't seem out of place. Hadn't she asked herself that?

"Maybe I was a little eager. I wanted to be married, have a family. My friends are married. I'd never had brothers and sisters. Randy and I shared that—we were both only children. Life seemed to be getting away from us. I hadn't done anything in particular, hadn't achieved anything, held a couple mediocre jobs. I lived like a nun to finish my master's in a year and a half." She paused, then followed a gut feeling that said it was safe to share with this man and added, "I had been engaged for a couple years, but it didn't work out."

"What happened?"

"The usual. We started to take each other for granted. He dropped out of school to work for his father. Eventually, I got dumped for someone new."

"So, it was Randy on the rebound?"

"No." She hadn't meant to say it so sharply; he hadn't said it unkindly. And, actually, she'd wondered herself. A whirlwind affair, a wedding—and now this. "I'm twenty-eight years old. It just seemed like the right time to get married. I wanted things in life like security, travel, a home and family, someone there for me. Things women are supposed to want. Randy could have given me all that. Or so I thought at the time."

"You haven't mentioned love."

She fished through the posole for a couple pieces of diced pork and didn't look up; she knew he was watching her. And what could she say? She thought she'd felt love because someone so overwhelmingly seemed to love her? But that had been a sham.

"Randy was unbelievably needy, emotionally needy. He had lost his parents as a teenager in some boating accident in the Midwest. His father had been a sales manager, traveled a lot. I think Randy had resented that. Relationships were difficult for him. Randy was a strange man. I don't deny that. I suppose the word nerd describes him best—a bit bumbly, but blisteringly smart. With so many hopes and dreams." She knew she was about to cry but somehow that seemed okay, too. She found a packet of Kleenex in her coat pocket and took time to blow her nose. "I thought I could make a difference in his life. I thought he loved me so completely that we'd grow close automatically." Her voice sounded small, choked.

Steve reached out and took her hand and held it and was quiet.

"It's tough when you have your chance taken away from you," he offered.

She tried to smile, let him know the fit of tears was past, but couldn't pull it off. "He'd spent so much time in the field. One project or the other. Becoming a partner grounded him. He had gone to school with Archer Brandon. So when Archer contacted him about forming a company in Albuquerque three years ago, Randy jumped at it. It seemed to be the answer to a prayer. He could stay in one place for awhile, invest some money, settle down. Guess that's where I came in."

"You met Randy through work?"

"Campus recruiter set up an interview. The company was looking for a technical writer. So, two days after I graduated, Randy interviewed me. He was attentive from the beginning. It was flattering. I got caught up in it. Marrying the boss was pretty exciting."

"I'm still not sure I have a very good picture of who Randy really was."

"I know. Maybe I don't either." Pauly took a sip of beer. "He was so easy to please. So undemanding. Spent a lot of time in the second story." Pauly tapped her forehead. "I had to remind him I was around. But I couldn't complain. It just seemed a part of being with this really brilliant man and I always thought I could change some of the relationship things—teach him how to be better in—" She looked up hurriedly, then dodged his eyes, finished her beer, and set the bottle on the table. She knew the red was creeping up her neck again. Had she said too much? She hadn't meant to share intimate details. But Steve didn't follow up, didn't make some inappropriate remark, and she was grateful.

"Can I get you another?" he said.

Her laugh was genuine. "Three?"

"I seem to remember I'm driving."

"It's bad enough that I've knocked back two, cried on your shoulder, and monopolized the conversation, let's not add tipsy to the act." She grinned. She suddenly felt good, and it wasn't a beer buzz.

"Now it's your turn. Why the tattoos? Why the carnival? Where's home? When—"

"Hey. Give a guy a chance." He laughed. "The body-art started with a dare, a spider somewhere on my posterior when I was in the service. Then I got into body-building, got good at it, competed, won a few trophies, sank my life's savings into a gym in California, and bounced back to earth about the time my partner cleaned me out. And ran off with my wife."

Steve paused while a waitress cleared their table and took his order for coffee.

"I learned a couple things about trust and my ability—or lack thereof—to manage a business. And then one night at a bar, I met Hofer and your grandmother, who sold me on how good carny life can be, and here I am, part owner in a Ferris wheel, bump 'em cars, various and sundry other midway rides, a couple snakes, and tents that seat hundreds. Hey, I'm a lucky man." He paused to smile. "Actually, I do consider myself lucky."

He was looking at her. Would he say something smaltzy about his luck at meeting her? But he went on. "Thinking I'd learned my lesson with the first business, I decided to be a working owner this time. So what you see are a few additional tattoos. Just part of the act."

"Are there a mother and father somewhere who won't let you in the house anymore?"

"Yup. A mom in Iowa who thinks I'm certifiable."

"And you? What do you think? Is the carny worth wall-to-wall tattoos and chasing around the country?" She said it lightly, out of curiosity. It wasn't meant to be judgmental.

He was slow to answer. "For now." He looked up at her, and seemed to be weighing something, then leaned on his elbows, hands clasped to support his chin. "If I wanted to be truthful—and maybe I want that from our friendship…want it to be healthy up front—I'd tell you that I got in trouble. I lost the gym because I was pushing steroids. I lost my wife because I did time."

Pauly caught the waitress's eye and ordered another beer.

Weren't body-art and prison synonymous? Couldn't she have guessed? What could she say? *Shit* came to mind.

"I'm sorry. I hope the truth hasn't cost me your friendship." He was watching her, waiting for her reaction. And looked stricken. He cared for her. She felt that. He'd taken a huge risk to say what he'd said. To be truthful. And that was a lot more than the man she had married had done.

"The way my luck has been going, I should feel fortunate you're not an axe-murderer." She grinned and heard the relief in his laugh as she held up her beer. "Here's to pals and the truth." She clinked the bottle against his coffee cup.

"Thanks." She knew he meant it. The confession had taken guts. "I guess I also want you to know that it isn't just your grandmother playing matchmaker, putting the screws to her partner to take out the poor, homely relative. I wanted to have lunch with you today." The teasing smile again.

Pauly crossed her eyes and stuck out her tongue. "Big of you to suffer in the name of free enterprise." She laughed and relaxed and tried not to think "ex-con." It felt too good to be sitting here away from the office…and the memories. She didn't want to pick it apart, but she was curious.

"How long were you in?"

"Six months—reduced from a year for a first-time offender. I might have pulled a suspended sentence if some teens hadn't become users as a result of the stuff being too easily available, though I tried to limit access to the fifteen or twenty of us who were into competition. Steroids give you the edge at shows. As long as you stay away from 'natural' contests."

"And your partner? Was he into the same thing? I mean did he compete?"

Steve seemed to be giving his answer some thought. "Jonathan? Not exactly the narcissistic type. He's five years older and a general pain in the ass. Did I forget to mention that he's also my brother?" Rueful grin.

"So now your brother is married to your former wife?"

"Just one big happy whatever, as the saying goes." He waited while the waitress filled his cup and brought another saucer of creamers.

"When I want to be truthful I admit that I knew the signs. And I also admit that they're better off together than Cathy and I ever were. Too young, too many dreams, not enough money...same old song and dance."

"Where are they now?"

"Still in California as far as I know. I don't check in very often. We skipped exchanging Christmas cards the last couple years."

"And carny life seems to be the answer?"

"For the time being."

"Will you ever go back to competition?"

"No. Not interested anymore."

"Maybe another gym?"

He shook his head, then asked, "How about you? You going to dive right into corporate life and make a career of boardrooms and fiscal planning?"

"God, I hope not. But there may not be anything else for awhile. And it's helping. The old saying about keeping busy seems to be the truth."

"I think you're doing exceptionally well." He touched her arm with his hand, left it there a moment, then drew back. "I didn't do half as well."

"Really?"

"Really. Fell apart probably describes it."

Pauly took another sip of beer. "It helps to be angry."

"That's natural. One of the steps everyone goes through when they lose a loved one. It's easy to feel slighted."

"No, not angry that way. Angry at the person, at things I've found out later. Things he'd done. Promises that could never have been kept."

"Tell me." Steve was sitting up straighter. She had his interest.

"I won't know whether I'm telling you the truth or not. I mean, I don't know what to believe anymore." She took a deep breath. "The one thing I do know is he'd had a vasectomy."

"I don't understand. Didn't you just say that you wanted children?"

"I thought we both did." Then she told him about the hospital, how she'd found out in a pretty dramatic finale with the urologist and his tech with a crochet needle that she and Randy would not be making babies.

"He never told you?"

"Never. But please keep this just between us. I mean I don't want Grams to know. She didn't like him anyway."

"No problem. It just seems that that's a pretty big thing to lie about. What could he gain by it?"

"Getting me to marry him."

"You wouldn't have if you'd known?"

"Maybe not...no, I've always wanted to have children."

Steve touched her arm again but this time left his hand there.

"There were even wills that I'd never seen before and a prenuptial agreement, and an affair with a woman at work who's now my secretary."

"The guy was a real winner."

Pauly nodded and then, after a moment's thought, decided not to tell him about the money, the almost million of unknown origin. More than anything else she'd shared, the money made Randy look guilty of something, some bribe, maybe connected with work. It was an area that she didn't allow herself to dwell on.

"Want to know something else strange? There was a child in the gondola."

"When?"

"When it crashed, a young boy tumbled out almost at my feet. He couldn't have been more than that far in front of me."

She gestured from where she was sitting to the wall. "Talk about strange. Poor thing was scared to death."

"Can you describe this child?"

"Hispanic. Probably seven to ten years of age. I remember him as young but wise somehow, worldly." Pauly leaned forward. "I'd never put it into words before but he had one of those old faces for a child. Knowing, like he'd been around."

"You're sure about male?"

"I think so. A pretty child, could have been female—but he ran like a boy. The detectives think he may have caught a ride, been stranded on a sandbar, and the pilot picked him up. He was lucky."

"Had you ever seen Randy with this boy before?"

"He wasn't 'with' this one. There's no connection with Randy. The pilot landed momentarily, taking the child on board...you make it sound...I don't know...like it was planned."

"Do you think it could have been?" Steve was sitting forward now, watching her.

"That Randy set up a time to meet this kid on a sandbar in the middle of the Rio Grande on a Sunday morning, the last day of his honeymoon? And...oh yes...told him not to bother to wear clothing in freezing weather? What do you think?"

She sounded snide, exasperated. She felt exasperated. She was getting tired of twenty questions and her watch said two o'clock. It hadn't been in her plans to take a long lunch the first day at work.

Steve seemed preoccupied on the way back, but dropped off at her car to change shoes and said he'd see her later back Grams. She ran up the front steps hoping the stick of spearmint masked any beer-breath. It'd probably be best not to breathe on anyone just as a precaution, wouldn't want to fuel any partner as souse' rumors.

She pushed open the door to her office. If anything, boxes had multiplied. It was almost defeating before she got started. She put her coat in the cloak closet and told

she didn't want to be disturbed in her best authoritative voice, and closed the door behind her.

Then she settled cross-legged on the floor, took a deep breath, and scooted the first box of folders closer. The going was slow. For some reason there was duplication of materials. She sorted through, stacking papers by topic in like piles before putting one set in the file cabinet. When the first drawer was full, she made tabs before going on. Three boxes contained legal descriptions and maps. She pulled out the ones she thought might be of real help to her and filed the others. The maps filled another drawer and a half.

Somewhere in one of the boxes marked "things from desk" Pauly found a packet of tracing paper. Old-fashioned, almost see-through, tissue flimsy—but just perfect for lifting a signature. Had he used this very paper for her will and the prenuptial agreement? He hadn't thrown it away. But why would he? There was every possibility that he didn't expect to be dead when it was found. Still, a packet of paper didn't really make him guilty—strong implication, but not a conviction.

If this were the movies, she could have a dialogue with the deceased. Yell a few obscenities, stomp around, get her anger out. She missed that. She was beginning to wonder if "just plain pissed" was one of the longest stages that she'd have to work through. And was there a short cut? If one party was missing, did the dissolution of a relationship go faster or slower? *Lots slower* was her guess.

"Will you be here for awhile? Should I leave the coffee pot on?" Noralee leaned in the door.

Pauly looked up from her barricade of papers on the floor. Was it five already?

"Yeah. I'll empty it later after I dig into all this. I'm going to make up a little time for having had a long lunch."

"Would you mind switching off the copier when you go?"

"No problem. Noralee, just out of curiosity, why do you think Randy kept tracing paper in his desk?"

"Beats me. Something to do with the project probably, reproducing a part of a map. Don't work too late." And she was gone. Pauly could hear the staccato click of her heels on the tile, then nothing as the carpeted area around the reception desk muffled her steps.

She got up to adjust the long green glass shade of the desk lamp so that its light was cast directly onto the floor and the stacks of papers in front of her. It was almost dark; going off daylight savings time did that—turned a nice sunny afternoon into dusk far too early. She wanted to go through five more boxes, at least five, before she quit. The more she did now the less she'd have to face in the morning.

It wasn't going as quickly as she'd hoped, but she had to be thorough, check every file, every folder. It would save her time later. And she was getting acquainted with the project. So when she came to the five by seven envelope addressed to a South Valley congressman, she set it aside. The correct postage had already been metered on. The machine-date on the envelope was the day before the wedding—Randy's last full day in the office. It was odd that Randy hadn't just left it in the mail room to go out with that day's business correspondence. Why would he run it through the meter and then not mail it? Could he have been a little muddled by the excitement and rush of those last couple days before he got married? It would have been easy to forget something.

And she could just drop the envelope in the mail now. But wasn't that stupid? She had no idea whether the envelope contained finished or unfinished business. Whether a month later it was still pertinent. She carried the envelope to the desk and picked up a letter opener. She was the partner acting on Randy's behalf, it wasn't like she was snooping. It would be a simple matter to check the contents and make a new envelope, if necessary. The letter opener made a clean cut across the flap. She pulled out the contents and stared. Then she let the photos drop onto the desk and reminded herself to breathe.

There were three photos. No note. No markings of any kind. She checked the envelope. The address label had been produced on a laser printer. Here at the office? There was no way of knowing. There was no return, nothing to link it to the corporation.

But the photos. Her mind was refusing to acknowledge what was in front of her. Two children. Males about eight or ten. Dark skin, dark eyes. Lithe frames. Frontal view. Both nude. The second photo, same children, both engaged in…what would she call it? Not sexual acts exactly. But highly suggestive, provocative posturing…and an older man in the background lying on a chaise, his face obscured in the shadows of an oriental screen. But older? Yes. There was no mistaking the thin ankles, mound of a pot belly, slack skin across the hairless chest, his full nakedness blocked by his companions.

Her hands shook. She gingerly aligned the pictures side by side and picked up the third photo, the photo of a dark, curly-haired child, nude, looking into the camera, coy, lips parted, tongue resting on small white bottom teeth. He was playing up to the photographer, giving the camera a come-on look, sultry far beyond his years. A worldly look. Certainly the sex of the apparition in the balloon was no longer in doubt because here he was, fondling his genitals and hugging his teddy bear. The teddy bear that now sat on her dresser at home.

What was it Steve had asked her? "Had you ever seen Randy with this child before?" And she'd dismissed it. Couldn't even think of a connection. Now this. It was pretty obvious that Randy had known this child. Maybe he'd known him in a little more complete sense of the word.

No. She stopped herself from thinking that. She couldn't have been so stupid, so blindly in love that she didn't see the signs. Randy simply could not have been a pedophile. But weren't there hints? His low-key sex drive, almost a lack of libido sometimes…not wanting children of his own unless he could adopt, not marrying until later….

But why had he married at all? She'd teased him about saying he'd "had to get married." Had she been the cover-up, something to divert attention from his real sexual preference? It was all here in front of her. What other signs had she missed—or ignored—in the name of love?

For a moment she was paralyzed. Then in a frenzy, she pushed the pictures together in a pile with the envelope and stuffed everything into her purse. Only after she had let the black shoulder bag drop to the floor did she take a breath, trying to slow her heartbeat. Relax. Breathe in. Breathe out.

She worked at keeping the questions, the whats and whys, from pushing to the forefront. Then finally gave up as they tumbled over one another for her attention. What if Randy was involved in child porn? Could he have been selling these pictures? What if he had a string of victims? The children in the other pictures, were they part of some porn ring?

The money. The million sitting in the bank. Her knees buckled and she clutched the edge of the desk. Could it have come from this? This perversion? Was this man involved?

The one who was supposed to receive this envelope, Congressman Sosimo Garcia, one of the state's political leaders?

Suddenly, a tiny, darting, pricking point of fear became insistent, pushing other thoughts aside. What were the consequences of her discovery? Would she be safe as long as people thought she didn't know? She rubbed her temples. Couldn't Randy have been killed because of this? Maybe because of what he was?

She'd have to be careful. There was little doubt that her life depended upon that. This was the stuff that ruined careers. And she could quickly become expendable. Of that, she was certain. She switched off the desk lamp and grabbed her bag. She needed to leave…the office suddenly seemed to be closing in on her.

"You're still here. I thought we'd missed you. I didn't see any lights."

Pauly wished she hadn't cried out when Archer opened the door.

"We didn't mean to startle you. I expected to find an empty office."

The light from the secretary's area pushed into the room and made the stacks of boxes and litter of papers cast elongated shadows up the walls. Didn't Grams use this same principle of lighting objects from behind in her haunted houses? The effect made everything loom up and appear ominous.

"Just leaving. I need a break. Wouldn't want you to think I'll work till six every day." She hoped she sounded light and chatty. She moved from behind the desk and didn't offer to turn a light on.

"Well, glad we caught you. Pauly, this is Congressman Sosimo Garcia."

Her heart seemed to stop. A small Hispanic man stepped into the room and bowed slightly. A bow—how provincial—but it didn't erase the feeling of panic. This was the man. The man who was supposed to receive pictures of nude boys. But more than that. This was the man in the photo, the man on the chaise. She'd swear to it. She smiled. Without thinking her hand moved to zip the top of her bag, her sweaty palm slipping across the leather. She had to protect the pictures, but for the moment she fought to keep the terror from making her nauseous. She set her purse behind her on the desk and stepped forward.

"Congressman Garcia. How nice to meet you." Was her hand moist? Shaking? Did her voice really sound tinny and forced?

"My pleasure." He was studying her. With small dark eyes that raked over her features. What did he expect to find? Somewhat boldly, she stared back. Intuition told her that this was a test of survival.

Archer seemed flustered. Nervous. He walked to the switch on the wall and squinted as a shock of fluorescent light glared down from the ceiling.

"Congressman Garcia was expecting a package. Results of a test on the community well south of Parjarito. Randy had promised that it would be in the mail. I don't suppose you've found anything addressed to the congressman?"

There it was. Out in the open. The congressman's eyes didn't waver, just continued to bore into her looking for one slip-up, one cause for suspicion. Pauly forced a laugh. "I apologize for the mess, but I've just gotten started looking through all this. It's my first day back." She paused to smile apologetically and prayed that she sounded sincere. "I haven't come across an envelope so far. When I find it, should I drop it in the mail or call?"

"Just leave it with me," Archer said quickly. "Sosimo and I have lunch every once in awhile."

"I can see why Randall was so bewitched. His widow is a very beautiful woman." Sosimo's voice was soft, caressing. Just the tiny hint of a lilt to go with his very Spanish features, the probably dyed, too-black hair and matching pencil-thin mustache. "I regarded your husband very highly. Truly a man cut down in his prime. You have my promise that I will do everything in my power to see his murderer brought to justice."

A lie. A lie from unblinking eyes and mask of kindness. Pauly wanted to scream, lash out, but she simply swallowed, looked down and murmured her thank you. She feigned collecting herself before glancing up and added sweetly, "It's important to me that justice is done."

"Have the police been helpful?" Suddenly all business, the congressman's voice had a clipped no-nonsense edge. "If not, I have some modest amount of influence. I could help, have my office look into the matter." He was watching her intently again.

"Modest influence is an understatement," Archer broke in good-naturedly. "I say this among friends, but Sosimo just about owns the cops around here."

Was that said for her benefit? *If you're tempted to go to the police, we'll know.* She was being paranoid; they couldn't possibly know that she had the pictures; still, the thing about the cops in his pocket was probably true. She felt cold, very alone, and crossed a call to Tony off her list of what to do. Ramiriz, and Garcia. Even if the one didn't own the other, there would be a sense of kinship linking them. And hadn't she always heard that Sosimo Garcia was more powerful than the governor?

"Perhaps my friend overestimates. But I am at your service." And still those eyes. Waiting to detect her duplicity? Her fright? Could human beings smell fright like animals?

"I appreciate your kindness. It's been such a—" It wasn't difficult to burst into tears. She turned back to her desk for a Kleenex. "I'm sorry. Maybe I shouldn't have tried to come back so soon." She wiped her eyes and blew her nose before pulling another tissue from the box.

"Pauly, please." Archer stepped forward, hugged her quickly. "We didn't mean to upset you. First day and all." He seemed to toss this last over his shoulder for the benefit of the Congressman. Emphasized *first day*, like a hint he believed that they were wasting their time, that she hadn't found a package. Her breathing evened out, sounded normal to her, and she picked up her purse.

"Could we walk you to your car?" Archer seemed just as eager to leave.

One more tissue for good measure and Pauly followed them out of the office, feeling she had escaped. Not been found out for now, at least. But the enormity of her discovery…Randy and the children…Congressman Garcia…she felt numb.

◇◇◇

They wouldn't follow her. She needed to believe that. They had no reason to. Sosimo had been solicitous, actually kind. He'd insisted that she use his first name. And Archer had offered to buy her a drink, but she had declined. Never had she wanted to get away from two people so much. She felt like the photos in her purse gave off a fluorescent glow, screaming to be discovered. Crazy…over-imaginative…but it probably attested to her state of mind. She needed a plan. Something that got her out of the loop, so to speak.

Wouldn't the safest thing be just to follow through? Put the photos in a like envelope, address it the same way sans metered postage, then pretend to find it sometime tomorrow?

It was obvious that Sosimo wasn't looking for the results of a water experiment. She could make a label on her laser printer at Grams', buy a duplicate envelope, and everything would be back to normal.

It was the next part of the plan that made her palms sweat. If she was so all-fired committed to finding Randy's murderer, to finding out why he was murdered, then she needed copies. Good, clear, unmistakable duplications of the very horror she wished she'd never discovered. She didn't know whether she could face it if Randy had been involved in something like child porn, but she had to treat this as evidence, a part of her investigation. And keep reminding herself that a person was innocent until proven guilty.

The pictures might give her leverage, though at the moment threatening someone like Sosimo Garcia seemed pretty far-fetched. Holding the pictures until he told her the truth about Randy? She almost laughed. There was naiveté…and then there was stupidity. A car honked. Had she really turned in front of him? She had to be careful. But as the neon arches over Central Boulevard came into view, she knew exactly where she was going and why.

The twenty-four-hour copying shop across from the University of New Mexico had parking in back. She pulled into a spot directly behind the rear entrance. Then sat a moment to collect herself before reaching into her purse. She needed to put the pictures back into the envelope. She glanced at each picture again. They didn't look any less pornographic than they had half an hour ago. And she felt just as sick, as disgusted as she had then. But tomorrow morning the original envelope and a set of copies would be in her safe deposit box at the bank.

She saw the gloved hand come towards the driver's side window and screamed. Then collected herself as the man jumped back, making motions for her to roll down the window. She cracked it a tentative two inches.

"Hey, sorry to scare you, but this is a delivery zone. I'm expecting a load of paper from the other store tonight." The man was young, earnest. "Could you park a couple spaces down?"

She nodded. Smiled her apology and started the car. If this was what it was like to be a fugitive, she didn't think her nerves could take it. She had to get over every shadow seeming sinister. After all, she chided herself, wasn't she the kid who had been practically raised in a haunted house?

But hadn't she squeezed her eyes shut every time Grams made her go through it? Some new skeleton that dropped from the ceiling, a wax figure that pulled a gun, goblins that suddenly screeched in her ear; she'd missed it all, only pretended for Grams' sake that the new addition had been particularly devastating. Suddenly she was making up for the sham of her childhood.

She nosed the car into an empty space, put the envelope in her purse, and didn't look behind her until she'd made it to the back entrance. Then she took a deep breath and pushed through the double glass doors. The large main room was glaringly bright. Along the north wall two young men were bent over a counter talking earnestly, their heads almost touching until one straightened to ring up a sale before continuing their conversation. The place wasn't busy, but Pauly checked out each patron, mostly students. No one seemed interested in her.

There was a row of self-help copiers along the back wall.

Pauly hesitated. They seemed so unprotected. But probably no one else needed a machine in a back-room booth. She told herself to act naturally and started in that direction.

"Can I help you?" one of the young men from behind the counter called out.

"No. Thanks."

She hurried to the copier on the far end. It was more or less isolated, but she glanced around just in case. Then she placed her purse on its side, eased one of the photos out, opened the machine's cover just far enough to slide the picture over the glass and align it between the arrows before she dropped a quarter into the coin slot, pressed start, and collected her change. The whir and back and forth flash of light was reassuring. One down. Her hand was steadier. Another coin, whir and flash—two copies of the same photo. Why? Pauly didn't really know, but the second copy might come in handy. A safeguard. Her hands trembled.

What she was doing was wrong. And it wasn't just having the pictures in her possession, there was some law about copying obscene materials. Hadn't some woman gotten fired for sitting on the machine's glass plate and copying her bare behind? What Pauly was doing not only fit into that category but was really far worse. There probably wasn't a single way to explain the pictures that didn't carry a prison sentence. She copied the other two, two reproductions each, willing the machine to go faster and grabbing the paper as it plopped into the basket.

They weren't perfect. But black and white photos transferred to black and white Xerox fairly well. Maybe the genitalia detail was a little fuzzy, but anyone looking at them would certainly get the idea. She bought two manila envelopes before she left and sealed each as she sat in the parking lot before starting the car. The one with the copies and the original envelope went into the glove compartment.

◇◇◇

She got in at ten the next morning, having called ahead with an excuse about some business that needed her attention. She had been vague and Noralee hadn't asked. There were no messages, no one who seemed to need her; no need to rush. Pauly just went to her bank and opened her safe deposit box and dropped in the envelope—nonchalantly left evidence that could rock the state's political system. Prove that her husband...but she tried not to think about that.

Everything seemed to be suspect. She'd spent the night wakeful, sorting through Randy's personality characteristics, searching for those traits that would make him a pedophile. She could hardly put the word into conscious thought. She could drive herself crazy with not knowing. But she had felt better in the morning. It was amazing how different things looked in the daylight. She felt calmer, braver—and had formulated a plan.

At a quarter to twelve, she "found" the envelope and told Noralee that she would be in Archer's office if anyone called. Fat chance of that. She had an office and all the trappings, but no credibility, no one clamoring for her opinion, hanging on her every word. If they only knew…she had become rather important to the future of this firm overnight.

She called ahead and Archer could barely conceal his relief. Offered to run right over. No, she mentioned some work in the firm's library, which was close to his office. It would be just as easy for her to deliver the envelope. Make him squirm. She could tell from his voice that he was trying not to sound eager.

"Is this what you were looking for?" She walked towards his desk holding out the envelope, but Archer was already standing and moving to intercept her. She wasn't invited but she dropped into a chair facing his desk. It was important to see the rest of this farce played out.

"I've looked for a duplicate, a copy of the findings on the Pajarito well. Sounds like it might be important to the project." She had brought the envelope into view from the folds of her skirt and placed it on her lap.

Archer cleared his throat. His forehead looked moist. "What are you saying?" He seemed at a loss for words but didn't take his eyes off of her lap.

"I would think that we might need a copy. I certainly feel it would be helpful for me to know what Randy had found out." Straight-faced. Just an idle statement that made perfect sense. She was beginning to enjoy this. Was Archer a sham, too? The same as Randy? A pedophile? He was divorced. Never dated that she knew of.

"Yes…uh, no, I don't think so. I'm sure we have a copy. Randy was never sloppy. You've just overlooked it." Dots of sweat were caught in his hairline.

"It would be such an easy thing to make sure. In fact, I'll just make a copy right now." Pauly leaned across the desk where an oversized coffee mug held an assortment of pencils and a letter opener.

Archer moved swiftly to stand in front of her. She drew her arm back and looked up expectantly. And innocently, she hoped. But her heart felt like it had leaped to her throat. What had made her play with him? What twisted overdose of curiosity made her bait him?

He calmly plucked the envelope from her hand but didn't move away. He leaned back against his desk.

"I don't know how to say this in any nice way. So, I'll just tell you. Until we get the results of the investigation—" he paused, "You're surprised? Tom said that you knew. I'm just sorry that he felt he had to lie about it. There was no need. You of all people should know that we can't take chances. Clients wouldn't stand for it. They'll demand to see your sterling character spelled out in black and white by a disinterested third party. Marriage to Randy didn't negate the necessity we feel to have you checked."

"Archer, how can you do this?" It was difficult to control her anger.

"Use your head, Pauly." Archer sounded exasperated, the "I'm really put out" voice one would use with a child. "For the most part this is a secured facility. Your present clearance limits you in what kind of material you can be involved with. We have to be careful. As a technical writer, you know that. We started the paperwork for a Q clearance for you six months ago, but it could take over a year. So, in the meantime, certain materials are off limits. For example, in this situation, in this room right now, I'm the only one who can open a sealed envelope that has been in the possession of a company principal."

His smugness was unbearable. But she played dumb and nodded and fought the urge to yell "bullshit" and worked on an expression that she hoped would look contrite.

"Archer, I wasn't thinking. Frankly, I'm a little miffed about the investigation, even if there is a reason for it."

"Look at it as a precaution. Do you know what kind of trouble we could get into? One suspect thing on your record and we're in for trouble."

"Such as?"

"A little pot-smoking, running your credit cards over the limit. God forbid you've ever been bankrupt. Those are red flags to the FBI, and rightfully so."

"May I assure you that the sum of my criminal life involves two unpaid parking tickets on campus?"

"I hope to God that's true. Nobody wants to see you be successful more than I. But I shouldn't need to remind you that the company is your investment, as well as ours. It wouldn't take much for us to lose a few government contracts. We simply can't be too careful."

Pot-smoking, credit cards? Wouldn't that pale next to child porn? She almost laughed out loud then caught herself. No matter how mad she got, she couldn't give anything away. And he was good, in control now that he had the envelope.

"I'd like you to think next time." The tone was condescending, still parental, a little slap on the wrist for the errant child. She wanted to scream. "If you run across anything else sealed, give me a call. Now if you'll excuse me." He walked back around the desk still holding the envelope addressed to Sosimo.

She stood. Lacking any clever comeback, she felt the power of the situation lay securely on Archer's side. But what had she expected? That he'd give something away? Really let her open the envelope?

He quickly glanced up at her. "By the way, where did you find it?" he asked.

The question caught her off-guard. Curiosity on his part? Or something more?

"In the box filled with desk items." Then gathering courage, she added, "Why do you ask?"

"Just wondered how it got mislaid, why it wasn't sent out when it should have been." He was staring at her.

She couldn't read his expression. Had she goofed? Did he know that she knew? Did the lack of postage on the new envelope give her away? But there was no reason to think that he'd ever seen the envelope before.

"I'd like to think that Randy was pretty excited about getting married. Wouldn't that be a safe guess as why he overlooked it?" She smiled broadly.

"Probably explains everything." Archer returned her smile.

But all the way back to her office, Pauly couldn't help but think her little plan had backfired. Archer suspected something. It didn't make her feel very safe. And Tom had lied. He had played so innocent, denied any knowledge of a check into her background…maybe her present…when, in fact, he was paying for it. With company money, but it was the same thing. Well, the first thing she'd do is break their date for Friday. Roses or no roses, she wasn't going out with a liar. And she wasn't going out with someone who might put her in danger.

Chapter Five

The four turkey carcasses on the sideboard looked like beached whales, picked clean, knobby ends of bones turning white in the overly dry room. On a full stomach the smells of dressing and gravy and candied sweet potatoes were oppressive. Pauly leaned on the table and played with the whipped cream on her pumpkin pie. Thanksgiving was always a production with a cast of thousands. Grams and Hofer had already loaded up the leftovers to share with a mission for the homeless down the road.

She smiled at Steve, who sat across from her. He could make a pretty good case for being ignored. She hadn't been very good company for anyone the last couple days. More than once she had wished that she'd just dropped the original envelope in the mail. But she hadn't, and now she wasn't sure what she should do. Tell the cops? No. Too risky. That was probably a direct pipeline to Sosimo. Tell Grams? And get her involved? No. She couldn't endanger anyone other than herself.

And she wasn't quite ready for Grams' "I told you so." Something like this would only give her ammunition. And Pauly wasn't ready to admit that her husband of one week had been a pedophile or child porn broker, or whatever they might be called. The shock still shot through her when she thought about it. How could she not have suspected? Didn't those kind of people give themselves away? Wear a scarlet letter on their forehead? Or bear some other noticeable brand?

And then there was Steve. Did she know him well enough to take him into her confidence? Could she trust him to not use the information in some way that might get people hurt? Sosimo was a powerful man. Steve was no match for him. Nor was she. And did she want the world to know that when Pauly Caton married, she had latched onto a sicko? Didn't know the difference and marched right down the aisle with a sterile man who loved children, but not in the way that she had thought.

And in all snobbishness, should the one-third owner of a prosperous company, who just happened to be under investigation herself, be seen hanging around a man covered with tattoos who also had a record? That would give the PI something to report and fodder for Archer's imagination. Another time, another place, and maybe a Steve could have been a part of her life. But not now.

Steve turned to hand off a piece of pie to someone sitting at the next table, and Pauly realized with a start that she was staring at his profile. He was so handsome. How trite. But that's exactly what she thought...almost breathtakingly so. It was difficult not to stare, not to want. She caught her breath. Not to *want?* Where had that come from? But if she let the thought surface, she would have to face her overpowering urge to get into bed with him. Willpower. He absolutely had to be off limits.

Maybe a walk. She pushed back from the table. The weather was glorious, staying in the low sixties. She had picked up a Spanish cross, punched tin rosettes stapled to crossed wooden stakes. She'd bought it in Old Town and had planned to place it at the site of Randy's death. It was tradition. Most highways in New Mexico were decorated with the like—crosses and bunches of plastic flowers, some at curves in the roads, others along a straight stretch—but all commemorating the deaths of loved ones due to accidents. The crosses marked the exact spots. She liked the message that a brightly colored cross gave out, that the deceased was not forgotten. And didn't she owe Randy something? At least a monument? His lies shouldn't keep her from honoring the dead.

"Any chance you'd like some company for the rest of the afternoon?" Steve asked.

She wanted to say, "No." Instead, she heard herself say, "Fine." When she explained what she wanted to do, he simply offered to help. No judgments. Just support. She wanted to hug him.

Grams' property extended to the edge of the Rio Grande, more exactly to the edge of the wooded area that became the bosque. The twenty or so acres that made up the grounds ran lengthwise along the river. "Superb frontal exposure. Perfect for sub-division." Grams would often quote the realtor who sold her the land, but always added, "Over my dead body." Sub-division just wasn't in Grams' vocabulary.

The dry brush crackled underfoot. Steve carried the three-foot cross even after she teased him about looking like a *penitente*. New Mexico was steeped in the folklore of pilgrimages. At Easter the highway to Chimayo would be filled with men carrying crosses. But maybe this was a pilgrimage of sorts, too. Her pilgrimage, a necessary part of healing, of facing the truth of what had happened.

This would be her first visit to the site since Randy had been killed. And it was great to have Steve along, she had to admit. Wasn't sure she could have done it alone. Even with him there she was beginning to have misgivings. So much seemed to have happened in such a short time. She longed for the safety of last summer, railed against the fact that her life had been turned upside down, would never be the same again.

If she hadn't walked it, she would never have realized how very close the site was to Grams'. Fifteen, twenty minutes away from the B&B at the most. They hadn't been walking very fast.

Had it only been a mile, just a little over to where the Rio Grande widened into an awesome channel? Even plagued by sand bars in years of little rain, the river pushed around and over to continue its journey along the border of New Mexico, Texas, and Old Mexico. It wasn't the Mississippi, but it was the biggest river in the Southwest.

She paused to listen to the gurgling roar, then looked up at the span of concrete, empty of traffic because of the holiday, and above it to the high wires, and blinked to keep the image of the red and yellow balloon from drifting across her line of sight. She felt Steve's arm go around her shoulders, but even his closeness couldn't keep the face of the child, the key to so much, from surfacing, staring back at her from the sandbar...he had been frightened that day, not sexy and alluring like in the picture.

"Where would you like the cross?"

She hadn't thought that far. She wasn't going to wade the river again to put it on a sandbar.

"Somewhere here. Maybe at the edge of the brush. There." She pointed and watched him slip the small axe from his belt and carry the cross to where she had indicated. She turned back to the bridge, then looking up swung her gaze in an arc to find the tree that had hidden the killer. With a shiver she realized that she had suggested Steve place the cross at the base of the only cottonwood tall enough or thick enough to have concealed Randy's murderer. But wasn't that appropriate?

Steve cut away the brush at the base of the tree before pounding the sharpened, sturdy, perpendicular end of the cross into the hard ground. Then stood back, glancing her way for approval.

"It looks great." And it did. A bright spot against the drab brown brush and tree trunk. Others would see it. Would they remember the balloon accident, the spectacular murder of the pilot by a sharpshooter?

The sun ducked behind a cloud, and a breeze sprang up. Pauly fumbled in her coat pocket for a Kleenex, then pulled off her gloves and blew her nose.

"That'll bring the geese."

She laughed. She was glad that Steve was with her, but she was through with this place. She would never have to visit it again. But this was the place to decorate, not his grave. And, at the moment, she wasn't sure how she would remember him...loving husband or con-artist. But she wasn't crying. She was past that. Maybe a few tears for herself now and then, but even those bouts were disappearing. Mostly she wanted the truth. Whatever it took—that was important to her.

She was quiet on the walk back. And Steve seemed comfortable with that, seemed to understand her need to be within herself. She wondered what he'd say if he knew that she wasn't mourning the loss of a husband, but rather the loss of trust. And trying to sort out what she should do.

The brush pushed into the narrow path in places closest to the river's edge. Steve walked beside her and took her arm once when she stumbled. She had quickly pulled ahead of him.

Touching was just too dangerous. Electrifying. And she didn't need a complication. She didn't glance back, but sensed that she might have hurt his feelings.

Something rustled upward from a tree to her right. She followed the raptor's ascent and watched the bird float across the low-slung sun, buoyed by breezes that gave the predator time to select his prey. A five o'clock shadow. Pauly shivered. The bosque was beauty and death together, rolled into one.

"*Accipiter Striatus,*" Steve called out, pointing above her head.

"What?"

"Sharp-shinned hawk. It has its eye on that flock of sparrows roosting in the cottonwoods."

They stood a moment to watch as the hawk pumped its wings then glided to the edge of a grove of young trees. Then it dove down through the center of a tree, turned and fought its way back up, oblivious to the branches, emerging at the top, a sparrow in its talons. Death to the unsuspecting. Pauly shivered. The symbolism wasn't lost on her.

They were in sight of the house and Pauly felt relieved. A hot bath and good book equaled an early night. A much earned mindless evening of relaxation. She had nothing planned for the next day.

"Want to come in for a few minutes?" he asked.

Said the spider to the fly, Pauly thought. He had the apartment over the garage and frankly, she was curious. She had always liked the bright, sky-lighted studio.

"I have a six-pack of Negra Modelo," he continued.

"Presumptuous of you."

"I'd call it good planning." He was grinning.

"Okay, one beer."

He walked up the drive ahead of her, the gravel crunching under his boots. It still wasn't too late to turn down the invitation. But…she didn't. She followed him thinking of how good he had felt against her when they had gone to lunch plastered together on the Harley. She promised herself that there would be only the one beer, then off to her own quarters. She looked to the side as he ascended the outside stairs. A great rear in skintight jeans wasn't helping her with abstinence.

"What do you think?" He opened the door and stepped aside for her to enter.

The large, single room was perfect. Gleaming hardwood floors, free-standing black-enameled fireplace in one corner, red and gold kilims, one of the Turkish rugs an easy twelve feet across. A futon, two floor-to-ceiling multi-media modern art pieces, and a framed stained glass featuring intertwining lilies hung in an east window. It screamed good taste.

"I love it."

She turned around in the middle of the room. She wouldn't change a thing. She stuffed her gloves in the pockets of her coat, and he helped her slip it off, then disappeared with it.

She heard the closet door in the hall open and close.

She walked over to look at an intricately carved screen of wild animals that separated living room from bedroom. The craftsmanship was perfection. The grain of the wood seemed to flow with the animals, move them along in their ascent up the side of a snow-capped mountain. The screen was big enough to offer privacy to anyone lying behind it on the king-size waterbed.

She turned to survey the room. It was mellow and warm with just the right splashes of color, combinations of wood and metal, but it didn't look lived-in. Everything had that too-new crispness of having been just delivered.

"How long have you been here?" she asked, keeping her voice casual.

"Couple months, a little less, shortly after I became a part owner in the circus." He walked behind a white oak bar that designated the kitchen and came back with a Negra Modelo and a small dish of lime sections.

She took the beer, squeezed two slices of lime directly into the bottle, and pretended to look closely at one of the paintings. Less than two months? She'd never asked, but she'd assumed that Grams had known him for some time. What kind of an endorsement could you give someone you'd known for less than two months? But, of course, with Grams a good set of buns was everything.

Steve excused himself and went outside for firewood, bringing back an armload of pinon. Pauly sipped her beer as he stripped to a tee shirt, throwing his ribbed turtleneck sweater on the futon. She wasn't sure what first caught her attention, mesmerized her, the inked mural that escaped up the neck and out the short sleeves of the tee shirt, or the muscle. Traps, deltoids, triceps, anything not covered by white cotton knit rippled with each movement. So did the tattoos that covered them. Oblivious of her open admiration, he stuffed newspaper under the grate, criss-crossed sticks of kindling, then placed two chunks of wood on top and lit a match. The fire crackled into life.

"Join me?" He had stretched out on the floor in front of the fire, a thick tasseled pillow propped under his head. Long shadows crept across the room, and without the light of lamps, the fire gave everything a burnished tint, glinting off the polished floors, even off the gold chain around his neck.

She didn't say anything but sank down beside him and stretched her feet towards the fire. Something had dropped her body temperature to a minus five. Or maybe it was anticipation? And she wasn't certain how she would react. Did she really want an affair with this man? Affair, hell. So far there was every possibility it would be a one-night-stand. And she couldn't afford to get involved, not until her life was a little more certain.

When he reached out to caress her neck, she pulled away.

"I don't want this...not now, anyway. It makes me feel cheap. My husband's body isn't cold yet and I'm—"

"I've read this plot before. Shakespeare, maybe?" He was chiding her, but he let his hand drop before saying quietly, "I don't think either one of us could back away right now, even if we wanted to."

She didn't say anything, just listened to the sizzle and pop of the fire, drew her knees up to her chin and hugged them. She didn't trust herself to look at him. But she didn't pull away when he took her hand, and Pauly knew before his arm came around her shoulders and he had tipped her head back what was coming next, and she knew she couldn't—wouldn't—stop him.

His lips touched her neck. She shivered and tried to choke back a gasp, a breathy, aspirated nanosecond of sound before it escaped to tell him more than a hundred words about how much she needed him—needed the physical closeness, wanted the touch, was drunk with the need before even finishing one beer....

Suddenly she wasn't thinking clearly and didn't care. A feeling of craziness hovered just out of reach and warmed by the fire and the tiny jolts of electricity that shot through her body with each touch of his lips, she turned to him and hoarsely whispered, "Condoms?" It was the only thing Pauly could think of that gave her a reality check, pulled her back from the brink of no return.

"Pocket full." But that wasn't the bulge that he guided her hand to feel. And suddenly his excitement was her excitement and she tore at her sweatshirt and Levi's and watched by the light of the fire as he pulled down his jeans and slipped the tee shirt over his head. The black thong and pouch combination was probably some leftover from days of competition and seemed to intensify the dark outline of the body art, the skin etchings that actually only covered shoulders, neck and arms.

She didn't know why this surprised her. She'd assumed there would be very little "plain" skin when, in fact, the perfectly tanned body was smooth, shaved and oiled like a bodybuilder—why?—and free of images.

"Will it be more exciting for you if I leave my socks on?"

Steve must have been watching her watch him, and he struggled to keep the corners of his mouth from turning up. Pauly laughed outright.

"I might be able to handle bare feet."

He pulled his socks off then pushed to his knees and facing her slipped down the thong and began unrolling the condom over his erection.

"How am I doing?" He paused.

Pauly realized she was still staring and blurted, "Fine." Again, the start of a smile played around his mouth.

"I'm not taking over a job that you'd like?" There was a sultriness about his smile, a certain amount of posing, she thought. More than a little narcissistic interest in how he might look. Pelvis thrust forward, shoulders flexed, Mr. January beside the roaring fire adjusting latex protection. And she was both excited and repulsed. She felt wooden, disconnected from reality in bra and panties and sweaty palms. Suddenly she didn't want this to happen, didn't want this calendar-perfect man swarming all over her saying all the words that he thought she'd want to hear. Or was she getting cold feet because she *did* want to hear them—but how would she know if he were telling the truth? How could she trust anyone again?

"Is it too late to order a drink?" Her voice sort of croaked over the words. He reached out and caught her wrist. Not roughly, just a little pressure to make her look at him. He didn't say anything, just studied her. A little spark of fear ignited somewhere within when she caught the tightening of his jaw, but he mastered his emotions, let her hand drop and erased any coldness that might have gleamed in those brown eyes.

He sat back, the condom forgotten as he pulled the thong back in place. He looked perplexed. There was a name for what she was doing, changing her mind at the last second, but she told herself that it didn't really apply. If she couldn't go through with it, she couldn't, and that was that. She scrambled back into her clothes as Steve rose, gathered his and walked behind the screen, the black strap of nylon separating two hard gluteals.

He didn't say anything. And she didn't offer an "I'm sorry." But then neither did he. The silence was awkward. He came back around the screen and padded barefoot across the wide room towards the kitchen, this time in a terry cloth robe, snugged in at the waist by a belt of the same material and color, a deep cobalt.

"Another beer? Sherry? Something else?" He leaned against the bar, his voice noncommittal.

"Sherry sounds good." She tried to match his tone.

She was still sitting on the floor when he came back.

He eased down to join her balancing two glasses of sherry.

At first she simply sipped her drink and watched the fire through the gold-brown liquid that swirled in the etched crystal. It was sweet and seemed to coat her tongue, felt good as its warmth slipped down her throat. She really didn't want to look at him. What was there to say? She had lost her nerve...that was a part of it.

But the bigger part was Steve's perfection, the almost unreal body parts and surreal art, and how he made her feel. She'd thought of Randy. Randy naked, the beginning of love handles, white skin, concave chest, runners' legs, sinewy and slight...how easily embarrassed he was by a hard-on. Would never think of posing in front of her while slipping on a condom. Always apologizing for wanting sex. Then coming in a breathless rush of thrusts and jerky movements that left her empty, wanting more, wanting something else. Or like now, *someone* else. How could she have been so willing to settle for so little? Had she really thought that children and house and security would make up for the lack of electricity between them?

"I'm good at back rubs, and listening, and holding. I'm also good at what you just passed up." He turned her head towards him, a finger under her chin. "But it's got to be when you want it. So, any of the first three interest you?"

"Holding?"

"You got it." He leaned back against the pillow, making room for her beside him.

She settled against him, still sorting through the mixture of thoughts. It didn't seem necessary to talk. She was glad of that. And leaning against him seemed okay, too. He put an arm around her as the tears came. Just tears. She took a shaky breath, and he looked down then reached across her to an end table for a box of tissue.

She dabbed at her cheeks and blew her nose and feeling spent and adrift in conflicting emotions, leaned against him and closed her eyes. He adjusted his weight so that she just fit there curled into his side. And she tried to close out all thoughts of Randy...all thoughts of anything...and just enjoy the fire and the rest of her sherry.

The room was pitch-black except for the glow of embers in the fireplace when she opened her eyes. She'd slept. For how long? There was no telling. She hadn't seen a clock in the room. She looked at Steve but could tell by the evenness of his breathing that he was still asleep. Maybe this would be a good time to go. She remembered all too vividly the scene earlier.

She didn't want to push her luck a second time. She'd backed out once—could she again? No, she shouldn't, it wasn't a moral victory.

She slowly sat up and wriggled an arm free. Steve didn't move. She stood, slipped on her hiking boots—she could worry about tying the laces later—and walked to the hall closet. She had to turn on the closet light to find her coat. If the room was sparsely and perfectly decorated, the closet was a cluttered disaster.

She found her coat towards the back, but not before she'd knocked one of his jackets off its hanger. That wouldn't happen if he'd zip them. She picked it up and paused to pull the zipper up to the collar. Now the jacket snugly hugged the wooden frame. And he shouldn't leave things wadded in his pockets. She could just hear Grams' voice. But it was true. It stretched the material into marsupial pouches that never bounced back, and the black leather jacket looked new.

She pulled the woolen mass out from under the left-hand button-down flap where he'd obviously stuffed it in a hurry. Not gloves but rather a single knit domed piece. She slipped her hand into the opening, pushed her fist against the top—and saw the eye holes light up with the paleness of her skin, the rounded double-stitched hole for a mouth puckered at her wrist.

Blow-ups of her photos flashed before her. The pictures taken from the bridge. The murderer in the top of the tree in a ski mask. This ski mask? The screams rode up the back of her throat, one on top of the other. She bit her fist and kept them rolling just out of reach, not breaking the silence. She had to leave. She pulled the chain on the light and fled. Closed the closet door, opened the one to the outside at the top of the stairs, and ran, slipping on the frosty wooden steps before bounding for the house and her room. And safety. Catching her breath, she stopped under the eaves of the house and glanced back. There was no light in the studio. No movement. Steve must be still asleep. She stared at the black, flaccid, puppet-like head still on her right hand. She was calmer, beginning to think rationally now, and wondered why she had taken it. Couldn't a man own a ski mask without being a suspect? Even a man whose move to this area coincided with the death of another?

Suddenly, she felt utterly foolish. But what if it was a link, another piece to the puzzle. Could Steve have had some part in Randy's death? She slipped the mask off her hand. She'd put it in the safe deposit box in the morning. One more unknown, one more what if….

◇◇◇

"Will you be closing out Mr. McIntyre's account?" The woman was walking ahead of her to the secured bank vault area.

"His account?"

"Safe deposit box. I'm sorry to have to bring this up. But under the circumstances, I just thought that's why you were here."

"I wasn't thinking. Of course." Actually, Pauly had no idea that Randy had a safe deposit box, too. Both of them had checking accounts at Sun Country Bank and Trust, two separate and one together, the household account, plus a savings. She'd put off consolidating them, didn't want to touch the suspect one million in savings. The police had warned her not to. But she needed to do something. Maybe if she turned Randy's personal account into another savings account. That would keep it intact. She'd ask Tony what would be best. She'd ducked him since the scare with Sosimo, but Tony already knew about the money. It couldn't endanger her.

"We would only need a copy of the certificate of death."

The woman pronounced the last like it was a worm on her tongue.

"I have one here." Thanks to Sam Mathers, Pauly added to herself. He had provided a stack of copies, apologized for appearing unfeeling, but told her to keep a few with her, said it would save immeasurable time, and he'd been right. Pauly pulled a file from her briefcase, trying to keep the ski mask hidden from view, and handed a crisp page to the attendant. It no longer bothered her, this one page that proved Randy was dead. It was now only a formality, as Sam had said, a "necessity."

"I'll be right back with the papers for you to sign. But let's get your safe deposit box first." Pauly followed the woman into the tight aisle between north and south walls of metal assurances, hundreds of peace-of-mind cubicles that held what? Jewelry? Deeds to houses and land and titles to cars?

Pauly walked to a table by a window, barred, two stories up, and opened the box registered to her, rented for one year.

Certainly, it didn't hold the usual assets. Wasn't it safe to guess that she was the only one with photocopies of nude eight-year-olds and a ski mask that was possibly worn by a murderer? She hurriedly rolled the knit headgear into a ball and pushed it towards the back, behind the envelopes. Then she shut and locked the box and waited, not allowing her mind to even speculate on what Randy had thought so precious that he had to keep it separate from his other "important" papers. Separate from her. As always, that was the difficult part, this something else she hadn't known about.

"Here we go. Everything's in order. A signature here," the woman pointed to an inked-in blue X halfway down the page, then pointed to an identical X at the bottom, "and here." Both signature lines were followed by the demand for a date.

"Do you know when my husband first rented this box?"

"Let's see. It should say somewhere." The woman peered at the single-spaced contract. "Just give me a moment. You'll have to excuse me, this isn't my usual area. Here. Looks like he's had this box for a little over five months." She looked up and smiled. "Well, I'll wait outside."

Pauly smiled her appreciation of the woman's thoughtfulness. She did want to be alone. And suddenly she had a case of cold feet. There was such a thing as knowing too much. And wasn't she just about at the saturation point? Did she want to know more? Her hands shook and it took two tries to fit the key into the lock.

The dark thick curl of human hair tied with a ribbon nestled on top of a stack of papers. She was stopped, reluctant to touch it, unwilling to think through the possibilities of what it could mean. A mother's memento? Randy's hair was a pale ash blond. And he had been an only child. The keepsake snipped from the head of an eight-year-old paramour?

The taste of bile gathered at the back of her tongue. She swallowed hard a couple times and forced herself to lift the lock of hair and gingerly place it on the table. Randy's passport was in an envelope underneath. She pushed past the picture in the front and briefly checked the stamped pages. It read like a travel log to Central America. Two trips to Honduras, three in one year to Guatemala, then Nicaragua, El Salvador, and Mexico. But then she remembered that rain forest project, an exchange program of experts that included research and a grant to offer classes at the local universities. There had been several trips in the months before the wedding.

It wasn't a surprise to find the title to the red four-wheel-drive truck purchased two months before the wedding and now sitting unused beside Grams' three-car garage. She should consider selling it. Pauly slipped the title into her purse and reached for the next envelope in the box. Immediately, she knew, felt, it was somehow different, maybe the reason it was necessary to have a safe deposit box that no one knew about. She unfolded the single eleven by seventeen sheet. It looked official with pale, almost transparent blue scrolling, Rococo twists and flourishes that trailed along the side of the page and gathered in feathery bunches in the corners.

She could only make out the names and a couple other words, Dr. Randall Vincent McIntyre and Pauline Lucille Caton McIntyre, wife...only she wasn't a wife at the time of the dates on the document. The rest was in Spanish. But the word *adoptar* was difficult to misinterpret. They were adoption papers, official-looking, drawn up by an *agencia* called Amistad...but, perhaps, not quite legal; Pauly couldn't tell even though they had been issued by a court. What was clear was that Randy was trying to—or did—adopt a child, a certain Jorge Roberto Suarez Zuniga born nine years before on the fifteenth of January. The orphan from Honduras had become the son of Dr. Randall McIntyre approximately one month before they were married.

Pauly sat back and looked out the window, not even seeing the criss-crossing of wrought-iron bars that interrupted her view. She just stared at the pale watery-blue sky and thin bank of cirrus clouds that were moving ever so slightly to the right. The powdery rim of the lead cloud touched the edge of a wrought-iron post before pushing slowly past to encounter the second metal bar, and so on. Somewhere beneath the surface of rational thought, a voice prodded her to acknowledge what she knew. What had to be true. But she fought to silence it and continued to sit there.

Finally, when she turned back to the open metal box, she was prepared for the picture lying in the bottom. Somehow she knew there would be one, a snapshot of a happy man, blond hair tousled, standing beside a dark-haired child. The child dressed in the pressed shirt, short pants, anklets and oxfords that said he was not American or, at least, not being raised in this country.

And she couldn't help comparing that photo to the others she had seen of the same child…and even to those minutes, two or three or four, when he had tumbled out of the smoking gondola in front of her, staring at her, frightened beyond his years. Randy's adopted child, Jorge Roberto Suarez Zuniga McIntyre. The child who had flown in a balloon with his father and almost died with him.

Calmly she transferred the adoption papers and passport to her safe deposit box but slipped the picture into her billfold. Finished, she locked her box and left Randy's now-empty box open before she pushed the buzzer that alerted the attendant to come for her.

She called Tony when she got back to the office. He sounded happy to hear from her and advised her to leave Randy's bank accounts untouched, not to consolidate or close them until the investigation was over. But he couldn't tell her when that might be. She detected sounds of his moving to a more private location and after what sounded like a door closing, he continued.

"Did you find any surprises in the safe deposit box?"

"No." His question had caught her off guard. Had she answered too quickly?

"I don't know how we missed the fact that he had one. In a case of wrongful death, the contents could have been subpoenaed."

"There was only his passport and title to his truck. Do you need to see them?"

"Probably not, but keep the passport handy. There might be questions about travel."

Pauly thought Tony seemed hesitant, like he was holding something back. Did they have new evidence?

"I've been wanting to call you. I'd like to think that once this investigation is over, you might want to go out. I mean, it's tough right now, rules and everything. We're not supposed to date anyone who might be involved in an investigation. But later?"

Pauly sighed. Aside from making her feel like pariah of the month, it was cute. And he was cute. At the moment she could do a lot worse.

"Let's see what happens. I appreciate your help in all this."

"Hey, it's…" He stopped short of saying "just my job" and amended to end with "my pleasure." He admonished her to stay in touch before hanging up.

She sat for a moment twisting in the swivel chair, then pulled the photo out of her billfold. Randy and Jorge. Father and son. What would Tony say about that? But she knew she wasn't going to find out. She might as well add a couple more pieces of withheld evidence to her growing cache.

Chapter Six

The tambourines gave her a headache. Pauly tried to pay attention, but the jingle-jangle of sound coming from the stage in front of her drowned out any attempt to think clearly.

"Aren't they just wonderful?" Grams leaned across to whisper, the sequin-encrusted fringe on her violet suede western jacket tickling Pauly's arm.

"Who are they?" Not that Pauly cared, but a line-up of four six-year-olds was suspect, even if they were girls.

"Carny kids." Grams turned back to applaud wildly at the finish of the number, which included a tap dance of sorts and the waving of miniature American flags.

The banner that stretched across the tent some ten feet above the stage read: "Clowns for Christ." At first, Pauly thought it was a joke but was quickly set straight by a miffed grandmother.

"We've done this once a year now for five years. Of course, it's immensely better now that Hofer's here. He's a natural leader. Usually two or three of the leading evangelists in Albuquerque join in, bring their flocks, kids and all. It's always a nice combination of entertainment and sharing of Christ's word."

Pauly still marveled at Grams' having embraced religious life. It was difficult to get used to. Her grandmother motioned for Steve to join them, and Pauly found herself uncomfortably sitting next to the man whose ski mask was in her custody, but whose touch still sent shock-waves through her body. How could she still be drawn to this man? A case could probably be made for it being plain old deprivation. What would she do this time if he made a pass?

But he didn't push it. He leaned over once and asked if she thought avoidance behavior ever solved anything. She had thought a moment and whispered back "maybe" and watched him return her own smile that she couldn't keep back. She shivered. It wasn't cold in the tent, yet she couldn't help but think that, perhaps, she was having lewd thoughts about a murderer. For the thousandth time, she admonished herself for not sharing her suspicions and findings with Tony. But she had no reason to think he wasn't owned—one of Sosimo's cops, as Arthur had put it.

"I don't suppose a six-pack of Negra Modelo will work again, get you back to the apartment?" he asked. They had both stayed seated during an intermission that divided two musical numbers from the main program. They were alone. Grams had said she was needed backstage.

"Probably not." Pauly hoped he knew that she was being serious. She hoped *she* was telling the truth.

"I blame myself for going too fast." He turned to face her. "Damn it, I want you to like me, trust me. I want to at least be a friend." Then he lowered his voice. "Did I tell you too much about myself?"

How did he mean that? Actually, that wasn't far from the truth.

"If you mean the part about doing time, no, that doesn't bother me. I know I'm beginning to sound boring, but I can't seem to just jump back into a relationship. Trust is an issue all to itself. One I can't seem to ignore. Sort of an internal chastity belt." She smiled ruefully and watched him shrug before he turned back and asked, "What are my chances for a friendship?"

"We'll see." She knew her turning him down bothered him. But she was saved from saying anything further by the overhead lights being flicked on and off. Those gathered at the refreshment table in back began finding their seats.

Pauly was amazed that there were over two hundred people in the audience, men, women, and children. The blue and white striped circus tent had been set up behind Grams' house in a leveled, graded field that offered ample parking, and not far from the rows of travel trailers and motor homes that housed the carnival troupe. And if she could believe the crowd's enthusiasm, this was a much-anticipated event. By now every child was hanging onto a helium-filled balloon. Blue and white balls tethered by ribbons tied to wrists or clutched in small hands bobbed and bounced around her.

"Kids love it," Steve said as if reading her thoughts.

"But what's it for? I mean, is Grams raising money for some worthy cause?"

"You could say that. She offers the circus for any number of fund-raisers. Clowns for Christ helps your grandmother's missionary projects in Mexico and Central America."

"I had no idea." And she didn't. Pauly was amazed at her grandmother's altruistic leanings.

"She's invested rather heavily in missions and church groups down there that help the poor. Probably one reason she continues to get a permit to cross the border and perform. There's got to be something in it for them." Steve paused to rub his thumb back and forth across middle and index fingers—sign language for "money."

Pauly nodded. Of course, that made sense. And she was beginning to get a picture of Grams, one that she hadn't had before. Funny how as adults it was so easy to just drift away, get caught up in one's own life, not really knowing relatives, even close ones.

Whatever else she might have learned was put on hold as amid horns and streams of water squirting from plastic flowers on lapels and hats, clowns crowded onto the stage, one on a unicycle, two on tricycles. Orange hair, purple hair, red cheeks, mouths outlined in white, tall hats, crushed hats, iridescent baseball caps, hoop-embellished skirts, baggy pants—it was all there. And at first it was a free-for-all. Posturing for effect, twenty-five clowns pushed and shoved and somersaulted, all in good fun, and to the supportive shrieks of the audience.

Pauly used to berate herself for not liking slapstick humor. But in reality, she hated this sort of thing. She didn't watch cartoons. An Elmer Fudd or Roadrunner left her unmoved. She never wanted clowns for her birthday parties, and her grandmother had almost never forgiven her for turning down a trip to Disneyland. Could she pick out Lulu? Odd—when it came to business, she thought of her grandmother by her stage name.

"Not exactly your thing?" Steve whispered.

She nodded. Was it that apparent? She consciously tried not to frown. Actually, Lulu was difficult to spot. Makeup hid a lot. Things like years, Pauly decided. The four-inch false eyelashes batted against the pink stars of rouge on her cheeks. The wig was violet, a bushel-basket-sized mass of curls, some sticking straight out from her head. But she was amazingly supple as she twisted and turned, feigning her disgust at being shot with water.

"Your grandmother's pretty good at this."

"Yes." She didn't offer more but gave her attention to the stage. The first group of clowns had finished their segment with a finale and were high-kicking off stage, trying not to interfere with a new bunch who bounded forward to set up for what appeared to be an animal act.

Bright red and green, two-foot-high plastic tunnels were laid end to end near a slippery slide and next to a miniature merry-go-round. Once they were snapped together, they snaked across the edge of the stage. Then came the vaults, bars placed at different heights, some with streamers and balloons tied to their wooden frames.

A piercing whistle brought the terriers, Jack Russells mostly, some with bandannas around their necks, others with bows, ten in all. She didn't see the monkey until it circled the stage right in front of her. She hated monkeys. This one was small, gray, with a long tail and a wizened, know-it-all face. It rode on the back of a small, black and white spotted dog that raced around darting into the tunnel only to emerge with its rider still aboard.

"Great, huh?" She wished Steve didn't feel that he had to comment. It was obvious that he was enjoying himself. But a part-owner probably had to look enthused. She didn't, and it had crossed her mind to excuse herself and walk back to the house. She had a big day at work tomorrow. And she wasn't looking forward to listening to Hofer's sermon, which came next according to the program.

The dogs were continuing to jump and tumble, being directed and encouraged by handlers, all in costume. Some were obviously children. Suddenly Pauly leaned forward. A lithe child in fuzzy spotted leotard and matching mask intended to make him a human terrier had stepped forward from the shadows to replace a bar in one of the jumps. He was maybe fifteen feet in front of her when their eyes met…and held.

Those dark, expressive eyes fringed with lashes were the only part of his body not covered by the costume. But she saw the terror. This time not because he had just fallen from a burning gondola, but because she might recognize him. He dropped the bar and darted backstage. Pauly stood then, fumbled for her purse under her chair, and scooping it up pushed along the row of seated onlookers to her right, stepping on toes and mumbling "excuse me" but not slowing until she had thrust aside the canvas flap that opened to the outside.

The night was clear and cold. Even Pauly's down vest didn't keep her from shivering. But maybe it wasn't from the temperature. She paused and searched the columns of trailers for movement. There wasn't any. Lights gleamed from curtained windows; some trailers were dark. The yip of a dog from somewhere by the river encouraged a sleepy half-hearted answer from a cousin towards the end of the first row.

The strangely reassuring sound of traffic roared in the distance from the freeway a couple miles to her left. Behind her was the muffled clapping and cheering of the crowd inside the tent, nothing else; the moonlit night was quiet. Could he have stayed inside, the child in the dog suit, recognizable only by his eyes? Was he hiding among the clowns watching as she left? Or had he already disappeared somewhere along the long row of portable homes that stretched in front of her?

Someone pushed out the tent in back of her.

"Are you all right?" Steve was at her side, taking her arm, turning her towards him, concern in his voice.

"Flu. The tent suddenly got a little hot. I thought I was going to be sick." Would he buy it? More importantly, why was she lying? Why did it suddenly seem so important that he believe her stomach was queasy? She'd told him about the boy in the gondola. Maybe he could help. But then again, maybe he was part of the problem.

"I thought you seemed a little quiet. Let me walk you back to the house." His voice was sympathetic and he put an arm around her shoulders.

"Thanks."

At the door he waited to be invited in. Or, at least, it seemed that way.

"I'm not going to be very good company. I really need to get some rest."

Steve nodded. If he'd thought to kiss her, she didn't give him a chance. The back door was open and she slipped inside, hanging her vest on a peg before walking ahead and flipping on the kitchen light. A glass of milk? Cup of tea? Beer? She needed something. Then abruptly she switched off the light and inched back along the hallway to peer out a side window at the figure crossing the ground between house and tent. She felt better as she watched Steve reach the tent and disappear from view. Pauly went back to the kitchen relieved and more than a little thankful to be alone.

This time she left the light off, found a bottle of Samuel Adams in the fridge door, flipped the cap off, and went upstairs to her bedroom. She sat the teddy bear in front of her on the bed. Was she surprised to find its owner here, at Grams'? Actually it made sense to think of him as a carny kid, a kid lured to the river to watch a hot-air balloon, thrilled probably to be pulled into the gondola for that short, memorable flight.

She wondered when Randy would have told her about the boy, about his son—but then, what made her think that he would have ever done that? What need was there to spill the beans? Certainly not before they had tried to have a child of their own, of that she was certain, months, years maybe of frustratingly hopeless, fruitless longing…and her never knowing how futile their attempts were. But why did the child live here? Even if he was a part of the carnival, that didn't explain the other part of what she knew. The pictures.

She couldn't waste the night, couldn't run the risk of the child's getting away. She had to find out more. Quickly she slipped on a flannel shirt, pulled on a sweater, and grabbed a blanket and the teddy bear. It was her one link to this child, a peace offering, maybe the one thing that would get her close enough to talk.

She loaded her vest with matches and a flashlight, tissue, a scarf, and her trusty wool stocking cap. She'd be inconspicuous if she stayed in the shadows and found a place to wait. A place that would put her in full view of the back of the tent but keep her hidden at the same time.

She took the long way around. She wondered if Steve were watching the house, not even relaxing when he saw the light in her room go out. But she had no reason to think he'd spy on her. And, she reminded herself, no reason to think he wouldn't.

She stopped twice when she heard someone leave the tent. Both times it was parents with cranky children. Nine o'clock was bedtime for most little guys. She came up behind the first row of ten trailers from the north and kept close to their metal sides as she worked her way closer to the tent. She had her eye on a truck parked with hood up and propped on blocks not far from the back door.

When she got close enough to inspect the arrangement, the truck looked sturdy enough for an adult to wiggle underneath and wrapped in a blanket keep completely out of sight. She dropped to all fours and paused to see if anyone was watching. So far, so good. She stretched out prone and pulled herself under, then towards the back, realizing too late that she'd put a mittened hand in something black and sticky. Oil. She allowed a short whispered curse under her breath and tried to wipe the residue from the wool by grinding it in the sandy soil. No luck. She carefully took the mitten off, turned it inside out, and stuck it in her pocket.

With luck, the child had stayed in the tent and was still there. The only good thing about being squashed under a disabled truck was the fact she didn't have to wait long. At somewhere close to nine thirty, cars and trucks parked to the front and side of the tent started to pull out. Pauly inched up on her elbows, banging her head on what was probably the axle. Would the clowns take off their makeup in the tent or go back to their homes first? She had no idea.

It proved to be a little of each. Some pushed out the exit in jeans and jackets, multi-colored wigs still in place, costumes slung over arms; others were scrubbed clean, clad in street clothes and shoes of normal proportions, nothing in polka dots or flapping soles.

Most of the adults had left walking close to her hiding place, then past. She heard bits of conversation: some performers were turning in, others were going into town. The cold, hard-packed sand was beginning to send shock-waves of chills up into her shoulders. Maybe this hadn't been such a good idea.

Then the double thickness of canvas was pushed aside and three young boys were silhouetted against the light from the tent before the weather-treated material stiffly closed behind them, leaving them standing in a patch of moonlight. Pauly strained to see their faces, but couldn't. But she knew the one on the right. There was no mistake. He was smaller and moved out ahead of the other two.

The three were speaking Spanish. And that came as a shock. What if he didn't speak English? Not at all? She hadn't even thought of that. Her Spanish was awful, almost non-existent, a lot of pointing and bastardized use of nouns.

The boys walked past her and she squirmed around as quietly as possible and watched as they stopped at the steps of the trailer opposite her. The three were laughing, the child she so desperately wanted to talk with pantomiming something that seemed to be hilariously funny to the other two. This was her chance. She backed out from under the truck and crouched at the bumper. She was a good thirty feet away and hadn't been noticed. The boys were still engrossed in conversation.

Waiting until a group of adults came out of the tent, Pauly used the noisy distraction to stand and moved in the shadows to the back of the trailer that was one down but across from the boys. She waited, afraid to move, and realized that her feet were numb with cold. Suddenly the door of the trailer opened and a heavy-set man yelled for the boys to come in. Two of the three scampered up the steps, leaving the third without so much as a wave.

She breathed a sigh of relief…he was alone. Pauly wondered what he was going to do, but she was poised to follow. She'd keep to the shadows of the opposite row of trailers and work her way along parallel to him until he did something, stopped or went into a trailer. She didn't have a plan.

What he did was duck between two trailers parked by a clump of trees. Pauly didn't even give it a second thought but hurried across the road, then, when she was certain that he had had enough of a head start, she plunged into the brush. She couldn't risk losing him. This might be her only chance.

Clouds obscured the moon, but a flashlight was out of the question. Something scurried away from her making soft, furry-body, scratching noises among the twigs and leaves. She didn't let her mind dwell on what it could be. Mice and rats were not favorites. The moon popped out of its hiding place and the stand of trees turned a shimmering silver. She shrank against a young poplar and listened and scanned the thicket. How could she have lost him already? He came this way. Had he seen her?

And then she heard the noise, the muted whoosh of water. Urine, if she didn't miss her guess. He was taking a leak before going back to the trailer. She almost laughed. It suddenly gave a human touch to this creature who haunted her. She waited, staying in the shadows of elm and poplar, then, guessing that she was beside the path that he'd use to return, she slipped to her knees and rocked back on her heels. She'd be less imposing this way. Didn't every elementary teacher intuitively know that he or she was less threatening when eye to eye with the audience?

He didn't stay long but was still zipping his fly as he came into full view. She waited until he was almost upon her, then she simply raised her arm and held the teddy bear in her bare hand out away from her body, offering it in a gesture of friendship. He stopped. She heard the soft intake of breath, saw in his eyes the flickering thought of flight. But he remained.

He was a beautiful child. Porcelain perfect, creamy-tan skin ringed by black-brown curls, hands delicate, not effete, perfectly balanced by a slim body with no hint of puberty. And he seemed naturally shy. There was none of the provocative posturing that she had pictures of. Maybe…just for a second…she could see why this child might be so prized. And then hated herself for thinking that way.

"I want to be your friend, Jorge Roberto Suarez Zuniga—" She paused, then softly added "McIntyre" and watched him. There was no reaction, maybe a slight widening of his eyes. Then keeping her voice low, she repeated "Amiga" and pointed to her chest and then at him. What would he do? Would he acknowledge his name, that she knew who he was? She waited. She could hear her own heartbeat bang in the stillness.

One minute. Two. Still he didn't move, didn't even blink it seemed. He stared at her, but the eyes had softened, lost their fright, their need to escape. Then he took a step forward and gingerly took the teddy bear.

"*Gracias.*" His voice was soft, a caress. She could see how small he was for his age. Words like delicate and frail came to mind. He seemed curious about her and she didn't really feel his hand on her face; it was just a soft tentative touch, the tip of fingers pressing ever so lightly to her cheek and then he was gone, looking back once from the edge of the trees. She waited long after she heard the door of a trailer slam shut.

She knew he wouldn't come back. But somehow it was the weight of all the other things that she knew that kept her from getting up—kept her oblivious to the cold. This child had been adopted by her husband...and maybe was more to him, meant more to him than she had. But the terrible secrecy—if there hadn't been some reason to keep the adoption from her, wouldn't Randy have shared the news with her?

Even Sam Mathers had known. "Hadn't you discussed adoption? Randy had looked into it recently." Weren't those his words? Pauly jerked forward. Sam Mathers. How much did he know about all this? She struggled to her feet, drawing the blanket closer. She'd contact Sam; if he knew about the adoption agency, had an address, she could go there.

And for now she wouldn't pursue trying to get the boy to trust her. She innately knew she'd earn his trust by not pushing herself on him, not making demands that might be misinterpreted. If she wanted to give a voice to what she really hoped for, then she'd admit that she wanted him to come to her. And maybe he would.

Tonight she'd given him the teddy bear. At their next meeting it would be something else. She didn't know what, but she'd think of something...and she wouldn't make him feel cornered. He seemed safe with the carnival; he hadn't tried to leave. But the pictures. Was he still being used? Posed and photographed by someone who was making a lot of money exploiting his vulnerability? Something told her she needed to find answers in a hurry.

◇◇◇

Sam had agreed to see her at nine, even personally met her at the door to the reception area and ushered her into his office. He stopped to pour each of them a cup of coffee at the bar in the back of the room. The scent of hazelnut was pleasing.

"How are you doing?" He was sincere and waited for an answer as he pulled a chair up to his desk for her. He had a way of giving someone his complete attention. It was difficult not to like this man, trust him.

"Better than I thought I'd be doing in this short a time period." Then Pauly filled him in on work. How she was getting involved in the Rio Grande Conservancy project as manager and tech writer. Things were going smoothly. Archer left her alone and Tom was being attentive and that made things easier, but she didn't tell Sam that. The business was flourishing and making her a very rich woman, Sam broke in to add.

"So how can I help you now?" His keen eyes held a wonderful fatherly twinkle. Pauly felt herself relax. She'd rehearsed this part and mentally crossed her fingers that it would work.

"When Randy talked about adoption, he was never particular about age or race. I mean it wasn't necessarily important to him to adopt the customary white baby under six months of age. I have to admit that I was the one who wanted to try to reverse the vasectomy, but if that didn't work, he felt we might not have to stand in line if we worked with a group who specialized in matching children from Mexico or Central America with interested parties in the U.S." Pauly waited and tried to read Sam's expression.

"Are you thinking of adopting a child?" He'd picked up a pencil and was gently tapping the point against the thick blotter in front of him. She didn't think his frown indicated approval.

"Yes. It may sound crazy to you. But I would be doing something that Randy wanted to do…actually, wanted us to do. I could complete something that had been important to him and help someone unfortunate. I certainly have the money—his money. It might be putting it to good use if there were someone to carry on his name. He even mentioned an agency, but I'm afraid that it wasn't important to me at the time. I'm hoping that you might know the name."

"Rings a bell, seems like he mentioned something. Let me check the files."

Sam left the room. There was no indication that he knew about the adoption sanctioned by a Mexican court in Chihuahua, after papers were drawn up by an agency called *Amistad*. She suddenly felt depressed. She had so hoped that Sam could produce the name and address, give her a place to start. She wanted the place to be legitimate, not some front for an operation that pandered to the tastes of lascivious old men, or youngish ones like Randy. But if there weren't a good reason for secrecy, wouldn't Sam have had the original adoption papers in Randy's file here, or, better yet, have been involved in drawing up the papers instead of this Mexican agency?

"This may be what you're looking for." That hadn't taken long, Pauly thought as Sam walked back into the room. "Randy had asked me to check the agency, make sure it was on the up and up a few months back. I'd forgotten about it; I'm afraid other things took precedence." Sam didn't say what "other things," but Pauly guessed that Randy's death was one of them. Sam referred to a legal tablet. "The agency is in El Paso and is listed simply as Amistad…friendship…appropriate name, don't you think? Looks like they have other businesses under the same heading."

"Is there an address or phone?" El Paso. This was better than she had hoped for. They would speak English, at least.

"Both. Let me copy them for you." Sam jotted down the information, and handed her the slip before sinking into a chair beside her. "I'd like to be involved." He waved away the start of her protest. "I think I need to be involved from the standpoint of protecting your interests. Some of these people can be unscrupulous, demanding unbelievable sums of money up front only to deliver a child who may have been abducted." He had leaned over to place a hand on her arm. He smelled crisply clean with a hint of citrus. "Taking them to court can be expensive and ugly. They can embroil you in legal hassles, not to mention the emotional stress and pain."

Pauly sighed. She needed to play along. "What do you suggest?"

"Let me make a few calls. There's a local agency that comes highly recommended. I have two clients who have used them with total satisfaction. Both became eligible within a year to adopt a newborn." Sam leaned across the corner of his desk to pull his Rolodex closer. "Here. Let me add their number." Pauly handed back the piece of paper with the number of the only agency that mattered. But she wasn't going to say that. It couldn't hurt to pretend that she'd do as he suggested.

"There. Now I want you to start here. I have to be frank. I really don't believe parent or child in a mixed-ethnic situation is really happy. My job is to look after you as well as your interests. So my meddling is perfectly within bounds." He smiled and sat back in his chair, steepling his fingers, elbows resting on the only part of his anatomy that might be considered rotund. "I really want you to give this some careful thought. You're still possibly reacting to Randy's death. I'm no shrink, but couldn't you be searching out a replacement for the love that you've lost? Rushing into a lifelong commitment on the strength of misplaced emotion?" He paused and leaned forward. "I hope I haven't spoken out of turn. I've grown to care for you. I don't want anything else to happen to you."

"I understand. I can't tell you how wonderful it's been, how much peace of mind it's given me to have you as both a legal advisor and a friend." Pauly hoped she sounded sincere. And, God knew, she wanted it to be the truth. She carefully folded the slip of paper and tucked it into her purse. She'd found out a part of the information she'd come for. Randy had shared the name of the agency with Sam. That gave a legitimacy to the adoption papers. Jorge was Randy's son. And after Sam's reaction to her wanting to adopt someone other than an Anglo baby, it made sense that Randy hadn't said more to his lawyer.

"Would you like me to make an introductory call?"

"Yes. That would be helpful." She knew he didn't mean to the firm, *Amistad*. And she'd have to play along in order to cover her tracks. It wouldn't hurt to visit a legitimate agency; it would give her something to compare with. "Don't make any promises that I'll see them until after Christmas. Things are a little hectic at work."

"I'll just tell them that you'll call; you can make the appointment. And, Pauly, let me know how it goes." He'd risen when she did and now took her arm and walked her towards the door. The quick hug before he opened it didn't surprise her; he wasn't out of line. Sam Mathers genuinely liked her.

◇◇◇

There were a dozen roses on her desk when she got back to the office—red, this time—and a note that said, "I won't give up." Pauly picked up the phone. This time she'd take the initiative, choose the time and place. Make certain that she would meet Tom in the daylight. Maybe a silly precaution, but lunch should be safe and short. She couldn't continue to ignore him. Not as a partner. Tom's secretary put her through, said she'd been given instructions to interrupt his ten o'clock meeting if Pauly should call.

"The roses are beautiful."

"I'm glad they got your attention."

Same old Tom, but he seemed happy to hear from her.

"What if I said I'd like to take you to lunch? 'Fessed up to feeling a little guilty about breaking our date?"

"Sounds like my lucky day." She could feel Tom relax and slip into his old bantering self. "My choice of place or yours?"

"Mine. I'll meet you at your office at a quarter 'til."

She hung up, then dialed the in-house library service and asked to have all the issues of the local paper that dealt with the water conservancy project sent over. Especially those from the last six months. Research needed to include local opinion, and there was some indication that all was not well. The project wasn't a popular one and wasn't improving with time. Randy had penciled in several questions in the margin of the proposal, and she would follow up. Starting with Tom. He'd offered to be a mentor, and she planned on giving him a chance.

Besides, the group that MDB was teaming with had its headquarters in El Paso. What better excuse to spend a week on the border looking into Amistad than a little legitimate work? She just needed to let Tom know, not necessarily to get his blessing, but to gain his support, if possible.

Then she dialed the agency that Sam had recommended. She might as well get a feel for what they had to offer. She was curious, and maybe it was important that Sam knew she'd taken his advice. He meant well.

At first the receptionist was reluctant to let her talk with a counselor, insisted, in fact, that she make an appointment. But Pauly persevered, dropped Sam Mather's name, said he'd recommended the agency and she only had a few questions, didn't want to waste anyone's time, especially this time of year. She was finally put through. Ms. Perkins sounded bubbly but older. Her own babies were probably grown and now she had an overpowering need to provide this gratifying experience to others. She rattled off her credentials, which included social worker, minor in psych.

"Am I to understand that you are currently not married?"

Ms. Perkin's voice was friendly, but reserved when Pauly mentioned being single. But Randy had been unmarried…at first. Maybe this was a stumbling block.

"I've been recently widowed." That sounded stilted. It was still a word that she couldn't get used to.

"Oh. I'm sorry. May I assume that there would be no financial worries then? Anything that would preclude your being able to provide for a child?"

"Financially, I'm comfortable. There would be no problems."

"We would, of course, need a financial statement."

"Of course."

"Our agency is more concerned with quality of care than having two parents. We all know the divorce statistics today. There are just no guarantees."

You can say that again, Pauly thought to herself but added aloud, "Do you only place babies?"

"Newborns, in fact. All adoptions are completed by five days after birth."

"Do you match prospective parents with the child in some way?"

"Absolutely. In addition to general physical characteristics, we wouldn't want six-foot parents to have a five-foot son, now would we?" Ms. Perkins paused to laugh good naturedly. "We also match for aptitude. We test mothers here at the facility. We hope to screen for any deformities in the genes someday soon. But right now health records are provided by both parties."

"It all sounds so complicated. How is the final choice made?"

"The mother herself. She will be given the scrapbooks of several appropriate prospective parents. She bases her decision on what she views as your potential to provide the kind of home she envisions for her baby."

"A scrapbook?"

"You would be required to put together a pictorial rendering of why you feel you would be a good parent. It's a sales tool. But if you think that's crass, look at it as a way of introducing yourself, showing your potential. They usually include pictures of your house, the baby's room, pets, relatives, anything that will help that mother choose you."

Fleetingly, Pauly thought of her room at the B&B, of Steve's tattoos and Grams' cosmetic chest surgery. And weren't there snakes in the garage? Pauly felt nervous laughter well up and threaten to burst into sound. She cleared her throat. No wonder Randy chose to take another route. She thanked Ms. Perkins and promised to call back after she'd thought about it.

◇◇◇

She'd chosen the Rio Grande Yacht Club for lunch, close enough to have walked, but Tom insisted on driving.

"I think I'm going to put it in the by-laws that the partners, minus one, must have lunch together on a weekly basis."

Tom was kidding but he was attentive, opening the car door for her, pulling out the wicker high-backed chair from the table by the fireplace, ordering two Samuel Adams. She could get used to this.

The waiter recited an incredibly long list of fresh seafood dishes. Tom chose a medley of seafood on a pasta bed; Pauly stayed with the spinach salad. She never ordered anything different. A real lack of risk-taking behavior or imagination— she preferred to think of it as the latter and only when it came to food.

"Noralee says you're jumping right in. Office in order. Staying late." Tom asked for another twist of ground pepper on his salad before the waiter moved away.

"Just trying to impress." She grinned and tried not to think of Noralee spying and running to tell.

"Is everything going well?"

"Actually, yes. It was a good idea to get involved."

"Not too much, too soon?"

"No. Not at all."

Pauly buttered a slice of homemade wheat bread and watched Tom finish his salad. Was she losing her nerve? She might as well just come out with it.

"Tom, I think I'm ready to do a little field work. The first round of reports on the Rio Grande Conservancy project are due the middle of February and I need to be in on the ground floor of the research, attend a few water board meetings in El Paso, that sort of thing. Oversee the hiring of two additional tech writers. It's getting close to Christmas, but I thought I'd go down this week and set up."

She couldn't read his expression. Thoughtful, taking his time, then waiting until after the waiter had set their plates in front of them to comment.

"Bet you wish you could change your order." Tom smiled through the steam that rose from the seafood. And it did smell good, she didn't have to close her eyes to imagine a salty pier jutting out into the ocean, but the calories in the cream-laden sauce weren't inviting. She let him savor a few mouthfuls before she tried to get him back on the subject, the reason she'd taken him to lunch, but, of course, he couldn't know that.

"Is there any reason that I can't just show up on their door-step? I mean after an introductory call? Or should one of you two set it up for me?"

"Do you really know what you're getting into?"

"What do you mean?"

"Well, for example, whose side are you on?"

"I'm not following."

"Do you think Texas or Arizona, or even California for that matter, should have a claim to New Mexico's water?"

Was this a test? Just a little check to see if her homework was done?

"First of all, a writer hired to report the project findings better be non-partisan." She paused to smile. "But, secondly, I think this is a landmark case. New Mexico's water rights have never been challenged before. The state has never been pressured into selling like it's being now. Our recommendations will get a lot of attention whichever way they go."

"Getting involved means a lot to you, doesn't it?" Tom put down his fork.

"Yes."

"Why? And don't give me some crap about carrying on Randy's work because I won't buy it."

Pauly tried to figure out what he was getting at. Maybe if she asked him about his relationship with Randy….

"Did you dislike Randy?"

"Dislike might be too harsh a word. He was Archer's friend, old school chum, and as you must know, it was Randy's money that got us started." That was a surprise, but she tried not to show it as he continued. "Randy was a taker, a user of people, almost flat emotionally—hey, I shouldn't be saying this. I apologize. I'm out of line."

"No. Please go on. I asked. I need to see him through others' eyes. I've found out that I didn't know him very well myself."

"I'll admit that I was shocked that you two got married so fast. I don't think marriage would have been what I would have predicted for Randy at any time."

"Care to share what you thought his future held?" She was curious now.

"Oh, a bachelor life, something sedentary with a stack of books." He looked away to catch the waitress' eye with a wave of his empty beer bottle, and Pauly knew he was lying. Tom had a good idea of what he thought would happen to Randy and it wasn't research.

"Pauly, I...." He had turned back, then stopped again as the waitress brought a fresh beer. He waited until she had moved on to the next table. "This project is controversial, you know that. I guess I've thought that some special interest groups might have wished Randy weren't involved, even taken measures to ensure that he wasn't."

"Including murder?" she asked.

He nodded.

Had he shared this with the police? Or was all this some kind of smoke screen for her benefit? Scare her off the project. She watched as he looked down at his plate, moved some linguini around, then speared a scallop and popped it into his mouth, swallowing before going on.

"There are some special interest groups that are pretty hot under the collar, scared to death that the project could divert water resources, cheat them with a rationing that would severely limit growth in their area, even make industrial expansion impossible. The politics have been just this side of nasty."

"Who seems to be the most vocal?"

"Representatives from the South Valley."

"Sosimo Garcia?" She took a sip of beer.

"Congressman Garcia is the leader. Have you ever met Sosimo?"

Pauly nodded, not trusting herself to speak. This was a new wrinkle—a very interesting one. Had Randy been in the process of buying the Congressman's support? Or tying him up politically with potentially dangerous material for blackmail? It put Randy in an unenviable position of knowing too much. And now her. And it could change what she'd suspected about Randy's being a pedophile. Maybe, just maybe she'd been wrong. But no. Before she got too excited, there was still his son....

"Have I lost you?" Tom was leaning across the table watching her intently. Had her face given her away? Registered the misgivings that she felt?

"The project isn't as straightforward as I thought," Pauly said.

"Exactly. Not when you're talking about life-sustaining resources and a lot of money invested. The Village of Corrales is still hassling Intel Corporation about water rights."

"You really think someone wanted to get rid of Randy?"

"I feel like I'm telling tales out of school here, but, yes, I think someone wanted to slow down the project. Taking out the lead hydrologist has done just that."

"Did you share your theory with the police?"

"Umhmmm. They seemed interested, took a lot of notes, anyway."

"What would the South Valley gain by slowing down the project?"

"Time to investigate on their own, build a stronger lobbying group, cross a few palms with silver. They could even woo industry now and put themselves in a position to have their resources already pledged."

"You really think the project is a dangerous one?"

"After Randy's death, yes. I'd like to dissuade you from getting involved, but something tells me you might be difficult to sidetrack."

She smiled. It was true. At some level this information about Sosimo only made her more adamant about finding answers. "So, I'm going to give you the old lecture on being careful, not overstepping bounds. That is, be exceptionally careful not to draw conclusions from any of the research. Let the guys getting paid for analysis do their job. You stick to the recording end of it."

Pauly thought he was about to say something else then decided against it. She waited, finished her spinach salad and ordered coffee.

"There's one other thing." Tom paused. "I don't want you to misinterpret this, but Archer prides himself on being able to oil the waters. He's been wining and dining Sosimo and feels he has the congressman where he wants him." I'll just bet he does, Pauly thought. "It might be best if you played dumb concerning the political side of the water project. I'm afraid it was my idea to share with you. Archer probably wouldn't be too pleased."

"No problem."

"And then there's the party. Sosimo is having a little 'do' this Wednesday, a holiday thing; he does it every year. It's not something we can get out of as representatives of the firm. I think it might be wise if we go together."

"Pretty slick way to get a date," Pauly said and they both laughed. But he was right; she knew she'd feel better arriving on the arm of Tom Dougal. *Better* in this case meaning safer.

Chapter Seven

It had been the fifteenth dress that Pauly had tried on, cognac satin above the knee and strapless, from one of Albuquerque's better stores, which made it far too expensive, a designer-exclusive wisp of material that fell perfectly, hiding a too-long waist and pushing up a chest that always needed help to be noticed. She hadn't wanted to wear black, not just because it denoted mourning, but because everyone wore black and the color of this dress matched her hair, seemed to lift the chestnut highlights and warm her skin.

Shoes were a combination of tiny, twisted, two-tone bronze leather straps that caressed her instep and tied around her ankle, tethering her to three-inch squarish, pencil-thin heels which boosted her to a whopping five foot eleven. How could Italian designers turn a few leather straps into something orgasmic? Americans couldn't do that.

The outfit had a little bit of a hooker flare to it, but she thought it would be perfect for Sosimo's party, a real attention-getter. She slicked her usual fly-away, fluffy mass of hair back into a classic bun at the nape of her neck, added diamond drop earrings—real, her grandmother assured her—a faux lynx jacket, and she was ready.

She hadn't seen Steve standing in the kitchen doorway while she primped in front of the hall mirror until she caught his reflection. And just for a moment before he whispered "knockout" she had seen the admiration as his eyes traveled down her backside, lingering a moment first on her legs and then the heels.

"Hot date?" Did he sound a little irked?

"Company obligation, stockholder shindig." She blotted her lipstick, bronzed peach, and hoped that Steve would wander off before Tom rang the doorbell. But no such luck. Steve seemed rooted until he heard the bell, and then he quickly moved to open the door.

"Well, if it isn't Prince Charming." Steve bowed obsequiously to usher Tom in. Why was he being such an ass? Pauly moved to intercept any more snide remarks. But Tom, impeccable in tux and topcoat, gallant in spite of his introduction, was shaking Steve's hand. Then turning to her, he said, "My god, you're stunning. The dress is perfect, the designer had to have had you in mind. No one else could wear it."

Pauly smiled her thanks but barely before Steve added, "Oh, I don't know, I thought I saw the same little number on the corner of Central and Carlisle the other night."

Tom's eyes narrowed at the obvious reference to the attire chosen by prostitutes. Pauly was appalled. And hurt. Was Steve drunk? One would think—and she hoped Tom didn't—that she was somehow important to this tattooed man who now, on some junior-high level, was marking off his territory by belittling her.

"You're out of line, Steve. I don't deserve that," Pauly said with just the right amount of frost. Then she picked up her jacket and started towards the door. Tom followed then turned and took a parting shot, "Hey pal, don't wait up for us." The smirk leaked through his voice.

Jesus, Pauly cursed to herself without looking back, why didn't the two just duke it out in the driveway. But she was more than a little flattered. To say the least, the dress was working, threw two males into an early rut.

◇◇◇

Albuquerque's South Valley was an enigma. And Pauly would be the first to admit that she could get lost even sticking to the major thoroughfares like Broadway and Isleta Boulevard. But in the center of his constituency, Sosimo's rambling adobe commanded attention. It was a walled fort. There was an entrance manned by armed guards, a winding mile-long drive through manicured lawns, valets parking cars communicating via walkie-talkies with the gate.

"Does it up right, doesn't he?" Tom slowed to pull into a line of cars inching towards the front of the house.

"I had no idea."

"You'll see everyone who is anyone here tonight. In addition to the company, I can vouch for the food and music, A-plus for both." Tom stopped and Pauly gathered purse and jacket as a smiling young man opened the door to help her out under the portico ablaze with light.

"Have I mentioned in the last half hour how gorgeous you look?" Tom took her arm as they started up the steps to the front door. "You know I'd like to beat out your tattooed friend for your favors, become the one and only."

Whatever else Tom was going to say was drowned out by Sosimo's booming welcome, which also saved her from trying to explain why an office romance, even among principals, wasn't a good idea. Pauly paused while the small man took her hand. She was a little sorry that she towered over Sosimo but knew that next to Tom's six foot two frame, they made an attention-catching couple.

"What a beauty you are. Thomas is incredibly lucky." Sosimo bent over her hand and pressed her knuckles against his lips. His mustache felt stiff and chafed as he murmured, "You do me a great honor." Then with a wink, he dropped her hand and moved on to welcome a couple in back of them.

Oily-smooth, used to being in control, the patron of all this. Pauly suppressed a little shiver of fear. This was a man who didn't let very much stand in the way of getting what he wanted. Just how much of a threat was the water project? If water was diverted from the South Valley, if his lobbying failed, would it be enough to strip him of his office, get him unseated? Maybe.

But the loss of power would be unthinkable. He would not allow that to happen, and to assure that it did not might mean taking drastic steps....

"Awesome, isn't it? I'll be right back." Tom helped her off with the jacket and walked to a coat check in a cordoned-off area on her left. The room Tom referred to spread out before her, opening to view flanked by two granite pillars. Six crystal chandeliers shot daggers of light across opulent pink marble floors laid in slabs with seams that were almost undetectable. An orchestra filled an area to the back that might normally serve as a sun porch.

As Tom took her arm to walk down the three short steps to the ballroom-sized dance floor, heads turned. Appreciative once-overs from the men, and a few barely veiled jealous stares from women. Pauly was beginning to feel that the dress was one of her best investments, and she began to relax. Tom, the ever-perfect escort, introduced her as a business partner and made sure she met the who's who of New Mexico. He reluctantly gave her up as a dance partner, but not often, and mostly monopolized her himself.

Was she surprised when Sosimo sent a servant to summon her to the study sometime before midnight? Not really. It was something she dreaded, being alone with him, but oddly something that she had expected might happen, a little chat to get to know her better. She thought Tom looked at her questioningly when he realized that the invitation didn't include him. But she smiled and whispered, "Must be anxious to grill the new partner alone." She barely caught his whispered, "Be careful," as she turned to follow the young man who was walking back along the edge of the dance floor.

The study had been professionally decorated for Christmas by a florist—or was there a Mrs. Garcia? One hadn't been present in the receiving line; Pauly must remember to ask Tom. But surely this mass of poinsettia, all whites, stacked ten deep around the fireplace and evergreen boughs chained together to loop across mantle and windows and French doors supporting golden angels with trumpets had a designer's touch?

"The room is beautiful." Pauly took Sosimo's hand as he chivalrously guided her over the threshold, dismissing the servant and closing the big heavy door securely behind them. Pauly tried not to flinch at the solid thud but continued to walk into the room marveling at the deep pile of the maroon carpet.

"Won't you sit with me by the fire?" Sosimo had pointed to two comfortable overstuffed chairs in an old fashioned chintz-inspired floral pattern. Now, that could be the touch of a woman. But that was about all. The fireplace, especially, in floor to ceiling rock was overwhelmingly masculine. She felt dwarfed by the room.

She sat opposite Sosimo and resisted the urge to tug at the short dress which rode high up her thigh. It was just a little more leg than she usually revealed, and wasn't this a business meeting? And he made her uncomfortable. That was the bottom line. Uncomfortable because of his vested interest in the project and almost manic when she thought of the pictures. Plain and simple, she knew too much to be here now, alone, trying to appear the gracious guest, play the naive widow. And he was studying her, brashly letting those small black eyes flit over her face.

"I've given much thought to why I've asked you to meet with me now. I need to be assured that I am doing the right thing."

Pauly waited. This didn't seem to be an opening to a business meeting. She watched as he stood and then moved to his desk, pulled out the middle drawer, retrieved something and returned to the fire. He hesitated only a moment before placing a narrow black velvet box on the coffee table between them. A jeweler's box, the kind that could hold expensive gifts. Was he going to bribe her? Dangle some bauble in exchange for promises to bend her findings in the water project? Was he about to buy her allegiance?

"I was forced to miss your wedding because of business. A group of congressmen were invited to tour a new power plant in the Virgin Islands, I was asked to go. There are some fringe benefits to government service." A wry smile. Pauly smiled back. But where was this leading? "My dear friend Randy asked me if I could pick up a piece of jewelry for him while I was there, knowing that there is usually more value for your dollar in the islands. And he had something very special in mind. It was a present for you. Actually, a Christmas present, because he was afraid that he would have to travel over the holidays. And since this would have been your first Christmas together and you would be spending it alone, the gift had to be extraordinary." His voice was soft; his face showed compassion.

Pauly hoped the incredulity that she felt didn't show. What a bunch of hogwash. How could he be so transparent? Randy asking him to buy an expensive gift? She doubted that. He had made a big deal over giving her his mother's pearls before the wedding. But he had never given her something expensive that he had bought. She realized that Sosimo was holding out the box, expecting her to take it. Well, why not? Why not carry this little farce to its limit.

The box had a gold clasp that could have been fourteen karat; Pauly couldn't tell in the light from the fire. But the case was expensive. If it was a foreshadowing of what was inside, she could be very pleasantly surprised. It took a little pressure to nudge the lid upward but when it sprang free, held open by hidden hinges, Pauly gasped. Nestled in pale gold satin was a diamond tennis bracelet. But not just any tennis bracelet. This one was seven inches of half-carat canary yellow diamonds. Not irradiated, she was almost certain of that, but the real thing, true deep yellow sparkling diamonds of top quality.

"May I?" Sosimo leaned forward and, slipping the bracelet from the box, encircled her wrist, struggling a moment with the clasp. The diamonds danced in the firelight, shimmering along her bare skin. And then she saw the note in the top of the velvet case, a holiday card with embossed gold foil bells in one corner, the kind that might accompany a gift. "Merry Christmas, darling. When you look at this, think of me and I'll be with you." It was signed simply, "Randy."

She felt her hands grow cold and shake just enough to wiggle the case. What irony. Like someone telling you to try not to stare at the left eye of the camel…of course she would think of him each and every time. She didn't need, didn't want reminders. So would she keep the bracelet? But how could she turn it down without raising suspicion? Without saying that even though it looked like Randy's handwriting, he would never call her "darling"—or, at least, never had.

But what if it were true? What if he had planned ahead, planned some incredible gift to sweep her off her feet when he wasn't there? A gift of apology, a gift he'd planned to give her two months into their young marriage because he was going to be off somewhere on business? There was a time when she would have believed that. But now? She didn't know what to believe. It was like a giant hand pushing up from the grave to clutch at her throat, suffocating her with memories and anger sparked by unforgivable lies. Who was it who had said that there was a thin line between love and hate?

"It's perfect for you." Sosimo gently turned her arm so that the firelight caught in the band and exploded into hundreds of tiny winking golden sparkles.

Say something appropriate, Pauly told herself, then get out of there.

"How did you know I love the color yellow in stones? I have an old topaz ring that I've practically worn out."

"Randy had an eye for detail, he took note of things. I'm only guessing that he may not have always been able to express himself, but Pauly—you were the best thing that had ever happened to him. He said that to me, over and over. He wanted this bracelet to be uniquely yours. I had explicit instructions as to what to look for, right down to the yellow diamonds."

Could it be true? Randy used to tease her about the topaz ring, made her toss it in a drawer when the band wore through. Who else could have known that she would have picked this very bracelet for herself? Purchased it, that is, if she had had an extra fifteen or twenty thousand in her pocket.

It was uncanny. But only because she'd buried any happy memories of Randy, not allowed herself to think that he might have cared for her. Not after what she'd discovered. And now? How did this bracelet change things? Because it did. And she couldn't help it. Suddenly the spirit of the man she'd spent two months learning to hate filled the room, hovered over her, beamed back at her from a couple dozen twinkling diamonds.

"Did I do the right thing? Perhaps, I should have waited." Sosimo was leaning towards her. He must have read the confusion in her face. Instinctively Pauly masked her feelings. Then, appearing to struggle for emotional control, she simply nodded, pressed fingers to the corners of her eyes to keep imaginary tears from falling, and swallowed hard. She squeezed his hand and was pleased with her performance when she felt him relax.

"Yes, you did the right thing. I appreciate your thoughtfulness. Randy would have been thrilled. I'm thrilled by your choice. But this is all so…overwhelming." Pauly rose, picked up the case but left the bracelet on her wrist. "Thank you." Sosimo didn't follow her as she walked to the door.

She let herself out and sought the first bathroom along the hall on the way back to the ballroom. Just in case she was being watched. It would make sense to collect herself, and maybe that wasn't a lie. She felt lightheaded, a little buzz of lingering shock. She glanced at the bracelet. It was the last thing she would have associated with Sosimo. But what was his relationship with Randy? She was already having to remind herself about the pictures, about Sosimo's sexual tastes, and maybe Randy's preferences as well.

She barely acknowledged her surroundings, more pink marble, walls, sink tops, sinks, and floor as she pushed open the restroom door and sank onto a settee. Automatically she started to unfasten the bracelet, then stopped. What if Sosimo saw her again before they left? How could she be so overcome with emotion and then race down the hall to take it off? She checked her makeup instead and tried to ignore the fiery blasts of color that bounced back at her from the mirror.

Tom looked anxious as she approached the table and slipped into a chair beside him.

"How'd it go?"

Instead of answering she simply held her arm up.

"What? If that's what I think it might be—"

"It isn't a bribe. But it's a long story." Suddenly Pauly realized how tired she was, fatigued, mentally and physically. "Could we leave?" It would feel good to get out of there.

"How about a cup of coffee somewhere?" Tom followed her across the dance floor. There was no Sosimo at the door and they got a valet's attention and were in the car without anyone saying good-by.

The "somewhere" turned out to be a posh little bistro on Central in the Nob Hill area, one of those quiet, white-table-clothed restaurants that stayed open until two a.m. and served fabulous dessert coffees. A jolt of espresso might be just what she needed.

They hadn't talked on the half-hour drive back into town. Pauly was thankful for that, but she didn't miss Tom's tight jaw when she glanced his way. Let him think what he wanted. She was still trying to collect her own thoughts, decide how she really felt and how much she wanted to share with him. All the time the diamonds lay coolly against her wrist, moving when she moved, catching in the plush of her jacket, a reminder of so much.

She waited until the waitress had shown them to a table in the loft. Then she drew the jewelry case out of her purse, snapped it open and handed it to Tom. She watched him read the note in the top. They both waited until the waitress had taken their order, then Tom said, "From Randy? I don't understand."

She explained. Told Tom exactly what had happened in Sosimo's study, no more, no less, pointedly leaving out her mixture of feelings. How she was becoming comfortable with Randy's deceit, how it had erased any feelings of love and certainly truncated the period of mourning. And now this.

"It's got to be tough on you. I'm sorry. This is like coming back from the dead." Tom reached over and took her hand, the one without the bracelet dangling from her wrist. "You must be wondering when it all will end. You've got to be reminded of Randy every day at the office. Now the bracelet." He went through combing motions with his fingers, trying to keep a lock of salt and pepper hair off his forehead, a nervous gesture done automatically.

"What are you going to do, Pauly? I don't think anyone can expect you to continue to be the martyr, try to carry on in Randy's place. It's got to be painful."

She was saved an answer by the waitress bringing their coffees, and Pauly took the time to run a twist of lemon peel around the rim of her cup. She was so tempted to share with him, just spill everything out on the table and for once have help in sorting the pieces. But how could she even consider such a thing? There was every possibility that Tom was into the child porn thing the same as Archer seemed to be. She couldn't take a chance. Instead she watched him wipe the froth of cappuccino off his upper lip.

"It's not the way I saw my life. That I'll admit."

"How did you see your life?"

"Babies. A big house. Lots of PTA and scouts. Junior League. Maybe another degree someday."

"Is that what Randy promised?"

She nodded. She couldn't read the look on his face. Did he know that that promise was a sham? He started to say something but instead bent his head over his coffee, this time removing the remaining foam with a spoon.

"I'm going to El Paso in the morning. I'll meet with the firm we're teaming with, see what they need, map out how we'll coordinate the reports."

"I wish you wouldn't." Tom put his spoon down and took both of her hands in his. "I see this as torture. Why are you subjecting yourself to this, forcing yourself to be reminded of Randy…putting yourself in danger, if my guess is correct about Sosimo? This is a tough project. I don't want you hurt."

Pauly mentally felt her heels dig in. She had such a difficult time with people telling her what to do, and she had to go to El Paso. Now more than ever. The Amistad agency might hold the answers. She prayed that it did. Who was the man who had ordered the canary yellow diamonds? Lover-husband? Manipulator? Sicko? She had a right to know.

"How can I assure you that I know what I'm doing, that it's important to me to be involved? I'll be careful."

Tom didn't look convinced, but he dropped the subject. They finished their coffees with nothing more than small talk. On the drive back to the house he tried one more time, almost begged her to become active in the company in some other way, said he had a couple of other projects in mind that could use her touch. Window-dressing, inconsequential tasks probably, something he'd consider a woman good at, Pauly thought. Their parting kiss lacked conviction. His heart wasn't in it. But neither was hers. The bracelet rattled around her arm as a reminder of other things, sort of a chastity belt worn on the wrist. It certainly put a damper on any romantic thoughts. He left without saying anything else about the trip to El Paso.

The house was dark except for a couple of strategically placed nightlights in the hall. She locked the front door before walking back towards the kitchen. Was she surprised to find Steve sitting on a stool at the butcher-block island nursing a cup of coffee and obviously waiting on her? Not really. She knew there would be an apology. And he looked awful; suffering didn't become him.

"Good party?" He sounded sober and looked unbelievably handsome slouched over the tabletop, a navy, loose-fitting cable knit sweater over a chambray shirt. The soft light coming from the hood over the stove muted his features and the ever-present art work. This was certainly her night for good-looking men. And it was almost easy to believe that this one really liked her. Didn't the boyish outburst earlier in the evening prove that?

"So-so." Pauly unbuckled her shoes, slipped them off, rubbed her right instep before pulling up a stool. She wasn't sure why it felt good to have a little company, but it did. It kept her from rehashing the evening, turning it over yet again in her mind—Randy, Sosimo, Tom's adamant stance about her quitting the project. She watched Steve's eyes rest a second on the bracelet but he didn't comment.

"Beer? Coffee?" he asked.

"I've probably had enough of both."

She got up and got a glass of water, padding past him to the sink on stockinged feet, and felt his eyes follow. The saltillo tiles were warmed from underneath, circulating hot water in pipes buried in the floor; it felt incredibly good on feet that had been pushed to their limits by fashion.

"I was really out of line earlier," he said.

She didn't say anything as she scooted her stool closer to the table.

"I was a jackass," he added, all the time watching her.

He waited to make eye contact, then held it. "The last thing I want to do is drive you away. And that's all I seem to be good at."

She heard the frustration in his voice and thought of the ski mask. She suddenly realized how much she wanted him to be innocent. But still, it made her wary....

"Any chance I might be forgiven?"

It was difficult to resist him; there was no way that she could stop the smile that tugged at the corners of her mouth. She reached across and took his hand and checked a tiny shiver of pleasure that shot up her arm and registered almost painfully somewhere in the pit of her stomach, but not before his eyes had given away the effect touching had had on him. Even knowing what she did, this man could still jolt her senses, weaken her knees, make her think of—damn...she needed to get out of here.

"Early day tomorrow." She took a sip of water, then pulled back and slipped off the stool, bending to retrieve her shoes. He followed her along the dark hall, the stairway to her bedroom being just beyond the back door.

"Thanks for listening. I wasn't sure what to expect," he said. She let him pull her around to face him, the narrow walkway making touching inevitable.

"Don't misinterpret forgiveness for an invitation." She was curt. But she must not have sounded too convincing because he laughed and brought her chin up so that he was looking in her eyes. Then he lightly kissed her forehead, waiting that split-second, letting his finger trace her jaw line before he kissed her on the mouth, hands suddenly pressing into her back, pushing her into him hard, his hunger raw and real, and she responding. Then he pulled away, both of them breathless, and forced himself to kiss her again on the forehead and just hold her.

"I don't know where all this is going to lead," he whispered with his mouth tickling her ear. "But we're not going to get there too quickly this time." He pulled back and grinned. "I'm impressing you with my remarkable restraint, right?"

She laughed. But she wasn't exactly feeling relief. She watched him put on his jacket and move to the door, open it and disappear into the darkness.

"Thanks a lot," she said, more or less in the general direction of the bracelet.

◇◇◇

She felt exhilarated; she'd slept longer than she had meant to. So much for the plan to head out at the crack of dawn. It was more like the crack of ten thirty before she gassed up the pickup and headed south on I-25 out of Albuquerque. With a couple of stops and depending on whether she saw a lot of patrolmen, the trip to El Paso would take about five hours.

But today was the day for solving puzzles. She felt it. The Amistad adoption agency would cough up some answers, and she'd be asking the questions. The red short-bed Chevy truck was a good choice of vehicle, but she was taking it mostly out of guilt for not having even started it in two months. If she was going to sell it, she needed to know something about it other than its color. Then again, she might take the time to go out to the project site or detour along Elephant Butte and check water levels; then she'd need its maneuverability. Whatever she decided, it felt great to have a day ahead of her with so much promise.

She'd slipped on a pair of Levi's, no hose or heels. She'd had it with dressing up, especially the heels part; her arches still ached from last night. But she fastened the bracelet around her wrist. How truly Santa Fean, a study in scruffiness, until the diamonds peeked out from under the cuff of her flannel shirt. Outdoor chic. She checked in the mirror, shaking her wrist to make the bracelet dance in the light, and thought she'd captured the look exactly, then laughed.

To save time she wrapped a couple of warm flour tortillas in foil, breakfast on the run, but it would do until she decided to stop for lunch. She'd try to get as far down the road as she could before her stomach started growling.

Socorro whizzed by after fifty minutes on the road and the landscape looked its bleakest. Of course, she reminded herself, it was late December, when the starkness of the flat browns became monotones until Elephant Butte Lake broke up the view.

She stopped for coffee in nearby Truth or Consequences. Strange how the town's one claim to fame was a TV show that few people now remembered. She chose a diner that inevitably reeked of cigarette smoke. She guessed it would be difficult to find a smoke-free place here. This was a retirement town for duffers. Duffers having coffee, reading the newspaper, arguing politics, poking fun at other duffers. This was real lakeside geezerville. She decided to get the coffee to go, then ordered a cheeseburger and sat down at the counter.

It had been a good idea to take a break. She felt invigorated once back on the road and welcomed the sight of the Organ Mountains outside Las Cruces. She kept on the by-pass and missed any college traffic from New Mexico State. The four and a half hour trip was just beginning to get tiring when the I-25 signs announced only thirty more miles to El Paso. She'd planned to stay the night, find the adoption agency as soon as she could check into a motel and shower, take whatever time was needed to find out what they knew about Randy and Jorge. Dinner might be someplace in Juarez, and then in the morning, she'd appear on the doorstep of the teaming firm bright and early.

A decent motel was easy to find. The one she decided on boasted cable, a hot tub, and a phone in every room. She pulled in more than a little pleased to see security guards walking the parking area along an eight-foot-high chain-link fence that defined the back and sides of the property. She wasn't worried for her own safety, but El Paso was notorious for offering an open invitation to car thieves. Living on the border had its drawbacks. And a brand-new red Chevy truck was pretty tempting.

Her room was on the back, ground-level, the usual shag carpet and swag lamps in greens and orange. But the shower felt good. It was early, only four o'clock, but already beginning to get dark when she pulled on a white shirt, tucked in the tail, and adjusted the silver concho belt over the broomstick-pleated red bandanna skirt. Black mock-cowboy boots, a red and black blanket-vest, and she was ready. Now she looked more than a little Santa Fean, but nice. There was a full-length mirror on the back of the closet door. She checked the hem; the skirt hung straight. She wanted to look good, but not necessarily bowl them over with anything too dressy or too casual. She tucked the bracelet out of sight under a cuff.

She hadn't decided whether to just show up or call for an appointment. There were pluses and minuses to each approach. Calling finally won out. She decided she could fake it, sound like someone desperate for their services, in need of a consultation. She was glad she'd called the other agency in Albuquerque and wondered vaguely if this agency demanded a scrapbook. Probably not.

She dialed the number that Sam had given her. On the third ring it transferred to electronic equipment that squealed in her ear and announced in a halting monotone that the number she was trying to reach was out of service at this time. She took the voice's advice and dialed it again, positive that, in fact, she had "reached this recording in error." But no, once again, the screech and voice. She hung up, then dialed the operator and asked for assistance.

Again, nothing. The number was not in service. There were no other listings for an Amistad agency. She even checked Triple A, thinking that there could have been an Americanization of Amistad Adoption Agency. But, no luck; she only got the auto service. Reluctantly, she put down the phone.

Then on impulse she dialed the operator again. Could she tell her when the Amistad agency's phone had been disconnected?

She couldn't, that information came under some privacy act. Pauly hung up. Did it really matter when? Didn't Pauly know for a fact that the agency was in service a scant three months ago? Didn't the adoption papers give the date as one month before the wedding?

She was kicking herself that she hadn't brought a copy of the papers. She wasn't sure why she hadn't. She had halfway planned on telling the truth—that Randy was dead, but she, the widow was very concerned for the child—if the agency seemed on the up and up. And if they were, wouldn't they have a copy of the papers? She had the picture with her of Randy and Jorge. That should jog some memories.

But now what? She could check other agencies if there were any. If one went out of business, would the owners consolidate services? Pass on records and business to another? But that could wait until after she'd checked the address. Maybe they were just closed for the holidays. But that didn't really explain the disconnection. Couldn't there be some kind of phone trouble, some reason she couldn't get through? Other than not paying their bill, nothing came to mind.

She walked out to the truck and got a map of El Paso from the glove compartment and spread it out on the bed. She had no idea where River Street was. When she found it, it looked like it was almost on the border; certainly it twisted along close to it. So much for the vague hope that she'd be trying to locate a plush office complex in the middle of downtown.

She folded the map; like parallel parking, it was something she was proud of being able to do. Sexist, but weren't those a couple of things for which her birth certificate somehow said she had no talent? The truck cab was warm. She rolled down the window, then decided to test the air-conditioning and rolled it back up. Air-conditioning in December at four-thirty in the afternoon. Even this far south of Albuquerque, the weather was unseasonably warm.

The tinselly Christmas decorations trailing across busy streets looked forlorn, with plastic snowmen and multicolored carolers hugging light posts. Maybe a foot of snow would perk them up. It was just difficult to get into the holiday spirit when it was sixty-two degrees outside. One thing was for certain, she'd never be able to live where they decorated palm trees for the holidays.

Pauly drove across town hoping she'd read the map correctly. It seemed like she was awfully close to the border. Then she saw it. River was the next street to the left. Pauly slowed, waited for the light to change, and then swung the red pickup into the left lane and through the intersection, noticing a Dead End sign on her right. There was very little traffic, probably because of the time of year.

River Street was in what looked to be an industrial part of town. Warehouses, barn-big metal buildings with ramps and turn-around areas, lined both sides of the street for the first block.

Except for a few parked cars, there was no sign of life. The second block held an assortment of businesses, but ones that needed storage, like a ceramic tile company, a paper warehouse, and a fenced area in front of a portable building that guarded a few thousand clay flower pots stacked one on top of the other, opening side down. Garden statuary, squirrels, rabbits, turtles, several supplicant St. Francises ringed the fence next to cement-mold fountains. All had the look of having been there too long.

The word "grubby" came to mind…maybe "dingy" was more descriptive. Everything needed a coat of paint and some caring. Trash, indiscriminate papers, food wrappers, fliers, sheets of newspaper were caught here and there along the curb. One company's driveway looked like an oil slick, which didn't say a lot for the condition of its trucks.

Pauly slowed to read the number on the business called Pottery Land. The Amistad agency should be in the next block, the last block before the street ended. She accelerated but kept an eye on the right-hand side. There—the yuccas should have given it away. It was the only building with any kind of planting in the front. A half dozen of the tall, spiked arid-land lovers stood as sentinels beside the entrance. As Pauly pulled into the empty parking lot, she could see that the middle one was dead and leaned precariously against the building. An evergreen bed of arborvitae shaggily spilled over a two-brick-high border that ran along the front then curved out of sight. Not much, but the touch of green had probably brightened things up.

At one time the parking lot had been a smooth layer of asphalt. But it had long since given up the battle with nature, and clumps of dried grasses erupted at asymmetrical intervals. Pauly didn't want to acknowledge the feeling of emptiness that the place exuded. She had come so far to be disappointed. She rolled down the window and slouched against the armrest. There was no sign of life, no human; she watched a yellow mutt lift a leg on the nearest yucca before trotting out of view.

The building was another portable. The street seemed to sprout them. This one had sage-green metal siding with a darker green metal overhang. The front door and the four large windows across the front were trimmed in brown. And all had bars, decorative, wrought-iron, sturdy, break-in-proof protection. And that didn't surprise her. This wasn't the most populated of neighborhoods nor, probably, the best part of town.

What a strange area to house an adoption agency. The entire office couldn't be more than twelve to fifteen hundred square feet, Pauly thought. Certainly in comparison to its neighbors, the place was dinky. But maybe she was jumping to conclusions. There were no signs proclaiming this was the right place, no name in gilded letters on the door; only the numbers in dimestore-cheap metal that had been nailed above the door matched the address Sam had given her.

The windows were bare of curtains and someone had tagged the panel by the door with graffiti. The building looked unused, looked like it had sat empty for a long time. But she just didn't want to give up, to have to give up hope, not yet. Five o'clock shadows pushed across the parking lot. The sun had almost set. Pauly shivered and started to roll up the window.

"Hey lady, me watch your car?"

She jumped. She had been too preoccupied to notice the slight brown-skinned boy who had walked up to the driver's-side window. She wasn't really certain what he'd asked to do, wash or watch? She asked him to repeat himself.

"Watch my car?" She said it once more to be sure.

He nodded.

"I don't see anybody around here who looks like trouble."

He shrugged, put his hands in faded jeans pockets and leaned closer.

"Sometimes biggest trouble you no can see."

He had her on that one. She agreed wholeheartedly. But he was assuming that she was going in, would be getting out of the truck. But to do what? Maybe to prove to herself that she hadn't wasted a trip, she should check out the facility, just look around. She was having a tough time overcoming her disappointment.

"How much?" She'd learned the hard way once to get prices settled up front. And she'd also learned that rejection of services could mean that your vehicle would be vandalized.

"Five." He held up five fingers, palm outward.

"And I bet not cents."

His look went beyond disdain. Like she had made the poorest excuse of a joke. So, five dollars it was; she'd spent more to probably get less and she was curious. She'd like to snoop a bit around the back of the building. Maybe the trash would tell her something. And it was getting dark. Knowing the truck had a miniature guard made her feel pretty good…five dollars' worth, at least.

"You pay now?"

"Do I look dumb?" She'd reached under the seat and felt around for the flashlight, put it in her purse, then got out of the truck, rolled up the window, pushed the door shut and locked it.

"I'll pay when I get back and see what kind of job you've done."

A sly smile bent the corner of his mouth.

"You pretty smart."

"Thanks."

She started towards the front door, then turned back.

"You know what kind of business this is?" She pointed to the building.

He shrugged, "Nothing now."

"But what used to be here?"

Again the shrug and a shake of the head. She couldn't tell if he knew or not; dusk had obscured his features. She watched as he ran around to the back of the truck, hopped onto the back bumper, swung a leg into the truck-bed and waved to her as he leaned over the cab. She waved back. Cute kid, not unlike a certain other dark-haired child who was the reason for her trip here, she thought.

She stood a moment to look at the building. There were no windows along the side. Odd. Must make the place dark inside. She picked her way over and around the jungle-growth of low-lying evergreens. The back of the building had two small barred windows, maybe bathrooms. And there was a Dumpster, close to the building just this side of the back door. Now that looked promising. She hoisted the lid but a quick swish of light told her it had been recently emptied.

It wasn't until she stepped around the Dumpster and let the flashlight play along the windows and door that she noticed the back door didn't have bars. As she got closer, she could see that the bars had been pried off and had been left hanging to one side. The back door, in fact, was open, not by much, maybe two inches, but the invitation was there.

Pauly didn't listen to any of her customary inner voices. There was no excuse for what she was doing; trespassing might be the least of what it could be called. But she had to know. If there was any shred of information, anything that gave legitimacy to the adoption, any hint of where the agency might have gone, she had to find out.

At least she was smart enough to nudge the door open with her purse and not touch anything. She'd make sure she didn't leave fingerprints. She fumbled a moment with her flashlight; it didn't want to stay on. It was so dark, she needed it. Not only were there very few windows, but there were no skylights, either. She wasn't an expert but the place seemed cheaply made. Thin, plastic fake wood paneling lined the hallway, buckling slightly in a wavy line where it pulled away from the wall. And the linoleum squares on the floor were chipped, the pattern worn smooth forming a pathway down the middle.

The first room to her left was tiny, and very empty, more like stripped. The blinds had even been pulled off the window, leaving gaping screw holes where the valance had been. A pile of what looked to be discarded diapers filled one corner, so old that any odor had long evaporated. A door on her right proved to be a bathroom, horrible with scummy, brown to black dried waste clinging to the commode, the sink broken, dangling away from the wall. She backed out and walked towards the front.

Each room she glanced into gave evidence of owners being long gone and current occupants being transients at best. Maybe the young man watching the truck stayed here sometimes. But the place had been picked clean. Whatever had been moveable or useable had also found its way out the door. There was a draft in the hallway, not a surprise since the glass in the front windows had been punched out; her light vest was ineffectual in the chill of early evening. She folded her arms in front of her, clutching her duffle purse, and pushed open the next half-closed door with her foot. The light from the flashlight arced into the room then fizzled. Damn. She rattled the batteries and the light flickered, weaker, but still on.

"Who you looking for, honey?" a slurred voice demanded.

Oh my God, someone was in the room. Pauly couldn't control her heartbeat. The flashlight went dead. Taking a deep breath, she stammered, "Amistad agency." There was silence.

"This ain't it." A muted belch, then the sound of someone turning over.

"How long have you been coming here?" Pauly was calmer now. She'd regained her nerve but didn't try her light again. She stayed in the doorway and could make out the huddled mass in the far corner. A woman, she thought, but the throaty voice, gravelly as it was, didn't give away the sex of its owner. There was a metal grocery-store cart parked just inside the room, overflowing with collectibles including a good-sized plastic garbage bag of aluminum cans.

"Who wants to know?" The voice had an edge of belligerence.

"Forget it. Sorry I bothered you." Pauly backed away. What a stupid idea this had been. Suddenly all she wanted was fresh air and lights, traffic and people, civilization. The flashlight was now utterly useless. She felt her way along the wall towards the back door, hurrying, stumbling over a loose tile. How could she have allowed herself to believe that she'd find an agency full of helpful people who were just waiting to allay all her fears and misgivings? People who would offer realistic answers, explain away any doubts? Exonerate Randy. The sting of tears blinded her before she blinked them back. She still, even with all the evidence, couldn't believe Randy's duplicity.

She reached the back door and stopped. Something was different, wrong; it was closed. She hadn't shut it, of that she was certain. Of course, it could have been the wind. Foolish, probably, to be so jumpy, she admonished herself, it was just easy to get spooked in a place like this. Screw worrying about prints—she turned the knob and pushed. It didn't budge. She pressed her weight against it and shoved. How could it be locked?

She threw a shoulder into it, grimacing with pain and fighting the claustrophobic panic that grabbed at her senses. It moved a half inch. So it wasn't locked; it was blocked. Something had been moved in front of it, wedged there and not about to be pushed away from the inside. She was trapped in a building with bars at the windows.

Suddenly she stopped her futile pounding against the door. An odor, familiar and unmistakable, was trying to register on her brain as it wafted towards her down the hall. Gasoline. She jerked her head upright. Recognition zapped through her nervous system, sending shock-waves across her body as the explosion rocked the building. Flames engulfed the front rooms, sending an exploratory tongue of fire curling along the ceiling to within twenty feet of where she stood.

Get to the floor. Stay under the heat and smoke. Where had she learned that? Who cared? Pauly jerked off her half-slip and wound the nylon around the lower part of her face and cursed the skirt she was wearing. The walls in the hall were melting, bubbling, popping, and then turning to liquid. She inched her way to the right. The bathroom, could she find it again? It had a window. Maybe, just maybe, the bars were loose.

"Lady. *Aqui. Aqui.* Over here."

The roar of the fire drowned out all but its own sound. But hadn't someone called out to her? She made it to the bathroom and closed the door.

"Lady. Here. I help."

There was a small face at the window about six feet up from the floor. The truck's protector was working on the bars with a tire iron. Pauly slipped once but finally stood on the toilet's porcelain rim, her slick-soled boots not gaining a hold until she balanced a foot against the tank. The room was filling with smoke. She coughed and sputtered and lent her weight to the stubborn bars. But at least there was air. She pushed her head through the opening gulping the outside air that already was acrid from the fire. No glass, no screen, just bars. She was beginning to feel faint.

"Push here...*aqui.*" The boy was pointing to the top corner of the window. Then he pulled and she pushed. A bolt snapped free.

"*Aqui.*" Now he pointed to the lower corner. Another bolt fell away. But the fire was at the door, five feet from where she hung grasping a window sill, her feet slipping and sliding over the tank of a toilet. The paint was blistering, then oozing down the inside of the bathroom door. How long before the entire door simply melted and the fire burst through? Seconds? She was mesmerized, staring at the killer so close.

"Lady. Lady. Now you come." Suddenly the child was leaning into the room. He grasped her around the neck, then pulled her arm, desperately trying to get her to follow, to understand that she was free. The bars had fallen away. In some gargantuan burst of adrenalin Pauly struggled to force her body through the small opening, using the toilet tank as a springboard just as she felt a burst of intense heat engulf her backside.

She fell hard. Dazed. Not comprehending at first that she was on top of the Dumpster's lid, she lay there gulping in lungfuls of air. Stunned. Something hurt. Her shoulder. Broken? She didn't know, but her purse seemed to have cushioned her head; she'd tossed it out first.

"Please, you come. Hurry. No is safe." The eyes peeking up over the rim of the receptacle were wildly large with fright. Another explosion somewhere to the side. Flames darted out the bathroom window. Panic. This time Pauly rolled to the edge and, dangling her feet over the side, jumped, then crumpled to the pavement. Small brown hands tugged her upright, pulled her to follow him back around the side, giving the burning building a wide berth.

They rushed for the truck. Fumbling, she found the keys, dropped them, scooped them up, opened the truck's door, pushed her rescuer in first, slipped behind the wheel, turned the key in the ignition and gunned the truck back over the low curb to bounce into the street with a screech as she rammed it into first gear and floorboarded it.

She made it the three blocks to the main street before she heard sirens in the distance. She pulled into the Allsups grocery-mart and gas station on the corner. Her passenger gripped the edge of the seat and watched her wide-eyed as she parked along the side of the building. She didn't turn the truck off but just sat there, fingers locked around the steering wheel, eyes closed as she tried to regulate her breathing, keep her heart from racing.

Then she looked at her passenger. He hadn't taken his eyes off of her. There were no words…just the fear. A fear that had become an entity poised between them, a shared thing that neither one cared to comment on. She had been so close to dying. He had risked his life. The sound of labored breathing filled the cab.

Finally, she said, "Thank you." It was all she could think to say. Maybe it was all that was needed. He nodded. She still didn't turn the truck off, just sat there feeling numb, not being able to sort through the thoughts that swarmed, no, swirled through her mind—the transient who probably hadn't gotten out, the Dumpster that had been pushed to block the door…which was good because it gave her rescuer access to the window. She reached in her purse and brought out her billfold. She owed him for watching the truck, but how much was life-saving worth? More cash than she had, that was for sure. She held out two twenties. She didn't have any more unless she went to an ATM. She showed him the empty billfold.

"I can get more," she said.

He stared at the money. Reluctant to take it? Sobered by it being so little? It had been his life that he'd risked. Was she insulting him? In a flash she knew what she had to do. She put the money back.

"*Muy caro.*" She pointed to the bracelet before she unfastened it and held it out. His eyes sought hers, then strayed to the sparkling diamonds. Had she used the right word? Wasn't *caro* the word for expensive? She repeated the phrase and emphasized "very." Still nothing. She wanted him to take it. It seemed fitting, a good ending for a piece of jewelry that reminded her only of deceit. It was interesting to muse that Randy had inadvertently purchased her life.

She nudged the child's arm. "*Por favor,*" she said gently. This time there was no delay. He simply reached out, snatched it from her hand, unlocked the passenger-side door and slipped away into the darkness before she could call out. The quickness stunned her. But what had she expected? That he'd wait around and chat?

A hook-and-ladder truck screamed around the corner, followed by an ambulance and two patrol cars. She shivered but her hands were steady now. She locked the passenger-side door, slipped the truck into reverse, then pulled forward and headed back to the motel.

Chapter Eight

Dinner was two packets of peanut butter and cheese crackers and a Diet Pepsi gotten from machines in the motel lobby. Pauly sat cross-legged in the middle of the bed, television on but muted, and tried to think. Rational thought. Somehow it was eluding her. What she couldn't quite seem to erase was the stabbing fear that someone had tried to kill her. But wasn't that irrational? No. Her escape had been blocked; the fire set.

She got up and checked the door, twisted the doorknob, all the while knowing she'd locked it and put the chain-bolt in place. Then she called the front desk and left a wake-up call and set the alarm on the clock-radio beside the bed. Doubly sure. No harm in that. She didn't want to spend one minute more than she had to in this place.

Her shoulder was killing her. She grabbed her purse and went into the bathroom. The half-full plastic bottle of Advil was fuzzy to the touch from being buried under gum wrappers and whatever else inhabited the bottom of her purse. She unscrewed the cap, dumped three in the palm of her hand, ran the cold water tap a moment before filling a glass and chugging them down. She should have thought to do this earlier, when she first got back. The shoulder wasn't broken, but promised to be stiff and painful by morning.

She looked in the mirror and found the reflection difficult to recognize. Terror stared back at her accentuated by blanched, too-white skin, lips devoid of color. Dark eyebrows, akin to two slashes of a magic marker, sliced across her forehead. She couldn't turn away. So this was what it looked like to be lucky to be alive. She shivered, closed her eyes, and stepped back. She needed a shower. Her hair stank.

She dropped all of her clothes in a pile by the sink, then walked to the closet and pulled out one of those complimentary plastic clothes bags and brought it back to the bathroom. She stuffed everything inside, the skirt, the hundred-dollar vest, the blouse, pantyhose. Not a lot was salvageable. The skirt torn, the right sleeve of the blouse shredded below the elbow, the vest stained across the shoulder, and all smelling so badly of smoke that she'd almost gagged. Luckily she'd packed another skirt and blouse combination and a jacket, something appropriate to wear to the office. The pantyhose were a loss, but she could always buy more of those. Even if the things hadn't been ruined, she suddenly didn't want to see any of them again. It didn't make sense, but if she could have buried the lot in the back yard, she thought she would have.

Finally she stepped into the shower. The water pulsed against her head and neck. She turned, shook her hair away from her face, leaned back and let the water run down her back, pummeling her bruised shoulder. She was coming back to life. She lathered and rinsed her hair three times and reluctantly stepped out of the steam and warmth to stand shivering on the thick pile bathmat.

The knock on the door made her cry out, then quickly cover her mouth. How could she be jerked from security to danger so quickly? She froze, unable to think of what to do. The next knock resembled pounding and she wrapped a towel around her hair and grabbed another for her body.

"Miss? Security here." The voice was muffled. "Can you hear me?"

Security. But how could she be sure?

"What do you want?" She had to repeat her inquiry twice to make herself heard through the door.

"Left the lights on in your truck."

Damn. She probably did. Now what? She unlocked the door but left the chain-bolt in place. "I just got out of the shower. Could I ask you to turn them off for me? I'll just get the keys."

The officer was young and seemed more interested in the amount of bare skin that was showing where the towel didn't cover. She handed the keys through the four-inch opening in the door. Was she being foolish? She was silhouetted in the truck's lights, high beams no less, that penetrated the darkness and blasted the front of the unit. Talk about a beacon that might call attention to number twelve…how could she have forgotten the lights? But she thought she knew. She watched as the security officer opened the driver's side door and punched the knob that plunged both of them into darkness.

"I get off at nine. There's a pretty good band in the bar out front." He handed the keys through the partially opened door.

God, he was trying to pick her up.

"Early day tomorrow. But thanks." Did she slam the door? She hadn't really meant to.

She fluffed her hair, deciding to skip the blow-dryer, and slipped on the flannel nightie, the one Grams wanted to replace with something more feminine. The faded plaid night shirt was one of Pauly's favorites. She wasn't ready for the tufted mules and matching feathery peignoirs that Grams favored. She flopped back on the bed. Calmer, more relaxed, ready to think this thing through.

Who knew that she was coming to El Paso? Besides Tom and Archer, there was Steve, also her grandmother. Sam had given her the address but had had no idea when she'd check it out, or *if* she would. Had she been followed? She had no idea. She really wasn't being careful, noticing things, making herself aware of her surroundings like Tony had warned her to be. There was still a PI out there following her around as far as she knew. And whom did he report to? Archer, or Tom? Maybe both of them.

But why? She didn't think she knew anything. Wasn't she the one struggling to find answers? Someone must be worried that she was getting close. But to what? Or did they just want her out of the way on general principles—like the pictures in her safe deposit box?

She hit the volume button as a news bulletin came on the screen. A three-alarm fire on River Street had claimed the life of an as yet unidentified person, who it appeared had been caught inside. It was uncertain just what that person's connection might be to the tragedy, which had been orchestrated by someone dousing the building with gasoline. The arson investigators were on the scene and were already offering opinions that the blaze had been set. One man pointed to a gas can that had been found in the parking lot.

The news cameras panned the smoldering building, now without its roof, and returned to the reporter who was saying that the building had been empty for some time but had been headquarters for a U-Haul trucking firm. Not the Amistad adoption agency? Was she surprised? No. The reporter finished by saying it might be a few days before a positive identification could be made on the body found in the building.

Was someone listening to the TV report at this very moment who thought that body was hers? The thought was chilling; goosebumps rose along her arms and rippled over her thighs. She hadn't thought of that. Or did the arsonist wait around? Did someone see the boy lead her back to the truck? That seemed more likely, someone waiting in the shadows admiring his handiwork, only to see the intended victim escape.

And what had the boy seen? Had he been hiding somewhere, maybe still in the bed of the truck, when the gasoline was poured around the front of the building? Why hadn't she questioned him? It had been stupid to just let him slip away. It was possible he could have identified the arsonist.

She got up and checked the window; it had bars but with release snaps along the side. She tugged the drapes to overlap at the center. Was she safe here? Probably. And she couldn't panic and just rush off, go home in the middle of the night. She really needed to make an appearance at the teaming firm in the morning. She didn't want to have to answer the questions it would raise if she just headed for home now. How could she tell Tom what had happened? She'd made such a big deal about taking an active part. No, she'd stay. It'd be business as usual in the morning.

And she made a silent vow to Tony. She would look over her shoulder, at least be aware of her surroundings, and not be so trusting, not put herself in possible danger like snooping around deserted buildings alone.

◇◇◇

The company was easy to find. El Paso Energy and Engineering was in a "nice" part of downtown, on the second floor of a five-story building that had a granite facade and its own parking garage. She hadn't slept well, but makeup covered a lot and taking the previous evening into consideration, she looked better than just presentable. And she was alive, wasn't she?

She'd checked out of the motel after breakfast and planned to work the day at El Paso E&E and then head back. Nothing on earth could have enticed her to spend another night in a strange bed. El Paso had quickly become her most unfavorite place to be. She pulled into the underground parking at the rear of the building and parked next to the elevators. So she wasn't a compact car, she didn't see anyone who was going to make her move and she just felt better being close to the building's entrance. The elevator opened directly in front of the receptionist's desk on the third floor. The nice suite of offices had the smell of newness, sizing in the carpet, Scotchgard protection for the overstuffed furniture in the waiting area.

"Mrs. McIntyre? If you'll wait here, please." The receptionist was interrupted by an incoming call, but waved towards the denim settee. Then, after answering a brief question, added with a smile, "I'll ring Mr. Warner for you."

Pauly didn't have to wait. Mr. Warner seemed to lope down the long hall to her right, hand already outstretched in greeting.

He had that Ichabod Crane look of the too-tall and too-thin which meant that his clothes hung and didn't fit well.

"Uh, I just got off the phone with the folks from MDB and I…I don't want you to shoot the messenger but you need to call your office. There seems to be some problem, no, a holdup, just a delay…well, some question about your getting a clearance and I…I've told them that E&E isn't comfortable with the fact that you don't have one, aren't cleared yet, and now that you may not be able to be." He stopped short. His nervousness almost overcame him but he hastened to add, "That's not a personal policy. I wouldn't be doing this, but you've got to realize that we've got a governing board, pretty strict in their requirements. We're a young company; we can't afford a wrong step." A hesitant, apologetic smile jerked up one corner of his mouth.

Pauly thought she could read between the lines. Archer. It had to have been Archer. Mr. Warner was just a little too nervous. Had dear Archer put the screws to him? Made him be the bad guy so that poor Archer just had no choice but to remove Pauly from the project? She was so angry that she didn't trust herself to speak. How could he do this? Bypass Tom and yank her off the job?

"Could I suggest that you use the phone in the reception area?" Mr. Warner was almost blocking the hall now. The hang-dog look appeared real. But let him suffer. What had Archer said that she'd done? Sold secrets to the enemy, whoever that was this month?

But she wasn't going to waste time on some hackneyed phone conversation. The damage had been done. She was officially off the project. There was no doubt about that. And poor Mr. Warner wasn't really a player in all this. No, her fight was with Archer. And what she and Archer had to discuss, had to be done in person, face to face or not at all. Pauly didn't say anything, just turned abruptly and walked back to the elevators with a protesting Mr. Warner offering his apologies. What a spineless ass. But to be fair, Archer could be convincing, and El Paso E&E didn't know her, had no way of knowing that the information

Archer had given them wasn't correct. The elevator doors drifted open, then shut after she stepped inside and cut off any further protestation.

She made it back to Albuquerque in four hours and without a ticket. Anger blotted out any memory of the night before. How could Archer blatantly lie about her? Intimate that she was unfit? Exactly like he'd done. But had he initiated some kind of suspect information? Planted something for the FBI to find? Or merely passed on a rumor that he'd heard, unsubstantiated but devastating if it were true, and let the PI take it from there?

Now the PI thing really impinged on her freedom, her ability to work, have a life. Hadn't she taken this "snooping" too lightly? She had been naive enough to believe that they wouldn't find anything, but that didn't include trumped up evidence, something planted that would make her suspect.

By the time she pulled into MDB's parking lot, she knew what she was going to do. And she wasn't going to worry about how dumb it might be in retrospect. Archer Brandon had sullied her name, was squeezing her out of participating, would demand, no, pressure her into selling her one third of the business because she was a liability. And it was all a lie. She thought she knew why he wanted to get rid of her. And unless she played her trump, put a new spin on all this, he'd do just that.

Tom was sitting in Archer's office when she stormed past the secretary.

"He can either stay or go. It's up to you." Her voice was controlled as she pointed to Tom, her eyes locked on Archer.

"Pauly, there's no need to be upset. There's just been a little glitch…" Tom started.

"Glitch? Interesting word for 'lie,' wouldn't you say?" She pulled a chair up opposite the desk and beside Tom. "I don't suppose it's anything you'd like to share. Clue me in on what is serious enough to warrant getting me bounced off the project?" Both men were immobile. Tom looked at the floor. Somewhere behind Archer's eyes there was the hint of a smirk, just a little 'I've won but can't gloat quite yet' look.

"If anything, Archer, I'm surprised. Shocked that you would attempt to get rid of me, threaten me with some trumped-up accusation that could ruin my career when it might not just be my career that goes down."

Silence she could cut. The glimmer of enjoyment was snuffed out and Archer's eyes hardened, squinting as if trying to concentrate, understand what it was she was getting at, maybe not wanting to believe.

"Pauly, there's no need for ugliness. You're upset." Tom reached out to put a hand on her arm, then thought better of it and paused.

"I think we're past the condescending bullshit," she said. Tom's arm recoiled and ended up in his lap; he shifted uncomfortably in the chair. Sweat dotted Archer's forehead.

"You don't know anything..." Archer managed.

"That's pretty profound. Care to elaborate?" Pauly settled herself in the chair and crossed her legs. "What might I not know?"

"This is stupid. I'm not going to play games." Archer stood behind the desk in a dismissive attitude. Pauly didn't move.

"There might be a lot of people interested in the kind of materials that...how would I put it? Pass through your hands."

More sweat. Archer was beginning to look ill.

"What would they be called? Hobby materials? Or lifestyle preference materials? But somehow that doesn't quite capture it either, does it?"

"What are you talking about?" Tom looked at Archer and back at her. Incredible actor? Or was it possible that he didn't know? Archer didn't appear ready to divulge anything.

"Analysis of the Pajarito well. Was that a code name?" She asked and watched the corner of Archer's eye twitch. Tom just frowned, no hint of recognition, nothing to give away that he knew anything about the pictures.

"I won't clean out my office. I'm looking at this as an extended leave of absence until the investigation for a clearance is complete and you can call off your private dog. Then I'll return as an active partner. I suggest you hasten said investigation and attempt to undo whatever it is that you did. My lawyer will contact you regarding interim compensation. I expect amends to be made in a reasonable amount of time. Are there any other 'loose ends' that we need to discuss at this time?"

Still Archer didn't offer anything, but he was leaning against the desk's edge, propped there with locked elbows.

Suddenly she was tired of all the cat and mouse. They had the advantage. She was effectively off the project. She knew how the FBI worked. Slowly, at best. And if information had been leaked, intimated by more than one person interviewed, it would be researched ad infinitum, checked and double-checked for months even if Archer called to say he had been mistaken. And she had better things to do. Maybe she didn't know what those things were just yet, but after last night, life was precious.

She began to feel calm, which was odd under the circumstances. Someone had tried to kill her and now, for all intents and purposes, she was challenging the very men who were behind it—which made her feel good but put her on the defensive big time. Talk about looking over her shoulder—she'd just be glad if someone didn't fire-bomb her car. She rose to go. The threat had been made. It was Archer's turn now. She'd savor the fact that she'd called their bluff. But victory felt empty, and she knew the price would be enormous.

"I told you this wouldn't fucking work," Archer exploded.

The rush of anger felt like a burst of heat in the room, but Archer wasn't talking to her, he was looking at Tom. "I can't believe you took her off the project without discussing it with me first."

Pauly looked at Tom. Could this be true? Tom acted alone?

"I'm worried about your safety. The water conservancy project isn't made up of amateurs. The stakes are high. There's a lot to lose. I tried to reason with you at lunch and then the other night. When I realized that you wouldn't listen to me, I...I've probably prolonged the investigation for your clearance." He looked up sheepishly. "It's nothing permanent. A little checking and a lack of substantiation and you're back on board. In the meantime you're safe." He managed to look somewhat proud of himself.

Pauly sank back down in the chair. Shit. There was no reason not to believe him. Safe. What irony. She'd just done everything but tie on the blindfold before the squad took aim and he was babbling about her being safe. She laughed, a sharp explosive sound, not the usual reaction to something humorous. It sounded forced; it was. She looked at Archer. He wasn't laughing, but he had sat down. She couldn't read the closed look that veiled his features.

"I'll make it up to you." Tom turned towards her, his voice pleading. "I didn't think you'd be so upset. I just felt the need to slow you down. I wasn't sure you really understood the danger, that's all. There's been a lot of opposition to the project. You're trying to take on something that could derail some careers. I never expected you to react so...so...."

He left the sentence unfinished. Hadn't he really meant to say "overreact"? Would she ever be able to work on an equal basis with chauvinist assholes? Even if she could change them, would it be worth it? Did she even want to try?

"I know this will cramp your style. But if I were you I wouldn't do anything rash." Archer broke his silence, back in power, unconsciously steepling his hands, index fingers tapping together in a point. He wasn't putting a description with what he might consider "rash." But it had the sound of a threat. So, what was new?

Pauly took a deep breath. "I'm taking thirty days leave. I'll be back the last week in January. We'll sit down and discuss what progress has been made at that time." She rose to go.

"Pauly, I did what I thought was best for you. Once you've calmed down, I think you'll see that," Tom said.

"It will never be your place to make decisions for me."

She didn't react to "calmed down," even though it made her bristle. It was going to feel good to get out of there. She walked to the door and turned to look back at Archer. He seemed deep in thought, removed from the scene around him, but the skin of the lip pulled over his lower teeth was splotchy white. What would he do now that she'd played her trump? One thing she was certain of, she needed to be prepared.

She didn't go back to her office but kept walking, past the receptionist and out into the parking lot. It was colder today but she hardly noticed the lack of a coat. She sat a minute behind the steering wheel of the truck. What was she going to do? Formulate a plan, for starters. She had one month to solve the mystery of Randy's death. And she had a good idea of where she'd start.

The child. Who else had the answers? He was the only one who could tell her about Randy. But how did you start a conversation with a child porn model who was supposedly the adopted son of your dead husband and didn't speak English? The last thing she wanted was to spook him, chase him away for good, never to have any chance to question him.

Had he seen something on the morning of the accident? Murder, she corrected herself. She needed to keep reminding herself of the severity of it all. Murder. Randy's—plus the attempt on her own life. That was her reality, the reality of the situation and not something to be taken lightly. And until she had some answers, she'd be looking over her shoulder. And being careful. Not trying to second-guess how Archer might use the fact that she knew how he pandered to Sosimo…maybe shared Sosimo's tastes…and all to keep the perks flowing to MDB.

She'd wrestled with how she could approach the child. It wasn't going to be easy, and it would be better if they could have an interpreter. She didn't feel that she could walk down to the trailers and make inquiries. Why did she want to talk with him, if someone should ask? And they probably would. Nothing really plausible came to mind. She'd stayed away from the carnival and it would seem suspect, perhaps, if she suddenly showed up trying to get information. And she couldn't involve Steve. That would lead to too many questions. And could she trust him? The ski mask rose to mind. She started the truck and pulled out of the parking lot.

◇◇◇

The cardboard sign tacked to the telephone pole at the edge of the drive was homemade, a child's block letters in black, large and slightly slanted uphill. Pauly had just slowed to make the turn onto the winding dirt road that led to Grams' B&B, when she saw it and slammed on the brakes.

CHRISTMAS PUPS-J.R. TERRIERS
AND ONE SPADE FEMALE OLDER

The misspelling of "spayed" didn't even bother her editor instincts. This was a godsend. Of course she'd want to see puppies. The excuse to visit was perfect. Was it premature to think her luck might be changing?

She parked the truck at the far end of the triple garages. She'd change clothes and walk down to inquire. Some of the carny kids were playing softball in a field to the left of the trailers. They'd be able to direct her to the puppies.

"And just where are you going? We haven't seen you for two days and you're running off again." Grams was standing in the kitchen doorway as Pauly was going out the back. "Will we see you at supper tonight?"

"I'm planning on it." A quick peck on the cheek seemed to appease her, but out of guilt Pauly followed Grams back into the kitchen. She hadn't spent much time at home, and with Christmas just two days away, she felt really guilty. "I'm going to go down and try to find the puppies that are advertised."

"Oh, Lord. That's all we need, something that isn't housebroken and cries all night."

"I didn't say I would get one."

"I've never known a bigger sucker for something small and furry than this one." Grams pointed her way, and it was then that Pauly saw Hofer sitting at the island cradling a cup of something steaming.

"Hi," Pauly said. He nodded. She'd never seen Hofer in the house before—when he wasn't there for meals, that is. If the romance was as hot as Grams had hinted it was a few months ago, wasn't it strange that they didn't spend any more time together? But, then, maybe things had cooled. Pauly had suspected the religious thing might turn out to be a problem.

"What are we having?" Pauly asked and walked closer to the stove.

"Are *we* suddenly particular?" Grams laughed and threw her free arm around Pauly's shoulders, not missing a turn with a long-handled wooden spoon that was cutting circles in something that looked like green chili stew. "Be ready by five. Early night tonight. Everyone's getting ready to pull out in the morning."

"The carnival's leaving?" Pauly asked.

"Yep. The whole kit an' caboodle pulls out Christmas Eve morning for a couple days' stint in El Paso."

"Will you be going?" She addressed the question somewhat generally to either Grams or Hofer. Hofer just shook his head and reached for the evening paper. What a conversationalist.

From the pulpit he was the silver-tongued orator—but not in the kitchen apparently.

"Not this time, honey. I've never liked to spend the holidays on the road. Done it plenty of times, though. Guess I've earned a break." Grams opened the fridge and squatted down to pull out five packages of flour tortillas and tossed each up on the oak island. She stood, then with two more packs in her hands, bumped the refrigerator door shut with her hip. "Besides, I thought we might want to do something together tomorrow night. Take the luminarios tour, spend a little time in Old Town. You just name it, sugar, and we'll do it."

Pauly realized that Grams was making herself available because she thought Pauly might feel down, first holiday after the death of her husband.

"Oh, Grams, thanks for thinking of me. Let's talk about it later. Maybe the tour would be nice. I haven't been for a few years." Pauly started out the door.

"I was only teasing about a puppy. It might be nice to have a little guy around the house. If you see one you like, we'll just consider it a little something from Santa," Grams called after her.

Was the puppy ruse beginning to backfire? Pauly didn't really want a puppy, the responsibility of feeding and housebreaking. There was recent evidence that she wasn't taking care of herself very well.

"Thanks. I just want to look." Pauly walked back to hug her grandmother and promised herself once again she'd spend more time with this pretty woman who cared for her so much. This time she meant it.

"See you later," Pauly said, including Hofer in her wave. The slight nod in return seemed forced. Yet, she'd felt his eyes on her when she'd talked to Grams. Hard one to figure, she guessed.

"Remember, supper's early tonight. Don't be late, you hear?"

Pauly smiled. The warmth of the kitchen, the tantalizing scent of green chilies, pork, and potatoes simmering in a kettle—it would be easy to be lulled into feeling safe in the big, brightly lighted room. She hung back a moment before going out in the cold, reluctant to begin her search for the child, afraid that she might not find him. Or was she afraid of the answers that he had? Wasn't speculation less hurtful than hard evidence? How badly did she want to know? She sighed. She didn't have to rehash. Didn't her life now depend on finding out?

She pushed the back door open, pulled on gloves and started across the driveway. She could see the group playing ball and headed in that direction. She found herself hoping that Jorge might be with them. But he wasn't. She scanned the backfield. No familiar small child. These boys seemed older, pre-teen but closer to twelve.

"Do you know who has the puppies for sale?" The boy nearest her was more interested in the game than in giving directions, but he paused long enough to say, "Second trailer on the left." She headed that way. The big tent no longer separated the playing field from the housing units. It must be dismantled somewhere, ready for the road trip to El Paso. It left a gap, a big trampled, mussed-looking area of flattened brown grass and gravel.

Pauly walked slower when she came to the trailers. They looked different in the day. Bleaker somehow, but was that just her prejudice? Her dislike of small closed-in spaces? It took three loud knocks on the tinny door before anyone answered.

"Don't tell me you're here about the puppies?" The woman was in her thirties, mousey hair pulled into a ponytail, a cigarette in her hand. "I told Davy to take the sign down. We only had three and they were gone before noon. Christmas and all. Sorry." She shut the door. It wasn't so much in dismissal as from the need to keep the cold out.

Pauly stepped back. Now what? No puppies. It was difficult to fight off the overpowering sense of defeat. She looked down the two facing rows of trailers and motor homes, some twenty in all, with the carnival paraphernalia parked in two fields beyond. It was quiet where she was; everyone seemed to be working with the equipment out back. Shouts of directions, pull this, push that, drifted her way. The size of the caravan that would be leaving in the morning would be enormous, some half dozen eighteen-wheelers plus the company living quarters.

She buttoned the top button on her down jacket. The sun was low in the pale turquoise sky. There was maybe an hour before it set. The hum of the generators that provided electricity to the makeshift community seemed unusually loud and intrusive. Pauly looked across at the trailer where Jorge had gone that night. Did he live there? She couldn't be sure. The curtains were drawn; there was no sign of life.

"Lost?"

Pauly jumped, then laughed. She hadn't heard Steve come up behind her.

"Trying to become a parent but they're all sold." She pointed at the sticker-picture of a Jack Russell terrier in the trailer's window.

Steve was beside her now squinting into the sun, a padded flannel jacket in a red buffalo plaid accentuating the size of his arms and chest. He smelled good, soap-fresh, like he'd just stepped out of a shower. And it was difficult to concentrate.

Pauly hated the way he made her feel. Well, only the part that made her feel not quite in control.

"Do you have to work tonight?" God, that sounded like she had something in mind for the two of them instead of just friendly conversation.

"Probably, unless I have a better offer." He was grinning, sure of himself. "You know, I was hoping to see you tonight. How would you like to spend a one-of-a-kind Christmas?"

"Doing what?"

"Traveling south with a carnival."

"Are you kidding?"

"Couldn't be more serious. We're heading out for El Paso in the morning."

"Grams told me."

"Did she tell you it was a virgin tour for the newest partner? A couple special performances Christmas Eve for the Ronald McDonald's house and a Shriner's parade on Christmas Day?"

"She and Hofer said they weren't going."

"Yeah, the new kid is on his own." Steve's lightness sounded a little forced.

"You'll do fine."

"I think I'd feel better with a little moral support." Imploring, sincere? Both, Pauly guessed. She could sense his nervousness as he waited for her answer.

"I'm driving your Grandmother's motor home, you can have that and I'll bunk with one of the mechanics."

"How long will you be gone?"

"We'll head back the day after Christmas."

Two days. She could find out a lot in that time, and not be suspect. And there was a certain safety attached to being out of town right now, even if it meant going back to El Paso; it made her harder to find, if anyone was looking, and they just might be. It wasn't difficult to conjure up an image of an irate Archer. And there was the fire. Wasn't Steve the lesser of a half dozen evils? And she could watch him. Surely there was safety in numbers. And he would be working.

"I'd love to." She smiled; he smiled back.

"You're serious?"

She nodded.

"I thought I'd have a real battle on my hands. This was too easy."

She could tell how excited he was. It was just as well that he didn't know the real incentive. But the invitation was perfect, perfect timing, perfect excuse for her to be involved.

"I won't handle snakes." Mock-seriousness on her part as she watched him pause.

"That may screw the whole deal." He played along.

"Actually, I'm halfway serious. Is there anything I could do to earn my way?"

"Is joining the clowns out?"

"Yep."

"How 'bout working with the monkey?"

"No way."

"Guess you're just going to have to be a guest and one-person cheering section. Hopefully, there'll be something to cheer about."

"What should I wear?" Pauly dared him with a glance to say something about pasties and G-string, but he was serious, wasn't kidding around anymore.

"Dress code is pretty lax, jeans, sweatshirt, warm coat. We could have dinner across the border. Have you been to Juarez before?"

She shook her head.

"Border towns are fun. Great places to eat. I'll show you the sights."

He was serious. She knew it, could hear the absolute happiness in his voice. She felt a twinge of guilt. Here she was plotting how to question Jorge, rejoicing at having two full days in the child's world, time that would surely give her an opportunity to interact normally without scaring him, and Steve could have no idea of her selfishness. But the prospect of finding answers—she could be within days, maybe hours of finally knowing the truth—was exhilarating.

◇◇◇

Three was just too early to get up. Pauly felt drugged even though she'd gone to bed at ten. Her clothes were packed—the casual stuff that Steve had recommended—but warm. She carried her bag down to the kitchen. The yard was ablaze with lights and activity. Grams had set up a table with stacks of foil-wrapped breakfast burritos and two restaurant-big urns of coffee just inside the back door. At the moment it was the place to be.

She dropped her jacket and bag in the hall and helped her grandmother hand out breakfast.

"I'm glad you don't mind my going. I feel rotten promising to be here for Christmas and then running off."

"Darlin', I'm thrilled that you'll go with the carnival. I always hoped when you were a child that you'd grow to like all this. And don't you say otherwise, I know that handsome young partner of mine had something to do with it."

"But what about you? Isn't there a special someone that you'll be spending holiday time with?" Pauly was tempted to go further. Maybe now was a good time to find out about Grams' love life.

"My special someone will be doing just what I'd like her to be doing...." Grams gave her a little conspiratorial wink and squeeze around the shoulders just as Hofer walked up. Was it Pauly's imagination or had Grams ducked the question because of him?

Pauly idly wondered how early Grams had gotten up to look that "together" in the middle of the night. Smooth skin, maybe a little puffy around the eyes, glowed with the expert application of foundation and blusher. The false eyelashes, short thick ones for street wear, framed violet eyes. Violet? Pauly looked closer. Grams was wearing colored contacts. The lightning-white hair was piled on top of her head, difficult to tell what was hers and what was a hairpiece. A wide violet scarf seemed to anchor everything in place. And other than looking like a leftover from *Dynasty*, Grams looked pretty good. Maybe she'd just stayed up, hadn't gone to bed at all.

"The motor home is parked out front. Here are the keys. I'll tell Steve that you've gone on over. It'll take him awhile to get this show on the road. Here, let Hofer hand out the rest of these burritos."

Pauly started to protest.

"Go on now. We can handle breakfast. You have just one bang-up Christmas, you hear?"

Was there a little extra emphasis on the "bang"? Pauly wondered. But Grams had quickly hugged her and hadn't said any more. She was obviously pleased that Pauly would be spending the holidays with Steve.

Pauly grabbed a burrito, her bag, and a jacket, pausing only to slip it around her shoulders before she walked back through the house and out the front door. The motor home sat in the semicircular gravel drive close to the house, and loomed up to block the circular rock garden that defined the driveway's inner edge. The coach was a boxy thing, a rectangle on wheels in varying shades of pinstriped brown. "The Southwind" was stenciled artistically along the side amid one-dimensional cacti and yucca in yellows and greens. The artist had even signed his work.

Pauly unlocked the side door and, tossing her bag ahead of her, climbed up the fold-down steps. The living area was deceptively spacious but crowded with ugly overstuffed flowered velvet furniture in wine tones. The interior paneling was dark, fake walnut Pauly guessed, while the short hall leading to the one-piece, molded plastic bathroom had speckled rose wallpaper. A bedroom just as garish, if Pauly remembered correctly, was a cubicle beyond that.

The whole thing had a little old Mom and Pop feel to it, something to tool around in once the nest was empty. It needed a bumper-sticker that said "We're enjoying our kid's inheritance." Depressing, but Pauly was too tired to care. She stretched out on the sofa. She hadn't slept well the night before in El Paso, and the fight with Archer had robbed her of energy. Now she felt safer, locked in a motor home. Only Grams and Hofer and

Steve knew where she was, and she could keep an eye on Steve. She'd wake when he got there.

But she didn't. It was nine thirty and they were almost to El Paso before she sat up, trying to get oriented.

"I figured you needed your rest." Steve glanced back at her in the large rearview mirror.

"My God, I must look terrible." Pauly quickly tried to fluff her hair. "How long before we stop?"

"We'll be taking over the National Guard Armory. It's across town, not too far from the border. We're probably talking an hour, maybe forty-five minutes before we get there."

Pauly pulled back the curtains from the square picture window to her right. The sun flooded in, high in the sky, painfully bright. Pauly blinked, then squinted at the landscape, the outskirts of El Paso. A metal building on River Street floated into her consciousness, the fire, a young boy, the transient; she turned away. Could all that have happened just night before last?

"Think I'll brush my teeth." There was no answer from Steve. He was concentrating on keeping his place in the convoy of trucks, motor homes, and trailers as they pulled single-file onto the first exit ramp.

Pauly had time to buy a newspaper when Steve stopped to gas up. She bought a cup of coffee and leaned against the counter. They'd be here for awhile. She scanned the front page, then leafed through the first section. She was looking for something in particular and almost missed it, the article was so small. Thursday's fire that had claimed a life in the industrial area of River Street was attributed to arson. No surprise there. The body still had not been identified, other than to announce that it was a woman somewhere in her late fifties. The article went on to say that authorities suspected it was the body of a transient often referred to as Maxine who frequented the area, and asked that anyone having information about this woman to please contact local law enforcement. There was a phone number.

Pauly wished the woman had remained anonymous. Now it was like she knew her, this Maxine who had accidentally gotten in the way, in the way of Pauly's death, and that made her feel responsible. She was the last person that Maxine had spoken with. Could Pauly have saved her? In all honesty she didn't think so. She could close her eyes and smell the gasoline, see the fire shooting down the hallway. The fire had simply exploded and burned so hot and quickly. She had been lucky to have escaped.

"Ready?"

Pauly crumpled the paper, then wished she hadn't started so violently when she saw Steve's quizzical look. She tried to wipe any semblance of guilt off her face. She'd just been reading the newspaper. Not a crime. Or maybe it was if you were withholding information.

"Want me to drive?" She smiled brightly. Change the subject, keep him from wondering what could possibly have been of such interest to her.

"Maybe later. Thanks."

She sat by the window again and watched as they worked their way across town.

"We're almost there. We'll set up in the parking lot of the Armory. It gives us bathrooms and showers, a real luxury. Steve turned at the next corner and followed his entourage to the back of a two-acre lot.

"This is where it might get a little boring. We've got less than six hours to turn this area into a midway with rides and shows. You can watch, or stay here and rest. Take a walk, if you'd like. I wouldn't wander far to the south if you do. That's where it starts getting rough, about two blocks over. A little close to the border. But there are some shops to the north, a shopping center with a grocery store."

Pauly checked her watch. Eleven-thirty. "I think I'll just wander around here, see if I can help anyone. I promise to stay out of trouble."

She smiled and hoped she sounded casual and not like someone with a plan to find a child and question him. She couldn't wait to seek out Jorge. At least find where he was staying. It had never dawned on her that he might not be with the group. It was unlikely that he'd stay in Albuquerque. She assumed from the number of people involved in the show that he'd be one of them.

But she felt a twinge of apprehension. She had so counted on this trip for answers, what if her time was wasted? But she didn't know that for certain yet, and she had the next six hours to hunt unobserved.

"I'll meet you back here at six." Steve pulled on a flannel shirt and tossed her the keys to the motor home. "You know you can always come back here before that if you want. Fridge is stocked, beer, sandwiches, help yourself."

"Great, I will." She watched him leave, trotting across the asphalt towards the eighteen-wheelers parked single file along a chain-link fence.

Pauly opened the fridge. Steve wasn't lying. There was more food than could possibly be eaten in a week, let alone a couple days. Grams' doing? Probably. Pauly pulled a sandwich off the saran-wrapped stack on the shelf nearest her, then searched for a baggy or foil, pulling out three different drawers under the counter before finding a selection of food wraps. On impulse, she added a second ham and Swiss on rye to the plastic bag that she dropped in her purse. She'd eat later, maybe find a picnic spot in the park across the street.

The afternoon promised to be warm, high sixties at least, but for now her down vest felt good. One more look around the motor home—did she have everything she'd need? Or was she just stalling? Being this close suddenly had given her the jitters.

Pauly took a deep breath, opened the motor home door, hopped to the pavement, and turned to lock up. This was it. No turning back now. She started towards the activity and quickly realized that she could get in the way by not knowing what she was doing. A Ferris wheel was being pulled into place with a winch and crane. A man yelled in her direction, warning her to stay back. It would be safer if she walked close to the trailers and motor homes and away from the trucks.

Pauly wandered behind the line of parked living quarters and next to a ten-foot fence with round loops of razor wire lacing the top. The area looked deserted and Pauly was about to turn back when she heard a trailer door open and close. The woman who had had the puppies for sale was setting up exercise pens behind her trailer and came back down the steps with an armload of newspapers.

"Hi. Need any help?"

The woman looked startled then relaxed.

"You're the one looking for a puppy. Lulu's granddaughter?"

Pauly nodded.

"I was real sorry that we'd sold them all. They're so cute. Sorta sell themselves. People watch the act and expect them to somersault off the divan at eight weeks and play dead. Actually they can't do that until ten weeks." She grinned and Pauly realized she was kidding. "You know if you'd like to help, you could set up another pen and put some papers down. Davy, that's my son, promised to help but he's disappeared somewhere."

"That'd be fine. I'm Pauly."

"Brenda." The woman lit a cigarette, offering the pack to Pauly.

"No thanks."

"Willpower? Or did you just never have the habit?"

"Maybe a little of each. I tried it in high school but didn't like it."

"That's amazing. You know now people can sue the tobacco companies for withholding evidence? Keeping people in the dark about how addictive this shit is. Guess they even upped the nicotine levels to keep people hooked. I've tried to quit. About a hundred million times." She smiled ruefully. "I've been hypnotized, stuck with needles, gone cold turkey. Nothing works. You think people are going to get any money if they sue?"

"I guess I'd doubt it. Too many of them."

"Davy." The woman suddenly yelled and motioned for a pudgy youngster to join them. Pauly watched as the young boy sauntered across the lot towards them. He was a pretty hip-looking pre-teen with initials carved into his hair on one side, baggy shirt spilling over baggy jeans that flared over the tops of unlaced sneakers.

"This is my son." Her pride was as obvious as Davy's embarrassment. He stared at the ground as his mother made introductions. "Now you help Pauly here and be quick about it. I need to let those little buggers out of their crates."

Pauly grabbed one side of a folded wire enclosure that leaned against the side of the trailer, Davy hefted the other. It was quickly apparent that he had done this before, so Pauly followed his instructions; they were more or less monosyllabic but helpful. Between them they flipped the four-sided pens open before placing them on the ground. Davy grunted his approval when she did it right. Teenagers were a trip. Had she been this insolent at the same age? Probably.

"Clip that corner." Davy pointed then clipped the corner nearest him.

Pauly found a metal snap-looking thing hanging on the side and snapped it into place, securing one end. Brenda had disappeared inside. This could be her chance. Wouldn't Davy know all the kids who helped with the dogs? Probably. He might be the one who could help her.

"I'm looking for a young boy named Jorge. I think he's from Honduras." Pauly watched Davy, who was spreading newspapers.

"There's no Jorge here."

Pauly fought back sickening disappointment.

"Did he stay in Albuquerque?"

Davy paused to look at her. "I don't know no Jorge."

"Wait. I have a picture." Pauly walked to where she had tossed her bag by the trailer's steps and, fumbling for her billfold, produced the snapshot of Jorge and Randy standing side by side. She handed it to Davy.

"That's the child I'm looking for. I've seen him work with the dogs before."

"That's Paco. Yeah, he works with the dogs."

Paco? Not Jorge? Of course, Paco was a nickname. Pauly put the picture back in her billfold.

"I'd like to talk with Paco. Is he here?" She held her breath, slowly releasing it at Davy's nod.

"He don't speak very good English."

"I'd need an interpreter." She had Davy's attention now. It hadn't dawned on her, but the job of interpreter probably needed to be worth something.

"How much you gonna pay?" Davy was obviously thinking the same thing. But why not? This was perfect.

"The job pays ten for bringing him to me and another ten for helping us talk."

"Twenty?"

Pauly nodded.

"Twenty-five."

Pauly got the distinct feeling that bargaining came naturally to Davy.

"Okay." She wasn't going to quibble about five dollars. "Is your Spanish good enough to be the interpreter?"

"Yeah. I learned from my dad. And, I help out sometimes with the kids around here. So, when do we do this?"

"Will everyone knock off for lunch soon?"

"About one-thirty."

"How about meeting me over by that bandstand in the park after the lunch break but before you have to be back."

"Okay."

Brenda pushed open the door to the trailer, carrying a Jack Russell under each arm.

"These guys are about to burst. I don't like to make them wait to go potty longer than six hours and it's been almost nine." She put the two dogs down in the nearest pen and went back inside.

"I've got to go now. You won't forget?" Pauly asked.

"Not for twenty-five." A kid's grin, pleased with himself, already counting the money, maybe planning on another haircut; those couldn't be cheap.

Pauly leaned over to pet the terrier leaping at the side of the pen.

"See you in a couple hours."

◇◇◇

Pauly crossed the street early, fully intending to try and stake out her territory. She wasn't sure what she'd do if someone was already sitting on the steps of the grandstand. But the steps were empty. She'd been too excited to eat but now spread a couple of Kleenex out and placed the two wrapped sandwiches on top. Maybe he'd be hungry, or maybe Davy. Kids were bottomless pits. She was glad she'd brought food.

She was having difficulty referring to Jorge as Paco. But she'd soon find out that the name was an alias. What other questions would she ask? She'd rehearsed her part. She thought she was ready.

The boys didn't keep her waiting. Next to Davy, Randy's adopted son looked diminutive. But so beautiful. Again she was taken by his frailty, unblemished skin almost translucent making the dark curls surrounding his face stand out in stark contrast.

Both boys seemed bashful at first and eyed the sandwiches.

"These are for you." Pauly handed one to each and motioned for them to join her on the steps. Paco sat next to her on the same step. Now that he was here beside her, trusting, at ease, munching on a sandwich, it seemed difficult for her to begin.

Pauly took a deep breath.

"Ask him about his parents."

Or parent, singular, she thought to herself. Was the question too direct? She needed to know about Randy, up front, at once…no putting it off with small talk first. They probably didn't have too long. She felt a need to make the most of their time.

Davy repeated her request and Paco stopped eating and looked away. Then slowly he answered, taking his time. The answer was a long one and Pauly fought an urge to fidget. Finally Davy explained.

"He says that his parents are very poor and that he came to the United States to work in the carnival. His uncle brought him here. His uncle got him papers so he could stay and make money to send back to his parents."

"What's his uncle's name?"

Pauly almost held her breath. Did he call Randy by name? Was "uncle" some euphemism for adoptive father? Or was there some special name between father and son? Or maybe a secret name, one used with the other while…. She couldn't let herself think of that, those moments when Randy might have touched the child, fondled him…or more.

"Preacher-man," Davy said.

"What?"

"The name of his uncle."

"But who's that?" Pauly was dumbfounded.

"You know, that old guy that gets up and talks about Jesus all the time."

"Hofer?"

"I guess so."

This was crazy. Was the child mistaken? How could Hofer be this uncle? Unless as an owner he took care of the paper work in order for Jorge to work with the carnival. But what kind of papers let a nine-year-old work? You didn't get a green card at this age. Pauly leaned forward.

"Ask him if his name is Jorge Roberto Suarez Zuniga McIntyre."

But the child looked up and shook his head. He seemed to understand some things.

He pointed to his chest and said, "Me llamo Paco."

"That's probably a nickname. What's his full name?"

Again before Davy could translate, the child said clearly, "Me llamo Carlos Zapata Chuc."

Pauly sat back. Chuc? Not Zuniga or McIntyre? What was going on? She stared at Paco, who had calmly taken another bite of sandwich. Was he lying? But why would he lie about his name?

"Was he born in Honduras?"

A quick conference between the two.

"Merida."

"Where's Merida?"

Davy shrugged. "Somewhere in Old Mexico."

"He's Mexican?" Pauly wasn't sure why she repeated that. But who was the child listed on the adoption papers? The age was right. But the country of origin, of birth, was Honduras. There was really only one way to clear all this up. She pulled the picture of Randy and Paco out of her billfold.

"How does he know this man?" She handed the picture to Davy, who showed it to Paco.

Paco shrugged but looked at the picture closely, turning it over then upright again before babbling excitedly in Spanish.

"He wants to know how you did that," Davy said.

"Did what?"

"Put him in the picture when he wasn't there."

Her heart began beating faster. *Wasn't there?*

"What does he mean?"

Davy questioned Paco, who emphatically shook his head, then pointed to Randy leaning against the brick wall in the picture and shrugged.

"He thinks you might be a *bruja*. He says that he only saw this man one time. He never stood by him like this and got his picture taken."

Paco had scooted away from her on the step, eyes round with apprehension but never leaving her face. He probably thought she'd give him the evil-eye. She had to go slow, smile, reach out and touch him. That would break any spell. He flinched but didn't try to get away.

"But is that a picture of him? It looks like he's wearing school clothes. Ask him when the picture of him was taken."

Davy conferred with Paco and pointed to the picture. Paco shrugged again and seemed agitated, a sneakered foot jiggled against the wooden step.

"He doesn't remember. He says maybe at school or maybe here. Sometimes his uncle takes pictures."

"Davy, this is important. Ask him when he saw this man."

Pauly pointed to Randy and watched Paco's expression turn to fear. She interrupted, "Tell him not to be afraid. I won't hurt him. I won't let anyone else hurt him."

Davy apparently repeated what she had said because Paco slowly began to explain but didn't seem to be any calmer. And he didn't look at her. The explanation was another long one and the jiggling was almost manic now. When he was finished, Davy didn't jump right in with the translation but seemed to be weighing his words.

"Davy, what is it?"

"Uh…he's not sure I should tell you."

"I promise. No one will get into trouble." She was almost holding her breath now. Why was he terrified of Randy? She was afraid to guess. Davy said something to Paco. Paco nodded.

"One time he was trying to run away from the carnival and he got lost down by the river and this—this sounds kinda crazy—this big clock on a balloon comes down out of the sky and offers him a ride." Davy stopped, broke into Spanish obviously double-checking his information but Paco only nodded again. "Like I said this balloon picks him up, but he's too heavy and just when the balloon gets back up high in the sky, it falls down to the ground and he almost gets drowned. But this man," Davy pointed to the picture of Randy, "was in the balloon and he was nice and Paco wants to know if you're going to report him for making the balloon fall out of the sky."

Pauly would have burst out laughing if Paco hadn't been so serious. He was looking at her now, eyes on the edge of tears. The child honestly blamed himself, probably thought others were looking for him because the balloon crashed. She turned on the steps and placed her hands on Paco's shoulders.

"You didn't hurt anyone. You weren't too heavy. Something very bad happened to the balloon, but it wasn't your fault." She talked slowly and Davy repeated each sentence. Paco seemed to relax but squirmed out of her grasp just the same. She sat back and smiled again. She couldn't move too fast.

Paco said something to Davy, pulled him over to whisper in his ear.

"He says that you're nice 'cause you found his bear and brought it back. He says thanks."

Pauly smiled at the boy, who shyly looked at her with lowered eyes. She said, "De nada."

"Ummm, we have to go now. My mom wants us to exercise the dogs." Davy looked at her expectantly.

"Yes, of course, here's your fee. And something for Paco."

Pauly held out a rolled-up twenty and five for Davy and a twenty for Paco.

"Great." Davy made a big show of putting the money in his jeans pocket. "Will you be needing to talk any more?"

"Yes. I might. No, I definitely will." Pauly knew she needed to ask Paco about the nude pictures. Surely those weren't in error. But should she show them to the interpreter? She needed Davy, but the second set of pictures could mean real trouble. At the very least a lot of teasing, embarrassment, maybe Paco wouldn't talk about it. But he knew who was taking those photos or at least where they were taken. Could she interview him by herself? And communicate at all?

"You let us know. We gotta go."

Before she could respond, the two bounded off the steps and took off across the park. She watched them cross the street and run towards the back of the parking lot and the commotion as the big tent was being raised. How could she talk with him again?

She'd have to find a way.

But this child did not know Randy. She wanted to scream it out, jump up and down, do something. All this time she had believed that Randy could be involved with a child. Only to find out the picture was a fake. She'd check out the picture the minute she got back to Albuquerque. Find out how it had been done. Some computer hocus-pocus, she imagined.

And the adoption papers, they were false, trumped up to look real from an agency that never existed for a child that maybe never existed either. Then the question of why interrupted her reverie. Why did Randy have that picture and document in his safe deposit box? Making it look like this was his family? Dear enough to keep safe…hidden and away from her?

She sat back down. It simply did not make sense. Did the fact that this child had only met Randy once make Randy any less a candidate for pedophilia? Not exactly. But a gut-level feeling said that it did. Something wasn't quite right. She just couldn't put a finger on it. But she was closer to the truth. She had to question Paco about the other photos.

Chapter Nine

She'd fallen asleep on the couch in the motor home and woke to the sound of Steve's key in the lock. It was late in the afternoon. She switched on two floor lamps and pulled the drape across the front window. Pauly couldn't believe how tired she still was. Trauma probably brought on by everything that had happened. And she felt safe here buried in the middle of a group of people, safe enough to relax.

"I tried to get out of it. Told them I had a hot date. But actually I really need to socialize." He was trying to explain why they wouldn't be having dinner alone later. And that was all right. In fact, it made things easier. She wouldn't have to make polite conversation, hide the fact that she was thinking of something else. She wasn't going to be very good company no matter how hard she tried. Steve had walked back to the bathroom to wash up. Pauly pulled a beer from the fridge and popped the cap.

"It's okay. Really. Do you know where we'll go?" She raised her voice to be heard above the tap.

"Shangri La. Chinese restaurant on the Sixteenth of September Avenue." He had turned off the water and walked back into the living area drying his hands. "I never asked if you liked Chinese. But this place is supposed to be great. Been there forever. Everyone recommended it. I just hate it that we won't be able to go until after nine."

"No problem. I'm anxious to see the show. Is everything set up?"

"Yeah. Even got a bunch of teenagers already on the rides and losing a few bucks trying to win stuffed animals."

"That's great."

"Wouldn't you think they'd have something better to do Christmas Eve?"

"Teenagers?"

"You're right." Steve laughed. "Now the show tonight's a different story. Good family entertainment. Something different to do on the eve of a holiday, sponsored by a reputable group. Should be a good money-maker."

"When do you have to get back?"

"Now, I'm afraid. Coming?"

"Just let me run a comb through my hair and grab a jacket."

She set her beer in the sink and went back to the bathroom, such as it was. She tied her hair back at the neck with a ribbon, a touch of blusher, a little lipstick and she looked human, not like some sleep-drugged zombie. She walked back out front and picked up the down vest she'd thrown on a chair.

Steve kissed her before opening the door. He slowly turned her so that she was facing him and leaned down to find her mouth, a finger tilting her chin back. She wanted to react, open her mouth, kiss him back, but she felt herself go wooden. She was still a little too preoccupied with the results of the afternoon's interview. If he was surprised at her unresponsiveness, he didn't say, just pulled back and smiled, didn't try again and didn't question. He was quiet as they walked back across the lot.

Pauly was surprised at how everything had changed. The tent was the center of attraction, highlighted by spotlights, and a Klieg light swept a hundred-and-eighty-degree arc across the sky. Parking attendants in uniforms and white gloves waved flashlights and directed cars into neat rows.

Pauly was amazed at how full the lot was already, and the show wouldn't start for another forty-five minutes.

"I didn't think there would be this many people."

"Supposed to have three hundred families." He paused to follow her through the flap into the tent. "At two hundred and fifty dollars a family, that's seventy-five thousand for charity."

"Not bad. But who pays the carnival?"

"Local businesses have pledged to match up to two-thirds of whatever we raise. And the parade tomorrow was a flat thirty thousand. Concessions and all monies from the midway go directly to the carny. Should be worth our while to come down. It'll put a couple thousand in everyone's pocket after expenses."

Pauly found her own seat near the back. Steve was paged to go backstage. She had hoped he'd invite her to go with him. But he didn't. Maybe she should have asked. She wanted to question Paco again but knew there wasn't a chance in the frenzy of getting ready to put on a show. She'd have to be content with trying to find him tomorrow.

She watched the audience file in. Families. Mothers and fathers and children talking excitedly, looking forward to a special treat on Christmas Eve. Pauly felt her chest constrict. Wasn't this what her dream had been? Her dream with Randy? The perfect family doing things together? Instead, she was looking over her shoulder trying to detect a killer by quickly scanning the group of people filling the tent. Tears stung her eyelids. She blinked and swallowed and the moment seemed to pass.

If the four or five instances of show-stopping applause were any measure of success, they were a hit. And after three encores for the dog act, it was finally over. Steve was beaming as he caught up with her by the back entrance.

"Not a hitch."

"I think you've earned your stripes."

"Still a parade to go. I've called a cab. No reason to take the motor home across the river. The guys are going to meet us at the restaurant."

Pauly wasn't sure what guys... no matter. The cab was waiting and she got in, thankful for its warmth. The evening had turned chilly. The clear sky was brightly decorated with stars and a full moon; beautiful, but there were no clouds to act as a blanket and keep the night from turning cold.

The moment the cab pulled away from the check points and started across the bridge at the border, Pauly felt she was in another country. It was too dark to get a good look at her beloved Rio Grande. But somewhere fifty feet below, its murky waters were flowing steadily towards the Gulf.

The shops that were clustered close to the bridge slowly turned into homes, tall green or pink or white stucco ones built flush with the street and each other, decorative iron gates enclosing carports underneath the second story. The street was paved but needed repair. The going was slow before the street turned into four lanes, divided by a sparsely planted median.

Street vendors pushed carts up side streets. Going home? Or just starting work. It could be either. Nine was a fashionable time to dine so lots of people were out. Buses traveling to the border from the interior tilted and rocked on bad suspension, belching black smoke from overworked engines as they tediously accelerated away from stop signs. The racks on top were packed with goods, some of it alive, Pauly noticed, as a chicken poked its head through the slats of its crate.

Suddenly the cab slowed, then darted to the curb. Pauly could see the Shangri La sign on the roof of the building. The restaurant looked upbeat. A red and gilt round doorway curved up out of an oriental landscape of bonsai evergreens and now-brown clumps of pampas grass.

The interior was red and black. What could be lacquered, was, including the arms of chairs, the cashier's counter, and the frames of delicate screens that separated seating areas. It was garish. Yet oddly pleasant, and smelled divine. Pauly's stomach gave a lurch as she breathed in the aroma of freshly grated ginger.

"Looks like they beat us here," Steve said.

The hostess was directing them to a table for four in a back corner. Two men were already at the table and both stood as they approached.

"Edgar Smiley, the carnival's bookkeeper. Chuck Bond, Midway boss. This is Pauly Caton, Lulu's granddaughter."

"Ed, how are you? Ed and I go way back."

"I knew Pauly when she kept her eyes closed going through the haunted house," Ed offered.

"And that was just last year." Steve threw in as everyone laughed, Pauly the hardest.

"I thought I had everyone fooled."

"Not this old goat. Your grandmother sure wanted you to be a carnival groupie, but I used to tell her it didn't look like it was going to take."

"She tried pretty hard to convince me." Pauly sat opposite Steve and pulled her chair close to the table. The shiny black armrests were just the slightest bit tacky to the touch.

"You can say that again. Got you to go to school at the local college, then got you a job that'd keep you from straying."

"Got me a job? I don't understand." Pauly looked at him quizzically.

Immediately Edgar looked like he could bite his tongue but was saved saying anything by the interruption of the waiter bringing water.

"Ed's the one who's been coming here for years. I vote we let him order for all of us," Chuck said.

"That's all right by me. How 'bout it, Pauly?" Steve was watching her. His smile seemed a little forced. Was he trying to get her to forget what Ed had said? Gloss over an obvious *faux pas* and get on with dinner?

"I think that's a good idea," she said.

The next few minutes were taken up by Ed's ordering. The waiter nodded and pointed to the menu every once in awhile, but it was obvious that Ed was in control. She tuned out and turned her attention to Steve and Chuck, who were discussing a problem with the Ferris wheel.

She didn't have a chance to ask Ed to explain until after the six courses including appetizer had been served, eaten, and empty platters removed. Conversation had been polite, funny even, when Ed and Chuck started telling carnival war stories.

Finally, Steve and Chuck excused themselves to go to the men's room. Even though Pauly would have liked to have gotten rid of what felt like an entire pot of green tea sloshing around inside her, she wanted to hear what Ed had to say.

"Hey kid, I was off base earlier. I think I assumed because of your grandmother's interest in MDB, that she might have put in a good word for you." Ed nervously took a sip of water, his Adam's apple jerking up and back quickly in his sinewy neck. "But I have nothing to back that up. It's just plain old assumption that just made an ass out of me."

Pauly ignored any veiled plea to put him at ease. She needed some more information.

"Is Grams more than an investor?"

"No, no. But she is one of those who bought in low and has done well. And here I am telling tales out of school again." Nervous laughter. "Guess it's okay to discuss business with a relative."

"It's fine, Ed." Pauly patted him on the arm. She really did have fond memories of this man.

"What's Grams' relationship to Hofer?" She hadn't planned on asking that, but the time seemed right and certainly Ed would know.

"Oh, on and off again friends. Your grandmother got into a money bind a few years back. Taking in a partner seemed the logical thing to do."

"There's nothing romantic?"

"Romantic? Between those two?"

"They're not planning on marrying?"

Ed laughed, a big guffaw of sound before he sputtered and had to take a drink of water.

"That's like throwing cats and dogs together. They've made the partnership work, but it hasn't been easy."

Pauly nodded. She could see why.

"You know, there was a time I fancied myself in line for the throne." Ed had leaned his elbows on the table.

"You mean with Grams?"

"Yep. Your grandmother's one pretty woman."

"Maybe it's not too late." Pauly was sincere. Grams could do a lot worse than Edgar Smily.

"Uh…helps if the current husband's out of the way, now doesn't it?"

Current husband? Who was the current husband if it wasn't Hofer? And he'd just said that Hofer wasn't a romantic interest…. So what was he talking about? But she didn't have a chance to ask as Steve and Chuck pulled out their chairs and rejoined them.

"Hate to break up a good party, but I need to be getting back. Midway's open another couple hours and if things are going to go wrong, it's apt to happen now," Chuck said.

"We'll share a cab. I'd like to check a couple rides before we call it a night." Steve helped Pauly with her jacket.

This time the ride across the bridge went quickly. She listened to the men talk business but tuned out to dwell on her grandmother. To say the least, Grams had a few secrets. Why wouldn't she have mentioned her husband? And what was this nonsense about getting Pauly a job at MDB?

Instead of being dark and vacant, the midway was ablaze with lights and probably a couple hundred people. Almost midnight on Christmas Eve, Pauly marveled, and all these kids and young adults were plunking down three to five dollars for rides or games of chance.

"I'll walk you back to the motor home." Steve helped her out of the backseat of the cab.

"Actually, I thought I might tag along."

"Are you sure? I'll be talking business. I won't be very good company."

"That's okay."

"Great. Let's go."

He seemed genuinely pleased that she wanted to get involved. And she was intent on finding Paco or Davy, preferably Davy, who could set up a meeting for the three of them in the morning.

She started to relax with Steve's arm around her. They were walking towards the Ferris wheel, which, it seemed, was giving the mechanics fits. Steve excused himself and said he'd meet her by the gate to the midway in fifteen minutes; if he wasn't there she was to come back and drag him away. He was starting to talk and act like a man with plans after the midway shut down. Plans that included her.

And maybe that was all right. Pauly liked being with him, liked the feel of strong arms…he made her feel safe. Somehow sleeping alone in the motor home wasn't looking too inviting. She felt a little thrill of excitement, just a tiny jolt that made her shiver. She'd never given Steve a chance. He'd been a truly great friend and she'd ignored it, pushed him away. She'd probably put too much emphasis on finding that ski mask. Well, maybe tonight would be different. Maybe she was ready now, was smart enough to keep an open mind.

She wandered over to a merry-go-round. The horses were brightly painted but looked pre-pressed, two-piece configurations that came packaged like that, ready to mount on poles and be set in a circle. The horses bobbed up and down to recorded calliope music and had only one rider accompanied by an older child who looked bored, but held his smaller companion securely in the plastic saddle. Next to the ride was a house of mirrors, then a booth offering chances for stuffed animals if a series of rings landed where they should. Beyond that a snow-cone vendor was packing it in, folding and latching wooden shutters across the front of his booth.

Pauly wasn't sure what first caught her attention. The sound, maybe. She was close to the back of the lot and the chain-link fence loomed over the tangle of electric cords and hoses that were half-hidden behind and under the tents and rides. A carnival was never very pretty from the back. But someone was near the fence and shaking it. Violently, it seemed. She slipped between a tent and the snow-cone booth.

What she saw seemed comical at first. There was Paco, his back to her, intent on lifting a loose piece of chain link near the ground to let an Hispanic youngster, maybe seven years of age, worm his way through. The two boys were digging furiously, not unlike frantic terriers, on opposite sides of the fence. Paco was excitedly urging his friend on, grabbing an arm and pulling, then trying to lift the fence up and away from his struggles. Finally the child emerged on Pauly's side of the fence, by way of the dirt tunnel, and Paco whispered something, then took off at a trot with the youngster following.

What should she do? Call out? She knew that there was a charge just to get onto the grounds, so this was a nicety, a treat for a less fortunate. No, she wouldn't get him in trouble. They were close to the border. It would be difficult for youngsters to see a carnival and not be able to take part.

But where was he going? He was hurrying along in the dark behind the rides. Pauly moved to see their destination and was surprised when Paco headed away from the carnival itself and towards the trailers. Then he disappeared. Quickly, she followed. What could he be doing?

Other than Davy's and Brenda's trailer, the others looked alike. There were lights on but it was impossible to tell which one they had ducked into. Pauly stood quietly and strained to hear any sound, talking, children laughing. But there was nothing. One trailer, probably not far from where she was standing, had simply swallowed up the two young boys.

She checked her watch. She'd been gone twenty minutes and needed to get back. Steve would be wondering. And she didn't want to say anything about Paco allowing a friend to come inside the enclosure. He'd probably get in trouble. And it was odd, didn't make sense that Paco would hide the child somewhere. Wouldn't the child be interested in the rides?

She'd barely returned to the asphalt path that wound past the merry-go-round when she saw Steve and waved.

"Thought I'd lost you." He put an arm around her. "I'm ready to call it a day."

She knew without checking again that it was close to eleven. The rides would be open another hour, but already a handful of people were heading towards the front gates. She snuggled closer and felt that familiar hint of excitement as they walked back to the motor home.

"Mr. Burke?" The man stepped out of the shadows from behind the motor home. Pauly gasped and hugged Steve. "Sorry to scare you, Miss. We've got a problem over here." The man motioned with his head indicating somewhere behind him, possibly the big tent.

"What's wrong?"

"Well, seems like a woman has lost her son. Swears that he's somewhere inside the grounds."

"Were they here for the show?"

"Uh, no, the woman's a Mexican National. She's pretty fired up. Says we're trying to steal her kid. She was screaming so loud that the guards out front went ahead and let her inside, thought maybe she'd shut up if they promised to help her find her kid."

"But she didn't?"

"No."

"Where is she?"

"Big tent. Thought it might be best to get her off to herself."

"Good. I'll be right over."

"I'm coming, too." Pauly wasn't going to be left at the motor home. Steve smiled and seemed glad to have the company.

Pauly could hear the woman's wails before they entered the tent, wails and accusations. The woman was probably thirty-five and poor. Her long hair was pulled back and tied at her neck above the ratty collar of a cheap cloth coat, one of those that discount houses on the border offered at inflated prices. Thin legs poked out from underneath a cotton dress that pulled tight over the woman's protruding stomach. She was pregnant, seven or eight months' worth, and looked weary as she leaned back in her chair.

Pauly watched as Steve moved to her side, dragged up a chair and sat down. She hadn't realized that he spoke Spanish, but from what she could tell, he was absolutely fluent. But then, being bilingual would be more than an asset if you owned a carnival that played to border towns; it was probably a necessity.

He was nodding every once in awhile, but the woman was speaking nonstop, taking a break to burst into tears before starting again. Finally, she seemed to run down and just sat rocking, gently staring into space.

Steve stood and conferred with two carny workers, who left immediately. Another man was offering the woman a glass of water and Steve leaned over to say something that made the woman shake her head. Then he stood and walked back to stand beside Pauly.

"Let's go outside."

Pauly followed him through the tent-flap and zipped up her jacket. Her breath turned white in the cold air.

"What's going on?"

Steve took a breath and looked out over the carnival grounds. Pauly could see spots of light being beamed under rides, flicked upward every once in awhile to check the roof of a low booth. Flashlights of a search party. Steve must have believed the woman.

"The woman claims that her son was enticed to run away. Supposedly a child from the carnival talked him into coming here tonight."

"But where did the carny kid meet her child?"

"The woman cleans houses in El Paso and has working papers to cross the border. She was cleaning up after a holiday dinner tonight for some people who live a few blocks over when she looks out and sees her son talking to this stranger in the backyard, a child that she's never seen before. When she goes out to check, her son shows her a carton of candy bars his new friend has given him and says that his friend lives at the carnival and can get him into the rides."

"Not a bad enticement, candy and rides."

"Yeah. Poor kids wouldn't need a lot. Her son begs her to let him go. At first she doesn't want to say yes, but she says the kid from the carnival was really nice. So, she says okay but tells him he has only one hour and then he has to be back at the house. Since it's Christmas Eve, they need to get back across the border to go to midnight mass."

"What time was this?"

"Maybe ten o'clock."

"And the child never came back?"

"No. She's adamant. She was busy in the kitchen later than she thought she'd be, but she swears that he never came back." Pauly was quickly calculating time. Was he the child that she'd seen crawling under the fence? Had he been lured there by Paco?

"Did she say what the kid from the carnival looked like?"

"Called him a pretty boy. Thought he was about her son's age, around eight."

Paco. It had to be. But wasn't that just like kids, showing off, trying to impress others? Living in a carnival would make Paco the envy of any child.

"Surely her son will show up once the carnival has closed."

"Let's hope. He's her meal ticket. She'll only be able to work another month or so before the baby and she needs his income to keep going. I gathered a big part of her anxiety had to do with money."

"He's a child. What does he do?"

"Washes cars. Cleans yards. He's the oldest of her children, there's no father. Even a couple pesos a day would keep them from starving."

"And she doesn't think he might try to run away? That's a lot of responsibility for eight."

"She swears that he wouldn't. She thinks we're keeping him against his will. She's heard stories of how Americans steal children. Her sister lives in Guatemala and has told her stories of how the *gringos* take the babies and young children for their organs."

"Their what?" Pauly couldn't believe what she was hearing.

"I'm afraid there was a documented case or two where young children were lured from their homes, murdered, and their hearts and livers and such flown to the states. Babies are usually taken for adoption and sold for high prices. It's a lucrative business. More than one ring has been busted operating along the border."

Organs? Adoption? Pauly's mind was whirling. Couldn't there be yet another reason to procure young children? Another lucrative business that might go best undetected if the participants were untraceable? Poor children from a poor country who wouldn't pass up a chance to see a carnival? What a great come-on. Probably irresistible.

"Have I lost you?" Steve was looking at her.

"Sorry. Guess I'm just getting cold."

"I wasn't thinking. You're an ice cube." Steve touched her cheek. "Let me walk you back to the motor home. I need to stick around, help with the search, but I could stop by later."

"I'd like that." Was that a look of surprise? She didn't blame him. She'd spent most of their time together keeping him at arm's length. Well, maybe she'd change that. At the door she put her arms around his neck and pulled his head down. His nose was cold but her frozen chapped lips probably left something to be desired, too. She laughed and stepped back. "I think I need to thaw out first." But he just smiled and gently pushed her against the motor home's metal side, kissed her, his tongue pushing into her mouth and she heard her own quickened breathing as she kissed him back, hard, searching, realizing her need, not even caring that it was so transparent.

"I want you." Pauly couldn't believe her own ears—was that her voice all croaky with emotion? Deprivation could make a person go crazy. Say crazy things. She tried to bury her face in his neck but Steve tipped her chin up and looked into her eyes. She couldn't read his expression. This time when she tried to wiggle away, he let her go and simply held her.

"I'll be back." A quick kiss behind her ear sent a shiver across her shoulders.

Pauly watched as he walked around the corner of the motor home and disappeared into the darkness. General MacArthur or The Terminator? Depended on your generation, she guessed, as to what image those three words evoked.

The motor home was cold. She needed to fire up the generator, which meant going back outdoors, but once done it would be toasty inside and she could grab a beer and wait for Steve. She paused by the bottom of the steps. Someone had turned several yardlights on over by the trailers. She could see a group of people gathered by the big tent; a half dozen more had fanned out to walk around the rides and booths. The search party seemed to be good size.

Pauly bit her lip. Should she have shared what she saw? Of course, she should have; but if Paco was reprimanded, she'd lose any chance she ever hoped to have of talking with him again. It had taken too long to win his confidence, if she even had it now. No. If he wanted to show off to a friend, sneak him into the carnival, then that was okay by her.

But what if there was some truth to the charges of procurement made by the mother? Wasn't it possible that this was how the children were enticed away from their families? A box of candy bars and the promise of free rides? Could this have been the way that Paco joined the carnival? There was no evidence that the children were being kept against their will. But there was no evidence that they were free to come and go, either. What was it Paco had said? The morning of the balloon accident he had been running away? And why wouldn't he try to leave? The pictures, maybe more.... Was it possible that someone had threatened him to get him to stay?

Pauly pushed the generator's starter button, waited for it to sputter to life and then went back inside, reminding herself to lock the door. The search could go on for some time. She stretched out on the couch. No reason not to be comfortable while she waited.

The light startled her. She hadn't closed the drapes and the sun's full strength was dazzling. So much for parking facing east. She bolted upright. What time was it? The travel clock on the coffee table said six. She was on the couch still in the jeans and sweater from the night before. And Steve? For all intents and purposes, it looked like she'd been stood up. A little teasing promise at the door of better things to come and then a no show. That could only mean something was wrong.

She looked out the window. Six floats were lined up on the street that ran parallel to the front of the armory. The parade. God. She probably needed to hurry. She pulled a clean pair of jeans and a sweatshirt from her suitcase that was still open across the bed in the back cubicle. She really needed to try sleeping on the bed one of these nights. The sofa wasn't doing her back any favors.

She turned on the shower. Maybe there was enough hot water. Then peeling off her clothes, she leaned over the molded plastic sink and about a nose-width from the mirror whispered, "Merry Christmas, Pauly Caton."

"Couldn't have said it better myself." Steve slouched against the doorway of the tiny room.

She jumped back. She tried to slow her breathing, but after mastering the onrush of fright, she found his presence pleasantly disturbing. Being naked probably helped. She suddenly wanted to be brazen, show him what he had passed up the night before. She wasn't dumb. Her boobs might be a little on the small side, not Grams' perfect fakes, but they were balanced on a figure that nipped in at a small waist above rounded buttocks and long slender legs.

"You could have knocked."

"I did."

She watched his eyes roam her body, flick over erect nipples, the wad of pubic hair, her long legs, bare feet with chipped polish on the toes. He started to say something, then closed his mouth. His eyes were a giveaway, just plain hungry. Pauly knew she was reading him correctly. But he stayed rooted in the doorway.

"Remind me to take your key away," she said.

Instead of reaching for a towel, she turned her back, stepped into the shower and pulled the cracked plastic curtain snug with the edge of the molded unit. She willed herself not to peek out; she knew he was still there.

"I need to get back." He raised his voice above the gush of water. "I'll catch up with you later."

And then he was gone. She felt it as much as heard him leave. She almost called out, swallowed her pride and invited him to shower with her. He looked like he'd been up all night, same clothes, stubble of beard, blood-shot eyes. She could have asked him to stick around to dry her back. "Damn." She really had been telling the truth when she'd said she wanted him. Or wanted someone? Was this just healthy hormones kicking in after a dry spell? She stepped out of the shower and turned the water off. Nothing could erase the fact that she'd stood naked in front of a man and he'd left, just walked away. That went right to the old ego and left a bruise. Still, she'd been less than an eager player before. She flashed to the late afternoon in his apartment. He was naked and aroused and she had chickened out.

She pulled a thick towel from a rack above the toilet, rubbed and patted her body dry, then wrapped it around her. She couldn't stop her thoughts from straying to Randy and how she'd thought Christmas would have been for a newlywed. Would they have had a new house by now? They'd planned on it. And there was going to be a tree, big and fat and decorator-perfect. There had been a bracelet, a reminder of what could have been. Of promises that weren't meant to be kept.

But instead, here she was in El Paso, Texas, with a carnival, lusting after a man with tattoos who didn't even make a pass when she stood in front of him naked. And the husband she should have been sitting across from at breakfast on Christmas morning, this morning, had turned into a dead husband who she was trying to prove wasn't a pedophile by paying a twelve-year-old child to interrogate a nine-year-old. Then to protect her source, she'd lied about seeing him spirit a youngster under a fence, hiding him maybe for illicit reasons. What a mess. She hated her life. Hated herself for what was probably grandiose stupidity or just a blindness, simply not seeing what had been right in front of her.

She couldn't stop the tears. She flopped the toilet seat down and sat there and cried, periodically blowing her nose on toilet paper that dissolved and stuck to her cheeks and upper lip. Why did her life have to end up this way?

This time she heard the knock on the outside door. Steve. At least he was back to say he was sorry, really sorry about last night probably, or for passing up his chance this morning. She grabbed a robe, splashed her face with cold water and ran to the door.

"Ed?" She couldn't keep the disappointment out of her voice.

"Sorry to bother you so early. Steve wanted me to bring this by." He handed her an envelope.

Pauly tore it open but some sixth sense already was warning her that it wasn't good news. She scanned the single sheet. Steve was renting a car and heading back to Albuquerque. Ed would drive the motor home back for her if she wanted. No explanation. No apology. She crumpled the paper.

"Let me know if you need my help."

"I think I can handle it." It was obvious that Ed knew what was in the note. Steve must have told him. But she wouldn't need his help. She'd driven the old boxcar around before. It had been awhile but it wouldn't be a problem. Ed had turned to leave and suddenly on impulse, Pauly blurted out, "Who's Grams married to?"

Ed stopped and turned around. She couldn't read his expression. But she was acutely aware of how it sounded to not even know the name of her grandmother's husband. Obviously, there hadn't been a big to-do. Maybe only movie stars celebrated after the first few times. Wore white even when the numbers would have put them in black. She hadn't been invited, but then she'd missed numbers three, four and five, too.

"Your grandmother's a private lady. And I don't think the marriage has worked out."

Pauly waited. So what was new? This still didn't answer her question. "I didn't catch a name, Ed."

"I'd rather you asked her." But the way he looked at the ground, hesitated to leave made Pauly think he wouldn't mind telling. Whoever thought women were the only gossips, didn't know men.

"I'd rather you told me." she returned.

"Well, I hope you take this right, but I think Lulu overstepped her boundaries with this one. I could see marrying him for status, legitimize her act, so to speak. But Lulu doesn't need to do that. I just don't think she realizes it though."

"Come on, Ed, the name."

"I told you, ask Lulu." He turned and walked away.

He could have struck her across the face. She bristled but thought of calling out to him, trying to soften his obvious anger at her persistence. But she had a right to know. Why wouldn't he share with her? And she should be the one who was angry—marrying for status—there wasn't anything wrong with her grandmother's status. Not now, not anymore.

On impulse, she yelled after him, "Thanks for offering to drive, but tell Steve I'll be heading out early."

A damn lot early, she thought as Ed didn't even acknowledge her. She wanted to talk to Davy, maybe get in one last discussion with Paco before she left. But there was nothing to keep her in El Paso. Probably lots to encourage her to leave if she thought of the other night.

She dressed quickly, bypassed making coffee, she could always stop on the road. She was eager to find Davy and almost missed him in his Power Ranger costume lounging against the side of his trailer.

"Nice," she said, indicating his costume.

"Yeah. I'm on a float."

He didn't seem too eager to talk. Strange. Maybe she should mention money again.

"I'd like to speak with Paco today."

Davy began to fidget.

"Could you help me again? I think we could make the same money arrangement."

"No."

He was standing now and she had the distinct feeling that he was getting ready to run off.

"Why not?"

"He's gone."

"Gone where?"

"How should I know? He ran away."

"Ran away?"

"That's what I said. You deaf or something?" Insolent. Pre-teen, but already had the mannerisms of surly sixteen down pat. She ignored it and plowed on.

"Why would he leave?"

"Maybe he got in trouble."

Trouble? Of course, the kid. The one she had seen crawling under the fence.

"Where did he go?"

Davy shrugged, "Home, probably. They always do."

Pauly was just about to ask who "they" were when Brenda opened the trailer door and walked down the steps.

"I hope this is our last Mexico trip. I'm sick and tired of having the bribes come out of my paycheck." She didn't have a cigarette in her mouth but she was smacking a wad of gum.

"What bribes?" Pauly was truly at a loss.

"To pacify the authorities. Keep them off our backs."

"But why? Did we do something wrong?" She fleetingly thought of Steve and the hasty trip back to Albuquerque.

"Oh, it's something different every time. Last time it was some new tax. Everyone had to chip in twenty bucks and show some fake permit in the window of their trailer. Just so much bullshit. One more handout in a 'gimme' world…free money while we enjoy the bad water and lack of facilities."

"So, what is it this time?"

"Oh, this time we're being accused of stealing children. They've turned this place upside down. Supposedly some kid sneaked in to make a few bucks helping us clean up and didn't go home. His mother is accusing us of hiding him."

"Has this ever happened before?" Pauly was trying to fight back the word procurement, but felt the goosebumps rise on her arms.

"Yeah, the carnival is a kid-magnet. How do you keep them away?"

"What usually happens?"

"The authorities check the trailers, detain us, then accept money to just look the other way. I'm sure the kids show up once we've left."

"So why is this time different?"

"The kid's mother is convinced of foul play. Says her son is no street kid, he goes to school and has principles." Brenda laughed, "Guess all moms would say that, right, Davy?"

Davy did not acknowledge his mother's humor. Instead he took off around the side of the trailer.

"Don't go far, you hear? This parade is going to start someday. I don't want to go looking for you." Brenda popped her gum, then fished the wad out of her mouth, tossed it, and reached in her shirt pocket for a pack of cigarettes. "I guess the kid's mother really fell apart. Had to be hospitalized. She's convinced he's dead. Just a lot of melodrama, but nobody asked me. Someone said the Governor of Chihuahua has gotten involved, turned it into a political issue. With our President due to visit the border next month, this is a perfect time for bad press." She shrugged and went back inside.

Discussion over, Pauly mused, but could sympathize with Brenda. This was not an easy life. But what if that child was never coming home? What if he hadn't run away, like the mother said. What if he had been kidnapped and used for—Pauly couldn't finish the thought. She was on to something. The pictures that she found addressed to Sosimo were of two other children besides Paco. Wasn't it reasonable to believe that others had been lured to the carnival and taken somewhere to be photographed? But where? And by whom?

Pauly felt numb. The pregnant mother who needed him. She felt tears fill the corners of her eyes. She could remember all too clearly the woman crying, her sense of desperation. Now what would happen to her? How would she cope? Life could be so rotten. Unfair beyond belief.

Suddenly, Pauly had lost all interest in the carnival. She wanted to get back. Maybe Paco was on his way home to Merida or wherever Davy said he was from. For that, she was relieved. If he wasn't, then he'd be discovered sooner or later with his new little friend. And Steve? No wonder he was detained. His first solo trip and now accusations of a kidnapping. He was probably being questioned by local authorities and would have to prove that the carnival had nothing to do with the child's disappearance. There would probably be another search before they were allowed to leave. She didn't envy his position. But she wished he'd told her—shared his problems with her. But had she ever really taken him into her confidence? Trust had to work two ways. And what could she really do? Offer a little moral support, for whatever that was worth.

But she paused. What if Paco had lured the child in and turned him over to someone? Was maybe paid to do so, but then what? Could someone be using the carnival as a base? Could there be a child porn ring operating under Grams' nose? It was time she talked to Steve and Grams.

◇◇◇

A breeze had sprung up that turned into a gale intent on separating the top soil on the east side of the highway and depositing it on the west. The motor home bucked and swayed and demanded two-hands-on-the-wheel attention. She could have done without shitty weather. It was Christmas, for heaven's sake.

She bypassed Truth or Consequences and stopped for coffee in Socorro. The McDonalds was only open on Christmas Day because it was serving meals to the homeless later that afternoon. A Christmas cheeseburger didn't sound appetizing. She pulled through the drive-up window and got the coffee to go, then nosed the "bus" back onto the interstate. The wind had backed off to a stiff breeze and she could relax a little, at least let her thoughts wander, go over what she'd found out.

The photo of Randy and Paco must have been pieced together. She trusted Paco; she'd seen his expression. She'd drop the photo off at a lab Monday morning and get proof. And if it was a fake? Maybe it wouldn't exonerate Randy of all wrongdoing, but she already knew that there hadn't been an adoption. And it was time to see Tony, show him the photo, tell him what she knew. And tell him what she suspected. To hell with Sosimo.

Chapter Ten

Pauly was glad for Monday morning. If Christmas Eve had been a bummer, Christmas Day was even worse. Grams and Hofer spent the day at a mission in the South Valley, services and dinner for the homeless. Presents were an afterthought, exchanged late in the evening with the ever-present Hofer slouched on the couch. If Pauly had wanted to question her grandmother about husband six, there was no chance. Her grandmother seemed tired, withdrawn. Pauly didn't have the heart to talk about the missing child and what she suspected. Not today.

The fire in the fireplace had been comforting and the Irish coffees, a contribution from Hofer, had almost made it worth having him around. But not quite. Hofer was livid about the police detaining the carnival. He ranted on about law suits and legal entanglements that could shut them down if the child wasn't found. Her grandmother didn't try to calm him. She, too, looked visibly upset, but promised to find the child's mother and make certain her immediate needs would be taken care of.

If Pauly had hoped that Steve might show up, that was another disappointment. He had been held up in El Paso, hadn't been able to come back to Albuquerque after all, and might be there another day or two trying to straighten things out. As of late Christmas Day the child that Paco had brought into the carnival had not been found.

Pauly loved her present of a fringed shearling jacket. Grams shouldn't have; it was far too expensive and made her own gift of pottery, serving pieces she knew her grandmother didn't have, look pale in comparison. Pauly had added a stocking-stuffer of Tea Roses cologne and a set of sequined bandannas. But it was a greatly subdued celebration that ended early. Everyone was in bed by ten.

When Noralee called at seven in the morning, Pauly was surprised. Her interest was even more piqued when she heard transports roar past. Noralee was using a pay phone. What was so "cloak and dagger" secret about meeting with her that she couldn't use her home phone or one at work? And her choice of restaurant, the Cantina in Bernalillo? Five miles north of Albuquerque? The nervous laugh said it all. Noralee didn't want them to be seen.

Pauly had hoped Grams would be up before she left, but at ten-thirty she was still in bed and Pauly was beginning to run late. Hofer was in the kitchen and muttered something about a sinus headache. She wanted to talk with her grandmother but it would have to be later. She'd make a point of being there at dinner.

Pauly dropped the photo at a lab, one specializing in enlargements and duplication. She was assured that it would be no problem to find out if the picture had been tampered with. Enlarged, any faulty alignment would be instantly apparent. The clerk promised an answer by early afternoon.

Pauly spotted Noralee's car when she pulled off the highway and into the sandlot parking area in front of the restaurant.

Not that a metallic blue Corvette would be inconspicuous anywhere, metallic blue and fairly new, Pauly noted.

The Cantina had great food and a fake Southwest atmosphere. Interior adobe walls were plastered blocks of plastic foam, but the vigas were real wood. She'd give them that much. The smell of fat-fried sapodillas filled the air. They were known for making their own. Another plus.

Noralee waved to her from a table by a window facing the patio. Her Angora-cashmere sweater matched the Vette in color and the jeans had been painted on. There had to be ten bangle bracelets on each arm. She must have been there for awhile, the basket of chips and cup of salsa had a serious dent in it.

"I'm glad you could come."

Nervous. Noralee's hand was ice cold and a little damp.

Noralee had offered first, but Pauly thought it was a little stilted to shake hands. What was their relationship? Secretary and boss? Secretary and boss removed. That was more like it.

Former girlfriend. Secretary and bosses removed twice. Noralee didn't have a very good batting average.

"How are you doing?" It didn't seem to require an answer but Pauly offered the perfunctory, "All right. And you?" Small talk was not Pauly's forte but she instinctively knew she needed to let Noralee take her time.

They ordered. Noralee recommended the blue-corn enchiladas, sour cream on the side. Pauly went along and added an ice tea. No beer today. Too many calories in addition to the grease. Noralee chit-chatted about her Christmas, which sounded better than Pauly's, a visit from her daughter who had a four-month-old baby, which made Noralee a grandmother. But who was into name-calling as Noralee referred to her new title? Pauly laughed and passed on dessert, ordering cinnamon-laced coffee.

"I hope I'm doing the right thing." Noralee tore open the second diminutive container of half and half. Pauly waited. "I guess you knew that Randy and I, uh, we had been together. We had even talked about getting married."

Now that was news. "Are you saying that I broke the two of you up?" Because if you are, I'll remind you that no one can break up a healthy relationship, Pauly thought. But her intuition said this wasn't a meeting to fling a few vindictive arrows. And wasn't it a little late?

"No, nothing like that. I mean you didn't do it on purpose. And it usually takes two people to make that decision. I was paid to get unengaged, to get lost. No one knew we were planning anything…at least, we didn't think so. But Randy had given me the car—"

"You were paid? By whom?" Pauly ignored the reference to the car.

"I'm not sure I know exactly. I was contacted by phone at the office. A man told me there would be ten thousand in an envelope waiting for me in my mailbox at home that afternoon if I agreed to disappear for awhile. I just needed to make it plain to Randy that our relationship was off. Well, my daughter was expecting in September and she'd been sick and needed me. Needed money. The jerk she was living with took off when he learned about the baby. She lives in Dallas." Noralee stopped stirring her coffee and took a sip. "Ten thousand was like a prayer answered. I guess I thought that Randy would always be there. That I could take the money and still…." She looked up apologetically.

"So you left in July?" Pauly watched Noralee nod. That was about the time that Randy began dating me, Pauly thought.

"I called to see if I could come back in October. I was really homesick."

"Who okayed it?"

"Tom. And, I guess Archer, too. But it was Tom I talked with."

"That must have been just before the wedding."

"Yeah. Imagine my surprise." Sarcasm? Pauly couldn't tell, then "I think someone made him marry you." Noralee blurted it out. "Paid him, maybe."

"That's absurd."

"Why? I was with that man off and on over two years. In all truthfulness, he wasn't going to marry me or anyone else. His first marriage was a bummer. There was no way he was going to do that again. I mean, we talked about it. I liked to think the Vette was an engagement present. But, honestly, I know Randy didn't think that way. Then in three and half months, he's married to you."

Four, Pauly thought, but was a half month important? And married before? Had she heard correctly? She was amazed at how well she was beginning to take these shocks.

"You said he'd been married?"

"Yeah, you know, Michelle, who couldn't be inconvenienced by contraceptives, and certainly wasn't going to ruin her body with pregnancy."

"So Randy had a vasectomy?"

"Um hmm. For a marriage that lasted sixteen months. Frankly, I don't think Randy ever wanted children. Not the type."

"No, he probably wasn't." Pauly paused. "You must have been shocked by our marriage."

"And remember, I had to get out of the picture first and fast. Someone paid me to disappear so he could do it."

Pauly thought of the unexplained hundreds of thousands of dollars, close to a million that just showed up in Randy's account—right before the wedding. A payoff of some sort, she'd always thought that, but not a payoff for marrying her. This was a swift kick to the old pride.

"Why are you telling me this now?"

Noralee fidgeted. "Because I think someone wants to kill you."

Pauly sucked in her breath, then forced herself to exhale slowly. She looked out the window. A pair of dark-hooded Juncos ate from a feeder of black thistle hanging from the edge of the portico. The sun was shining, peeking through a bank of ominous clouds. It was supposed to snow later and it looked like the weatherman hadn't lied. A couple laughed two tables over. She turned back to look at Noralee. But now it was her turn to have cold, clammy hands.

"How do you know?"

"I overheard Archer talking to someone. He said 'the stupid cunt'—"

"There must be more than one of those in the company." No laugh. Humor was wasted on Noralee.

"He called you by name. Said that you were getting in the way. That you were going to get hurt."

"When was this?"

"Friday."

The day of the famous dismissal.

"What made you think he was serious enough to harm me?" Pauly couldn't bring herself to say the word "kill."

"I don't know. His tone of voice. He was really mad. He kept saying that you needed to be taken care of—those were his exact words. And I don't think he was talking pension plan." Wan smile.

Pauly laughed. She had to take it back. Noralee did have a sense of humor.

"How did you overhear all this?"

"I had a migraine. No one was using the lab conference room so I stretched out on the floor of the projection booth. I had no way of knowing he'd use the phone in there."

Pauly believed her. She wasn't sure why, but she did.

"You didn't actually hear him be more exact as to what he thought should be done, or when?"

Noralee shook her head. "I guess mostly it was a feeling I got. You know how it is when you'd bet your life on something but can't prove it?" Pauly thought she knew. Noralee continued, "Maybe this was stupid to meet this way. But I thought I could warn you, encourage you to be aware, just a 'heads up' as they say in the biz." Another weak smile. Seeking approval?

Pauly smiled back. "Thanks. I really appreciate it."

A waitress filled their cups and Noralee fiddled with more cream and didn't seem to be in a hurry to leave. It might be a good time to get a little background.

"You helped Randy on the Water Conservancy Project?" Pauly asked.

"Yeah. Talk about a project being snake-bit."

"What do you mean?"

"Well, there's no winning. It would benefit the state— *beau-coup* bucks worth if it went one way—but screw over a powerful constituency in the meantime. But if the smaller group won, the state would get the short stick."

"What was Randy's position?"

"Governor's boy all the way."

"You mean he was prepared to 'screw over' the South Valley?" Noralee nodded.

"Was Sosimo Garcia aware of this?"

Noralee nodded. "They had terrible fights. No love lost there."

The bracelet. What was it Sosimo had said? "My good friend, no, my *dear* friend asked me to pick this up...." A lie. She had known that at the time. A beautiful golden bauble that did what? Confuse the issue for one thing. But how could he have made it so convincing? Picked the right color stones? Who would have known that? Besides Randy and…Grams. She hadn't thought of that before, but Grams knew how much she loved yellow stones. Could Grams have given out that information?

"You okay?" Noralee leaned forward.

"I'm fine. It's just that so much has happened." Understatement, Pauly added to herself. "Noralee, do you think someone had Randy killed? Maybe because of the water project?"

"I guess I've always thought that. It might have been worth it to some people."

Neither one of them needed to repeat Sosimo's name. But it was there all the same.

"Do you have to get back?" Noralee had glanced at her watch.

"No, I took off today."

Pauly took a breath. "What do you know about pedophilia?"

"Men who molest young children?" Noralee shrugged. "Not much."

"Is there any way that Randy could have been a pedophile?"

Noralee was looking at her like she was crazy. "I don't understand what you mean."

Pauly took another breath. She hadn't planned on this. But why not? What better person to check with?

"There was evidence that Randy was involved with a young boy, a Mexican national. I found a picture, adoption papers.... I even found pictures of nude children, more exactly, of the child he supposedly adopted and might have used for sex."

"No way." Noralee stared at her.

"I found an envelope of pictures in Randy's desk addressed to Sosimo." Pauly ignored Noralee's shaking her head but then she stopped—something had flickered in Noralee's eyes, fleetingly, before she looked down.

"Noralee, what is it?"

"Guess I'm not surprised. I've heard rumors. Randy referred to him one time as a 'baby fucker.' I didn't take it literally. Thought it was just more of his anger against the man in general."

"But you think it might be the truth?"

"Who knows? Does that stuff run in families?"

"I have no idea, why?"

"Well, a couple years ago Sosimo's brother was defrocked. He'd been the priest in a little community in northern New Mexico. Apparently he was diddling the acolytes. He was sent away for treatment. It was a terrible scandal."

If Sosimo wasn't a pedophile, he wasn't a stranger to the affliction, Pauly thought. And did she know for a fact that the man in the pictures was Sosimo? No. She didn't. What if the man in the picture was his brother? She sat up straighter. That could be. There would, no doubt, be a family resemblance. Had Randy been blackmailing Sosimo? Threatening to revisit a family scandal with new information? Pictures that would be far more than just an embarrassment? This was an interesting new twist.

"You didn't know about the vasectomy, did you?" Noralee leaned on both elbows, chin resting on clasped hands, and looked at her earnestly.

Pauly shook her head.

"Would you have married him if you had known?"

"I don't think so. Until recently I was into the American dream. Husband, house, two point five children."

Noralee's turn to nod. "You gave the impression that bagging the big one was more important than a career. I mean until lately." She looked pensive. "You know, I really think the lie about the vasectomy proves my point. Randy was set up to marry you."

"It doesn't make sense. Why?"

"Who knows? For whatever reason, Randy had to get married."

"Funny, he slipped a couple times and used those very words. I teased him about that being my line."

There didn't seem to be a lot more to say. Noralee reached for the check but Pauly grabbed it. Was seven ninety-five plus drink too much to pay for information? She'd paid forty-five recently to kids and still didn't have a lot of answers.

Noralee walked her out to the parking lot. She'd heard that there was some problem with Pauly's clearance and that she was on leave. Pauly made it clear that the delay had obviously been trumped up. Noralee agreed. It was one more piece of evidence that someone was manipulating Pauly's life. Neither could imagine why. She thanked Noralee for coming forward and after a quick hug, Noralee got into the Vette with a promise to stay in touch.

Pauly watched her go. The sky was gray now and faint pinpoint sized flakes of snow floated around her. It wasn't really serious about snowing, yet, but by late afternoon, this could turn into a traffic-stopper. The new shearling jacket was warm and she'd been smart to wear boots with heavy socks. You just never knew in New Mexico, sunshine to blizzard within an hour.

◇ ◇ ◇

Pauly walked through the door of the photo lab and took a place in line behind four other people standing at the counter.

"Be with you in a minute." The kid sounded apologetic.

Pauly wasn't in a hurry. Much. Curiosity was eating her alive. This was important. So much hinged on what these people could tell her. She hoped that they might have time alone. And then she didn't want to feel rushed. It seemed like the people in front of her were taking forever. But no one had come in behind her, so when it was finally her turn, the young man wasn't hurried when he pulled a large envelope from under the counter.

The enlarged copy of the photo was eight by eleven and made some of the features fuzzy. Paco looked morose, not just unsmiling. It was the shadow across his face. She bent closer, ignoring the jolt that seeing a robust, happy Randy caused...even with the distortion it was impossible to miss his carefree, grinning self. She straightened abruptly.

"Hard to see with the naked eye." The young man rummaged in a drawer under the counter and handed her a magnifying glass. "But on the enlargement, look here." He pulled the copy closer, adjusted a crook-neck light, and handed her the glass. He ran the tip of a pencil down the fuzzy shadow between Randy and Paco. It was not really noticeable in the small photo, but at this size it stood out sharply. It looked like tracings, a cut-line that followed the shape of Paco and one that outlined Randy.

"It's not a bad job, but no one used any sophisticated equipment, either. Anyone with a copy stand could have done it."

"But you're sure this is a combination of photos?"

"Absolutely."

"But the background. How could someone manage that?"

"I'll show you. See here and then again here?" The point of the pencil skipped over the foreground. "Both figures are standing in grass. A foreground that's easy to duplicate and covers all sorts of evils." He stopped to grin at her. "Whatever would have separated the shots is blurred, airbrushed to blend together. It could have been two entirely different buildings, trees, who knows? The sky was the easy part." Pauly followed the pointer-pencil again as it skipped across the top of Randy and Paco's heads. "The photo was pieced together, blended here and there and reshot to focus on the figures themselves, diminish the background altogether."

Pauly leaned closer. Now that it was pointed out, it was so obvious.

"Could someone then reduce the size?"

"Just paste-up and shoot. He could do whatever he wanted with the film itself, the negatives, that is. This could have been a poster or the size you brought in."

Pauly took a couple of deep breaths. The feeling of relief almost buckled her knees. She had wanted the photo to be a fake even more than she realized. Pauly put the original in her billfold, paid the man, picked up the blow-up that he'd slipped back into an envelope and left.

She hadn't felt this good since Paco had told her the photo was a lie. Now she had the answers in her hand and proof of Paco's trustworthiness. Randy had simply not been involved with this child, had only met this child minutes before his death. But why had the photo been made? And how did it get into his safe deposit box? She sighed, then reached under the seat and shoved the envelope out of sight.

She still wasn't sure where she was going to go with this evidence. It had some connection with Randy's murder. But she had no idea what. She started the truck. She really needed to call Tony. Just tell him all the things she should have been telling him all along.

A bright spot in all this would be if Steve had gotten back. Not that she'd share information with him, but that didn't mean she couldn't share something else. Like her body. Pauly grinned. She was on the verge of OD'ing on horniness. And it felt good.

Pauly turned into the gravel lane that would take her to the three-car garage beside the B&B. What was the motor home doing in the driveway? She'd left it down by the maintenance garage. Was there another trip planned? She didn't know of any. She was accustomed to seeing hive-like activity in the field out back, and the Carnival would have gotten back late morning, but why was there a crowd up here by the house? Something was very wrong. She saw the police cruiser in the rearview and slowed as the driver came up on her bumper and turned on his lights. What was going on? She skidded to a stop and jumped from the truck.

"Not so fast." The cop grabbed her arm. "Wait here."

"I'm not 'waiting' anywhere. I live here. What's going on?" She didn't try to disguise the anger.

"You'll end up handcuffed in the cruiser if you're not careful." The older cop was gruff but dropped his hold on her arm.

"That's her." Pauly turned to see Davy pushing through the crowd. Brenda was two steps behind, and from the look on her face, Pauly was being accused of something heinous. "She paid me to take her to Paco."

Whatever was going on, it had everyone's interest. But where was Grams? Or Steve? Wasn't he back? Pauly started toward the house.

"You can't go over there," an officer yelled.

Pauly paused, then saw Ed standing by the motor home. "What's going on?"

"Jeez. This is the pits." Ed was upset, running his fingers through thinning hair, then slamming his cap back on.

"Can you believe it? I go out to gas this ol' cow up and find a mess."

"What kind of mess? Vandals?"

"I wish it was just that. Pauly, I'm sorry. I had no idea. I didn't mean to get you in trouble. Listen, I know you had nothing to do with this. It's just that Davy there said you was paying him to bring you Paco. Asking all kinds of weird questions. And now this." Ed moved aside.

The smears of blood on the back side of the motor home door looked fresh. At the bottom of the steps was a child's tee shirt, crumpled and bloody.

"Oh, no."

"That's not the half of it. Those boys were kept hostage in this coach. And they were tortured." Ed looked her in the eye. "You was the last one to use the motor home. You was there when that kid disappeared."

"The coach has been sitting here for a day and a half."

"At the border they searched everyone else. Only you'd taken off. You never got searched, did you?"

"Ed, what are you saying? Are you implying that I had something to do with the boys disappearing?"

"Not saying anything. Just saying it looks strange. I found this." He held out the teddy bear.

Pauly took it but almost gagged. It reeked of Tea Roses—Grams' scent. Grams?

"Where's my grandmother?"

"Nobody's seen her this morning. Went into town, I think. We need supplies."

"I'll take that." The teddy bear was lifted from her hand.

A familiar voice, calm, steadying. "Tony. Thank God. We need to talk."

"Understatement. I would have thought you'd have called." He looked stern, none of the old flirtatious Tony in his demeanor. But hadn't she asked for this? Taking on the world herself and not including him?

"I should have called. I meant to."

"I'm not sure I can help you now."

Pauly suddenly felt chilled. How stupid to try to find the answers by herself. She put a child in danger, maybe two. But who would harm a child? What was Ed talking about? Tortured? For the first time Pauly felt the bone-chilling fear register, then overload her nervous system. It went beyond the unanswered questions. She couldn't let Randy's murderers win. Because she knew Randy's murder, the pictures, and the disappearance of two young boys were all connected.

"Pauly, I need to take you in for questioning."

"Take me in?" Did she hear correctly?

"Let's get in the car. Over there."

"I need to leave a note. Tell Grams—"

"You can call from the station."

"Am I being arrested?"

"Not at this moment."

"Then why—?

"Pauly, I hate this. Believe me." Tony gently took her arm. "Let's go. The sooner we get started, the sooner you can come home."

He was propelling her toward the first cop car in line out of the three that hugged the side of the drive. Tony opened the passenger-side door and she sank onto the plastic-covered front seat. Where was Steve or Grams? Or Hofer for that matter; she hadn't remembered seeing him in the group. She was beginning to feel very alone. Tony walked around and slipped in the other side behind the wheel. She assumed they would go over the motor home. What else would be found? Was there something Ed hadn't told her?

◇◇◇

Tony's office was a cramped corner of the new concrete block substation on Second Street, efficient, a handful of reference texts, a computer in the corner, new with blinking cursor, nothing homey or inviting, no philodendron trailing across the top of a bookcase. The gray metal desk matched gray metal chairs, prison-issue spartan and about as comfortable. But what did she expect? Taxpayers weren't about to keep their protectors in tufted leather. It was always tough enough to just get decent salaries. The cops had her sympathy.

Pauly excused herself to go to the bathroom, splash water on her face and comb her hair. Tony had shown her where the bathrooms were on his way to put on a fresh pot of coffee. He seemed tense, but said to take her time. Would he be standing outside the door when she came out?

He wasn't. And she felt relieved. She passed him in the kitchenette on her way back to his office. She was beginning to feel better. But not by much. She took a chair opposite the desk and couldn't stop her thoughts from straying to the teddy bear and the scent of tea roses. It wasn't a popular scent. She had to face it. It linked her grandmother to Paco or whatever child left a bloody tee shirt and who knew what else inside the motor home.

But she couldn't tell Tony that…couldn't implicate her own grandmother. She felt sick again. Had her grandmother just looked the other way when other young children were lured into the carnival? Used and controlled by violence?

No. Pauly could never believe that. Never. But didn't her grandmother seem as strongly implicated as anyone else? Grams had certainly kept things from her…had her secrets. Did Pauly have blinders on when she set out to exonerate Randy? She'd never thought that the seeming guilt of one person really might belong to another person even closer to her.

Her stomach churned. Hadn't Grams given them the balloon ride? Knew that Pauly would not be in the gondola…. And what was it that Ed said about Grams buying her the job at MDB? She leaned back in the chair and closed her eyes.

Tony pushed open the door, "I don't think I could find a couple aspirin around here if I tried." Apologetic smile. "But maybe this will work just as well." He stood in front of her holding out a cup of coffee. "Cream and sugar are in the top drawer if you need 'em." He indicated the filing cabinet in the corner. When she didn't move, he walked around the desk, opened the drawer and set a few packets on the edge of the desk before sitting down and sorting out two packets of Equal for himself. He looked strangely out of place in the small room; the image of paper-pushing didn't quite fit with his exuberance, his youth. Hopefully, he didn't spend much time here.

"Black is fine." Pauly found her voice with the first sips of coffee that warmly slid down her throat.

Tony was watching her. He didn't seem to be in any hurry; or was he just planning what he would say? But at least he'd softened. Away from his buddies, he was almost human again. Suddenly, he leaned forward in his chair, elbows on the desk.

"We received a call yesterday about a problem with the carnival. Two young boys disappeared and a pretty exhaustive search didn't turn them up. It was brought to our attention that you had returned to Albuquerque in a motor home that had not been searched. Then some kid came forward and said you had paid him to take you to meet some carny child. That you asked lots of questions—crazy stuff. I think he said you had pictures and kept calling him by the wrong name. This true?"

Pauly nodded. It was no use to lie now.

"The child's name is Paco?"

Again, Pauly nodded.

"This Paco was the kid who was in the gondola when your husband died?"

"Yes."

"Where did you find him?"

"He worked for the carnival. I saw him working with the dogs one night and I returned his teddy bear. That's all."

Tony was quiet a long time. There was a faint sound from under the desk of material being swished against metal. She guessed Tony's leg was nervously jiggling against his chair.

"Just like that? That's all there is to it?" he said. She thought he was fighting to keep his voice calm. "What about the accusation that you paid one kid to lead you to another? This Paco to be exact."

"I wanted answers."

"To?"

"Why he was in the gondola. Who he was."

"And what did you find out?"

"That he had never met Randy before the balloon ride. He was running away and the pilot put the balloon down long enough to pick him up. In fact, he was scared to death. He thought he had caused the accident."

"And what else?"

Pauly knew she couldn't tell him more. Not until she had figured out the place Grams had in all this. Anything she said now would implicate the carnival and its owners…and that, she realized, included Steve.

They both turned at the knock on the door. It opened a crack and an officer motioned for Tony to step into the hallway. "I'll be right back." He shut the door behind him.

Pauly couldn't hear what they were saying other than a couple expletives. She idly wondered if it had something to do with Paco and the motor home. She watched through the glass partition as the officer handed Tony a manila envelope and then showed him something in a crumpled paper grocery sack. They both stared at whatever it was. Tony looked upset and angry when he turned back towards the office. So, she wasn't surprised when he slammed the door.

"I don't think you're being very smart." He walked to the front of the desk, put the envelope down, perched on the edge and leaned over her. "I think you know a whole hell of a lot more than what you're saying. I guess I thought you would have called me when you found the boy, let us ask him a few questions."

"I'm sure I should have. But there didn't seem to be a reason. I just didn't find out anything other than how he came to be in the gondola."

"You're lying. You questioned that kid and decided for whatever reason to keep quiet. Questioned him about things other than just a balloon ride." His voice rose.

"He spoke Spanish, for God's sake. We didn't communicate very well." She could yell, too. And the possible language-barrier seemed to stop Tony. He was staring at her.

"What do you make of what was found in the motor home?" New tactic. She'd have to be careful. "Can you think of a reason someone in the carnival would want to harm a child? Torture him?"

Pauly shook her head. What had they found? She had seen the blood and could only guess what else there might be.

"Pauly, talk to me. Something happened. Maybe this kid got in the way of something. Panicked someone by knowing too much, threatening to tell, to run away." His voice trailed off.

"What? What could he have known?"

His eyes were on her, hands on his thighs, his face a scant foot from hers. This meeting was a far cry from the friendly chat over coffee they'd had a month ago. She had to be careful. Finally, he stood and drained his cup of coffee.

"Someone, most likely a child, was bound with ropes and gagged, kept in the closet of the motor home, and at sometime while he was held captive, beaten. If not killed."

"But they didn't find a body?"

"Are you saying there is one?"

"No, of course not. Paco was never in the motor home that I know of."

"Then explain what was found. The teddy bear for example, a bloody tee shirt, a pair of child's sandals. How did these things get into the motor home that you drove to El Paso, lived in for two days and brought back before it could be searched?"

"I have no idea. But the motor home has been parked by the maintenance garage since yesterday evening."

"Tests will show how old these stains are."

Was there such a test? Probably. But he could be baiting her. Hoping she would implicate herself...indicate she'd invited the boy in.

"Is there something you want to tell me?" He leaned against the file cabinet.

"No." She'd said it too quickly. She needed to take another sip of coffee, think before she spoke. She scooted her chair back. "It's just such a tragedy."

Again silence, just his gaze searching her face, then, "Who are you protecting?"

There it was. He sensed it. She had to go slow.

"No one. What makes you say that?"

"You left the carnival and rushed back to Albuquerque; but we don't know why."

Where was this leading? "I wanted to spend some time with my grandmother. It was Christmas."

Tony picked up the envelope he'd tossed on the desk and drew out a letter-sized piece of paper. The copy of the picture. Someone must have gone through the truck. She should have expected that. But now what?

"Looks to me like your husband knew the deceased rather well. Grown man, young boy. What sort of scenario comes to mind?"

She sat mute. She knew what he was getting at. But if she explained the picture, pointed out that it was a fake, she'd end up telling a lot more. And she just wasn't sure anymore that she wanted to do that. Not before she'd had a chance to question her grandmother.

"When did you suspect that your husband was a pedophile?"

"He wasn't." Her voice was raspy, high-pitched…. She swallowed, took a deep breath, then, "This picture is a fake. I can prove it's a fake." He didn't seem to be paying attention but stepped behind the desk.

"And these? I suppose you're going to tell me that these are fake, too?" Sarcasm dripped from his words. He yanked open the middle drawer and scattered four pictures across the desktop. All were the size of the one in her wallet, but these showed Randy partially clothed, Paco on his lap, Paco on his knees. Black and white, crisper than the one in her wallet. One was frontal, Paco by himself. A duplicate of the photo that had found its way to Sosimo.

"This is disgusting. And these are a lie." She pushed up out of the chair. She couldn't look at those pictures. They needed to be destroyed before someone, anyone believed they could be true. "Give me those. They're not real. They're lies. As much a fake as this one." She pointed at the enlarged copy she'd picked up just three hours ago.

She held eye contact, but knew that Tony didn't believe her. She made a swipe to scoop the photos up, but Tony was too fast. He pinned her wrist to the desk and held her as he carefully picked them up, then he fanned them out and feigned studying them.

"Is that why you had this Paco, what shall we say, detained? Make sure he didn't tell anyone about your husband? It was bad enough that he had to take the kid along on your honeymoon, give him a balloon ride instead of you. Did you want friends to know that you'd been duped, married some sick son-of-a-bitch? We know about the vasectomy. The doctor filled us in on how upset you were when you found out. You wanted children, he lied, then you found out that this very man procured innocent children for sexual acts. Did you decide to punish the evidence? Keep this Paco from talking by threatening him? Beating him?"

Pauly fell back into the chair. Her hurt Paco? What was he saying? This wasn't happening. It was insanity.

"Where did you get those pictures?" Her voice was a whisper.

"Where did you get this one?" Tony picked up the copy.

Pauly managed to mumble, "I found it. It was in a box of his things."

"Let's just say that these were a little gift, that in the interest of justice, someone thought that he or she could help us out. No name but someone who knew about Randy's interests."

"You don't know what you're talking about." She sighed. She felt absolutely drained. The hopelessness of the situation was beginning to dawn on her.

"Let me tell you what we do know. Then you be the judge. You were seen in El Paso questioning the kid. We know you used an interpreter and paid them both for information. Then on Christmas Eve you followed him late at night when he helped a young friend slip into the carnival. You confronted this Paco. Threatened to turn him in. The kids got scared. You wanted to keep this Paco quiet so you took him back to the motor home—maybe him and his friend."

"This is crazy."

"Oh yeah? What part do you deny? There are witnesses, Pauly. Witnesses that place you with Paco on Christmas Eve, in the afternoon and again at night. Do you deny following him after he let his friend into the carnival?"

Tony's face was flushed, but his eyes never wavered. She wanted to crumble. Instead, she straightened her shoulders.

"I did not take him back to the motor home. I don't know anything about…about any of this."

"Do you have an alibi? Maybe someone stayed with you overnight, Christmas Eve?"

It wasn't like she hadn't planned on having someone stay the night. Steve. Of course, he could get her out of this. They were together that night. For a good part of it. He could tell them that all this was some mistake. Unless…could Steve be a part of this? Her head hurt. She couldn't think straight anymore.

She needed to try a different tactic. Stay calm. Keep her voice steady. She took a breath, "Let's go back to that picture. It's an enlargement that I had done just today at the Camera Corral. Call them. A kid named Jeff waited on me. He'll confirm my story. Here." She fumbled in her billfold. "Here's the original. If you have a lab take a look at the pictures you have, they'll find that they're fakes, too."

Tony took the picture from her and looked at it before he handed it back. He didn't seem that interested. Must not be racy enough for him, Pauly thought as she tucked it away.

"That doesn't explain the things we found in the motor home."

"All of the pictures are fakes."

"Do you know that?"

"I'll bet my life on it."

"It's easy for you to say. Maybe, easy for you to have faked the pictures. But there had to have been some originals. Like this one. Who took this one?" He picked up the photo of a partially clad Randy. She looked away. What could she say? He went on, "Who would have a better reason to keep this Paco from talking than you? And who would have had a better reason to kill Randolph McIntyre than the one who stood to inherit and erase his past?"

What could she say? Pauly was getting tired of all this. She wanted to go home and confront Grams, get explanations of her own. She wasn't going to say anything else until she'd done that.

"Take me back."

"Sorry, I can't do that just yet."

"Am I under arrest?"

"Let's just say that you're being detained."

"I'm calling my lawyer."

"There's the phone." Tony turned the desk unit so that she could use it. "Dial nine." He leaned back in his chair and worked over a cuticle on his thumb.

"Any chance of getting a refill?" She pointed to her coffee cup.

Tony shrugged and got up from behind the desk.

"Oh yeah. I've been meaning to tell you I got the name of that PI hired by your business partners to keep an eye on you."

"And?" Pauly pulled a wad of business cards out of her billfold and thumbed through them looking for Sam's.

"His name's Burke. Ex-con. Real sweetheart from what I hear."

The cards scattered across the floor. She kept her head down and retrieved them. Steve? No. She couldn't believe it, *wouldn't* believe it. But how could she prove differently? And wasn't she being unreasonable? There wasn't one reason why it couldn't be true. He'd admitted to being an ex-con, so why couldn't he also be a private dick? When she'd met with Paco in the park in El Paso, Steve could have seen them. He'd certainly been in a position to know her every move. Had he informed Tony?

She clutched the cards and stuffed them back in her purse. A phone book. She sat up. There was one on the desk. She needed to compose herself while Tony was out of the room. Stop thinking about Steve right now. Sam had offered to be her friend as well as her lawyer. And it looked like she could use a friend. If she could settle this nightmare, she needed to take charge of her life. For now, she flipped open the phonebook and picked up the receiver.

Chapter Eleven

Sam's secretary had reached him on his cell. He was at the station in twenty minutes. Pauly had refused to continue the conversation with Tony and waited in the foyer next to some pretty sad-looking potted plants that obviously didn't want to be standing there any more than she did. Tony was irked, but what could he do? He must know that he didn't have enough to keep her. She had rights and wouldn't be bullied.

Sam's hug was the most caring thing that had happened to her in a long time. She reveled in it, clung to him, and he didn't pull away. Tony watched but didn't say anything.

"My client and I are going to leave now. I know and you know that you don't have any reason to keep her here." Sam was matter-of-fact, decisive, daring Tony to say otherwise. Tony only nodded. He looked grim-faced.

She couldn't help her spirits rising as she sank onto the navy seat of Sam's Jaguar and breathed in the aroma of leather, a far cry from the unyielding plastic of the squad car an hour ago…and the faint scent of someone's Egg McMuffin lingering in a door's side pocket.

"I think a drink's in order." Sam was smiling at her. Reassuring, calming as he started the car. "We need to talk. That young man wouldn't be threatening you if he didn't think he had something. You need to tell me what that something is and then we'll go from there."

Pauly stared out the window and tried to collect herself. To think, to even suggest that she could have hurt Paco was so hideous. But was it a stretch if you were in Tony's shoes? And those pictures. Obviously, there were more of them floating around. Another set of fakes. Of that she was certain. But who would believe her? She stole a glance at her chauffeur and savior. Was he her only chance? She shivered.

"Are you cold?" Sam must have been watching her.

"No. Just upset." She tried a smile that stopped with the corner of her mouth jerking spasmodically.

"Well, we're almost there and it's going to feel good to just get this whole thing out on the table. I can't imagine you're in danger of being charged with anything. It seemed like the usual bluff tactics to me. But we'll be prepared. I won't let you down, Pauly. I want you to know that. I've been involved more in contract law lately, but I can get the right lawyer for you in a second." The smile was genuine and warm, then he squeezed her arm.

Sam turned into the parking lot of El Pinto Mexican restaurant on Fourth Street. It had stopped snowing but the afternoon was bleak, heavily overcast and threatening to turn cold and wet. Suddenly a margarita in front of a fire sounded great. Finally, she could sit calmly and tell someone what had been happening. Turn over her evidence to someone who would know the right thing to do. Someone who would believe her. And he'd be able to explain Grams' involvement.

With a stab of anger, she thought of Steve. Had he really been hired to search her background? Work for Archer and Tom? But it went beyond that. If he had followed her when she talked with Paco, could he have followed her to El Paso on Thursday as well? Followed her to the Amistad address and set the fire that killed someone? Certainly Archer would have kept him informed as to her whereabouts. So, just maybe, Steve had tried to kill her. Anything was possible. How could she have kept quiet about the ski mask?

Sam asked to be seated in the bar. The tension seemed to flow out of her in the coziness of stained glass and red brick floors. The crackle of the fire in the corner fireplace was comforting. There was an array of chips and salsa, con queso and taquitos on a side table. Suddenly, she was famished.

Sam pulled out a tall stool at a table near the fireplace.

"How about something to eat? We can just have some munchies or order a late lunch. It's your call."

"Munchies will be fine."

"Consider it done." With a smile he walked to the side table and returned with a heaping basket of chips and bowls of salsa and cheese dip.

He ordered their drinks, excused himself to make a phone call that would clear his afternoon and give her time to relax.

By the time he returned, she was eager to tell him everything that had happened. The burden of not having anyone to talk with had weighed heavily. And this was her grandmother's lawyer, the one person who might tell her about her grandmother, if he wasn't afraid he'd breach client confidentiality. Wouldn't he know if somehow her grandmother might be caught up in something…something sinister and dangerous, something that had led to the murder of Pauly's husband?

"To what? This is your call." Sam held up his tumbler of scotch.

"Truth. Finding answers." They touched glasses. The lime-fresh taste of the margarita was reviving. But where to start? Sam was watching her, affectionately, being patient and understanding.

"Sam, I don't know how I can thank you for coming to pick me up. I so appreciate your thoughtfulness."

"There's no need for thank-yous. Whatever you have to tell me will be held in strict client confidence. But I want you to know that I'll do everything in my power to help."

She smiled. Why was she tongue-tied? Now that she had a chance to unburden herself? Was it because she might sound hysterical? Someone tried to kill her, frame her husband; maybe her grandmother, your client, too, is involved in a porn-ring.... Didn't it sound a little preposterous? She took a breath.

"After Randy's death I found out certain things that he'd kept secret. Things that would have torn us apart. Like the vasectomy."

"I hope I wasn't the one to tell you?" He leaned forward, concern in his voice.

"No. I found out in the hospital when I tried to have his sperm harvested for future use."

"I'm so sorry. I had no idea that he hadn't told you."

"Why do you think he didn't?"

"I don't know. Probably afraid that you wouldn't marry him if he did. He was infatuated. I've never seen him as happy as he was with you."

"So you don't think someone paid him to marry me?"

Sam stopped midway to taking a sip of his drink and put the scotch glass back on the table. He was frowning.

"What do you mean?"

"I have it on good authority...." Did Noralee qualify as a good source? She had made sense at lunch. "That someone might have wanted the two of us to get married badly enough to make it lucrative."

"Who said such a thing?"

"That's not important. The issue is why."

Sam shook his head. "I can only think that someone wants to hurt you, diminish what you had with Randy."

Noralee qualified for having a reason to do that all right, but Pauly didn't believe she was vindictive. Not after today.

"But let's say it could be true, for now, for the sake of argument. The story gets crazier." Sam took a big swallow of his drink but didn't interrupt her. "When the balloon crashed after the pilot had been shot, a child tumbled out, scared out of his wits, as you can imagine. I didn't try to stop him, and he was so freaked that he simply ran away."

"Did you report this to the police?"

"At first they didn't believe me."

"But later?"

"They thought I was telling the truth. They even searched the area and found a teddy bear and Randy's jean jacket…the one the child had worn."

"Mind?" Sam had pulled a pipe from his pocket. Pauly shook her head.

"Well, I didn't know it then, but this child would be the pivotal point to this whole thing." Pauly reached for her billfold and pulled out the picture of Randy and Paco. "I found a pornographic photo of this child and others in Randy's desk at work, and this photo and a set of adoption papers in his safe deposit box."

Sam picked up the picture.

"Where is the child from?"

"Mexico."

"And Randy never mentioned this child? You found out all this after his death?"

"You said yourself that Randy wanted to adopt a child. Did he adopt this child? Did he mention this child?" She eagerly sat forward.

"I didn't mean to imply that. Yes, he'd spoken of adoption. Must have known he'd get caught in the lie about the vasectomy. But, frankly, I discouraged him. I suppose he could have taken steps to adopt on his own." Sam studied the photo.

"I don't think he did. I think someone was trying to set Randy up as a pedophile, discredit him, smear his name after he was dead."

"Pauly, why would anyone want to do that?"

"I don't know why. One set of child-porn pictures I found in his desk was addressed to Congressman Sosimo Garcia. And because of the water project Randy was working on and its importance to Sosimo, I thought there could be a motive in there somewhere." Pauly took a sip of her drink, then two more. Didn't Sam believe her? He looked thoughtful, staring into space, sucking on his pipe. "But the important thing is this child." A vision of Paco's bruised body floated to the surface; she pushed it back. Had he been tortured in the motor home? "I found the child. He was working for Grams' carnival." She lowered her voice. "I have reason to believe that he helped procure other young children to join the carnival, maybe join a child porn ring. I think the carnival was used to attract children, sort of a front." She sat back. "Anyway, he's gone. I was being questioned because of what was found in the motor home. The police think he could be dead." She couldn't bring herself to say murdered.

"Whoa. What's this about a child porn ring?" She had Sam's full attention, that was for sure. He was frowning in his earnestness to make sure he understood.

"What other explanation is there? This picture is a family portrait compared to the others."

"And this is the child they think you tortured…that you hid in the motor home?"

Pauly nodded.

"They know that I interviewed him while we were in El Paso, that I followed him, saw him bring a kid into the carnival."

"That doesn't seem to give you a reason—"

"Especially not when he proved that he wasn't involved with Randy. This picture is a fake." Pauly was excited now. This was the most important information that she had. She picked up the picture. "The detective has three or four others, same size as this snapshot, but the others are suggestive, explicit even…." She thought of the one of Paco on his knees in front of Randy. Randy bare-chested but in the original picture must have had on shorts or swim trunks, before a little touch-up work made him look naked. She'd spare Sam a description of that one. "But they're all fakes. I just know it. If this one is a fake, I'll bet the others are too. I had this one analyzed at a photo lab. It's good but it's been pieced together. Look at this shadow, and here." She pointed with a straw at the shadows between the figures.

Sam took the picture and held it closer to the winking votive candle in the green glass container in the center of the table, then shook his head. "I'll have to take your word for it."

"Trust me. The lab will testify that it's been doctored."

She picked up her drink, flinching when the straw sucked air. She'd forgotten that she'd finished it. God, she'd almost gulped it down. And she had a slightly dizzying, exhilarated feeling from the tequila—or maybe from the unburdening? She guessed a little of each.

"This is an interesting twist." Sam was still staring at the photo.

"You know that adoption agency in El Paso? Well, not only did it turn out to be a false address, but someone tried to kill me. And the adoption papers were falsified—"

"Pauly, I had no idea. You've been in real danger." Shock registered on Sam's face.

"The name on the papers, Jorge Zuniga, wasn't the child's real name. I have no idea who this child Jorge is, but Amistad didn't exist. Probably never had. The office belonged to a U-Haul rental firm that had gone out of business. It was some trumped-up lie that I was supposed to discover, but I don't know why."

"I can't believe that you've been doing all this on your own. Analyzing pictures, snooping around boarded-up buildings. You've taken unbelievable chances."

"I had to know, Sam. I had to find out the truth."

"You're damned lucky that you weren't killed in that fire."

"I just didn't think at the time. Sam, I need to clear Randy's name." She sat forward earnestly. "I believe now that he had nothing to do with those young boys. I bet he'd be in shock right now if he knew what was going on."

Sam didn't say anything, just twirled the ice cubes in his empty glass. "You don't think he could have been a pedophile?"

Pauly almost gasped. Was Sam holding something back? He'd know, wouldn't he? He'd known Randy all his life. "Sam, was he? You've got to tell me."

Sam seemed reluctant, seemed to be choosing his words. She felt like screaming. Could she take the truth? Here she was faced with it.

"You can't deny that Randy was peculiar. Forty-one, never married. Pauly, I have to tell you that I wondered about his sexual abilities. No, no, not preferences, but just his libido in general. It seemed a little under-developed."

Not a confirmation. But not a denial, either. What was he really trying to say?

"You can't imagine how happy, no relieved, I was when you came along. I have to say I encouraged him in his decision."

She sat up straighter. "If he'd been interested in boys, there wouldn't have been a reason for the vasectomy. There wouldn't have been a first marriage." Her voice was no-nonsense crisp, a hint of exasperation. Then she sat back, arms folded across her chest. There. Didn't that prove something? She found herself mildly irritated. Because Sam hadn't jumped right in and sworn that Randy was hetero all the way? Maybe. But there was something else he had just said, a minute before. She'd meant to question him at the time, but it escaped her now.

Sam shrugged. "The marriage was annulled. I don't think it proves anything other than Randy made a bad choice. Let me get you another." He pointed at her empty drink glass. "I won't accept a no. Let's just say it's medicinal." He patted her on the shoulder before he walked to the bar.

Convenient time to leave the table. Was he dodging the issue? She seemed to have struck a nerve. Maybe, if she tried a different tactic. But what was it he'd said earlier? Something that struck her as odd…something that surprised her. She had no idea why she'd accepted another drink; her thinking was fuzzy as it was. But she thanked Sam for the second margarita and took a sip and waited for him to pull his chair closer to the table.

"Enough about me for a minute." Maybe if she changed subjects. "Sam, I have to ask, what do you know about my grandmother's involvement here, using the carnival to lure children into…well, some kind of porn ring?"

Sam's teeth clattered against the pipe's stem. She couldn't read his eyes but she felt his surprise.

"Your grandmother?"

"She seems to be at the center of all this—Grams and probably her sixth husband."

"There are always a line of those, aren't there?"

Did he sound irked? Maybe. he'd been one of the suitors.

"I know how it must sound…a granddaughter suspecting her own grandmother." She touched his arm, left her hand there for a second until he put his hand over hers. "I've found you very supportive. Thank you for listening…for understanding."

"There's nothing wrong with questioning. Pauly, your grandmother won't have a sixth husband very long. She's a very independent woman. It's difficult for her to have a partner…for her to accept business suggestions."

Pauly smiled. That was true.

"I've drawn up papers for an annulment. Her last marriage just didn't work out. Both parties will walk away no worse for wear. It's all fairly amicable."

But Pauly doubted that. Somehow from the way he said it, she guessed things had not gone all that smoothly.

Pauly leaned forward, "Sam, who is number six?"

"Your grandmother's my client. The relationship was an embarrassment to say the least. I'm going to have to tell you to ask Lulu."

Pauly sighed. Did it matter? Probably no…not unless…. "Sam, what do you think about my grandmother being involved in something illegal?"

She felt him go on guard, stiffen ever so slightly before he pulled his hand away.

"Could she know that young children are being lured to the carnival possibly to be used, exploited for child porn?"

"Lulu? Absolutely not. Surely you know your grandmother that well. I can't believe you even entertained the thought. And you have no proof that that's really the situation."

His sharp tone didn't surprise her. Recrimination, she deserved it. How could she suspect her grandmother? But that didn't explain the cologne-soaked teddy bear.

"What do you know about Hofer?"

A flicker of something passed across his eyes. Was Hofer her about-to-be annulled husband—despite Ed's disclaimer? She knew for certain that Hofer was the "uncle"—the man Paco had said got him a job, the "preacher-man." The one who might have taken the picture of Paco that was pieced together with one of Randy. She'd almost forgotten that. Maybe Hofer took other kinds of pictures, too.

"I guess I don't know much about him. He can't put two words together unless he's behind a pulpit."

She returned Sam's smile. It was true, but the idea that Hofer was the deviant made sense.

"Do you trust him?"

"Why do you ask?"

"I'm just trying to figure out who could be behind a child porn ring, someone also involved with the circus."

"Pauly, listen to me. I'm not sure you have enough evidence, proof, that such a thing exists." He sounded exasperated.

This was the lawyer talking. And he was probably right. Just because Paco helped a friend under the fence.... Still, someone had to have taken those photos of a nude Paco and the others, suggestive, provocative poses.

"Is there anyone who was with you in El Paso who could vouch for your whereabouts, give you an alibi for the time that this Paco or the other child might have been abducted?"

Sam was trying to bring her back to where this discussion started. And this was the immediate priority, wasn't it? Keeping her out of jail? She thought of Steve. He knew where she was, and she had been with him when the child's mother had been interviewed.

"A man by the name of Steve Burke."

"Your grandmother's newest partner?" Sam looked surprised.

"Yes. But that's not all he is." Pauly quickly told him what Tony had said.

"Are you mixed up with this Burke fellow?" He scrutinized her features as he tapped tobacco firmly in the pipe's bowl.

What was "mixed up"? Some euphemism for "have you slept with him"? It had been a narrow escape, but no cigar. She was thankful for that. Was she bitter? Yes. And angry, boiling over angry at herself...at how she'd let Steve get to her. How she'd trusted him. So would he be a good alibi? Somehow she thought not.

"No, not mixed up with him," she smiled.

"I tried to talk Lulu out of adding him to the team. One of our many disagreements." He smiled ruefully and sucked on the stem of the pipe. "Where is this Steve now?"

"Still in El Paso, supposedly."

"Think carefully. Could he vouch for your whereabouts on Christmas Eve?"

"For some of the time, up until about midnight."

"But not after that?"

Pauly shook her head and didn't elaborate about falling asleep waiting on him, standing in front of him stark naked the next morning before getting into the shower.... She was still smarting, but hey, she just decided she had been lucky. Fortunate that there hadn't been an affair? And wasn't there a ski mask and evidence that he'd given false information to the police—that should make her doubly lucky that she'd be able to just walk away.

She stretched her legs. She was beginning to feel numb. One fishbowl-sized margarita had gone straight to her head. She'd take it slow with the second, not compound the slight buzz she already felt. Because there were still questions that needed answers.

"Why do you think Randy was killed?" She'd always wondered about Sam's opinion.

"I'm not sure anyone's proved that the pilot wasn't the primary target. He was the one shot."

"True, but the police seem to think it was Randy."

"Why do you think?" Sam asked. The question was punctuated with a couple of quick puffs of pipe smoke.

"Uh uh. No fair. I asked first." Was she sounding a little slurred? She scooted the margarita out of reach.

"If your suspicions of pedophilia are true, that would give someone a reason." More puffs from the pipe as he watched her.

She could cut the silence between them. This wasn't what she expected him to say.

He continued, "I honestly don't have an explanation for the pictures. I believe that we have to take into consideration the possibility of Randy's being a pedophile, however distasteful that might be. But nothing's been proved. I want to caution you not to let your imagination run wild. And if the detective gets back in touch, don't meet with him without me there. That's very important. I want you to promise me. Do you understand?"

She nodded. Suddenly, it felt like she was getting a lecture. Did Sam believe anything she had told him? She had proof, for God's sake…the pictures were fake. Randy was not a pedophile.

"The same goes for this Burke fellow. If the company hired him to spy on you, you don't want to give them anything to use against you. Your grandmother said that she thought they were trying to squeeze you out."

Pauly was smart enough to know that; she didn't need him to tell her. She felt peevish. Uneasy. But she couldn't quite get her margarita-laden brain to work. But there was something just beneath the surface she needed to address, something that was important, if she could just think clearly.

"I should be getting back now." She shook her hair away from her face and tucked errant strands behind her ears. Whatever it was that was so important, it eluded her. She was just tired.

"Of course." Sam left a wad of four or five ones on the table and helped her on with her jacket.

It took an extra firm shove to open the restaurant's heavy wooden front door. The gust of wind was teeth-chattering cold, and the sting of sleet surprised her. Within the last hour the promised winter storm had descended on the city. Fourth Street was already glazed over. And it was dark now. Dark, but the street lights reflected brightly on patches of black ice. Thank God she wasn't driving. She hated this kind of weather. It didn't happen often in Albuquerque, but when it did, it was chaos; everything came to a halt.

"I hate to make you take me home in this mess."

"We're not that far away. I think we can get there all right. Maybe I'll impose on your grandmother to put me up for the night." A chuckle.

The Jag maintained traction up the short incline of the parking lot ramp that would put them on Fourth Street. Sam paused before turning to the right. Traffic was light, almost non-existent. The car slipped, then dug in and seemed solid in spite of the treacherous footing. They got on the interstate. He was probably going to take Paseo Del Norte. Pauly began to relax. He was a good driver and the sleet had turned to snow, big wet elephant flakes that collected along the wiper blades.

Half a dozen cars turned before they did, making slow careful arcs onto the four-lane. The uphill curve didn't bother the Jag. Sam straightened the car, settled into the middle lane and accelerated to twenty-five miles an hour. They were driving into the storm and the flakes stuck to the windshield, thickly limiting visibility.

The pipe was in a pocket somewhere and Pauly could see the line of his jaw, taut and determined. Sam backed off the gas as a tangle of lights appeared on the right. A fender-bender. Both parties were standing by their vehicles.

"Should we call someone?" His cell phone was on the dash.

"There are probably so many calls, you wouldn't be able to get through. They seemed to be all right."

Pauly turned for another look. Both men were obscured by a wall of dense white flakes.

"Damn."

Pauly turned back as she felt Sam start to tap the brakes. This time the accident was in front of them and stretched across all lanes. Pauly leaned against the dash, gripping its edge, and peered out the windshield. One car was on its side. Several others fit together in an accordion-pleated zig-zagged line, headlights aiming all directions.

Sam had almost stopped when the lights that swept across the interior of the Jag startled her, especially when they swung back to the right as quickly as they had first appeared. A car was spinning out of control, coming up fast behind them.

Pauly leaned over the back of the seat in time to see the whirling car sideswipe an eighteen-wheeler, which jack-knifed, skidding sideways, tractor and trailer skating across the highway in slow-motion accuracy aimed at the back of the Jag.

"Sam." The scream was useless. There was nothing he could do. No place to go. Sitting ducks. They were going to be sandwiched between the truck and the pile of already wrecked cars in front of them.

The squealing and gnashing of gears gave way to the grinding of tearing metal. At the moment of impact, the back window of the Jag exploded inward, spraying the interior with sparkling bits of glass. Then the back of the car rose in the air to perch against the truck's radiator. They were pushed like a cow-catcher on the tilting Peterbilt to ram anything in front of them. The headlights and grillwork of the truck seemed to inhabit the back seat.

Pauly hugged her legs to her chest, burying her head in her thighs, bracing for the next impact. She was beyond screaming. She opened her mouth but there was no sound. All of her senses were frozen. She didn't look at Sam. There was no time. Only nanoseconds before the truck ground them into the pile of already twisted steel—the barricade that had been a line of cars just moments ago.

Her seat belt snapped viciously into her chest and lap, but held, holding her rigid and upright even when the Jag's roof caved in dangerously close to the top of her head. And then there was nothing, no motion, no sound. They were stopped. She was alive. She gulped in air and tried to stretch her legs, but she was wedged between seat and dash.

Sam. He wasn't moving. Blood spilled over his forehead, trickling unnoticed across his eyes, down his face. The cut across his forehead looked deep. She had to stop the bleeding. She had to move. She frantically pushed against the dash, and the seat gave way a couple of inches, allowing the glove compartment door to flop open. But at least she could put her feet down a little ways.

She rummaged through the compartment's contents, intent on purpose, fighting the hysteria that threatened to sweep over her, trying to shut out the smell of wrecked metal, of gasoline and fear, the feeling of claustrophobia that could make her crazy, make her flail against the smashed door, the collapsed roof as she sought a way out. No. She was needed. Sam could be bleeding to death. She couldn't leave him. Surely there would be something, some piece of cloth she could use to stop the flow.

The compartment's tiny light was a help. She pawed at the contents. The gun nestled in the back was a semi-automatic with extra clip. No surprise. Lots of people carried guns. The car's manual was in a plastic zip-locked pouch, loose papers, registration, insurance papers on top of it, not even a packet of Kleenex. But there was a deck of playing cards rubber-banded snugly together.

Pauly started to toss them aside, then stopped. The card on top was face up. Hadn't she seen enough of this sort of thing? Numbly, she slipped off the rubber band. They weren't playing cards but carefully matted photos of young children. Ten of them, two of girls, maybe one was five at the most. They looked like miniature advertisements. The statistics on the back gave particulars about each child. Particulars that would appeal to someone interested in children for sex. She fought nausea, swallowed and thumbed through them again. She didn't recognize any of the children.

Suddenly the accident was forgotten. Quiet terror settled over her. Sam. With a jolt she remembered what he had said earlier. What had eluded her at the time, what she knew wasn't quite right because there was no way that he could have known unless he had masterminded the attempt on her life or was an avid reader of the El Paso newspaper. He had said she'd been lucky not to have been killed in the *fire*. He had used the word fire. How could he have known someone had torched the building if he hadn't been the one who had ordered it done? But why? Why did he want her dead?

Panic. She wanted out of there. She slipped the gun and clip in her purse and glanced at the man slumped behind the steering wheel. His eyes were closed and his chest rose and fell unevenly. The flow of blood had slowed, coagulating along the hairline. She fought back hysterics. She couldn't stand to be with him one more minute. She raised her two gloved fists and beat against the unyielding windshield, then screamed as hands on the outside cleared a rounded space and a face stared in at her.

"Take it easy. We'll get you out."

She hadn't heard the man crawl over the hood. He must be helping people.

"We've got to bust the windshield. Cover your face."

Pauly did as she was told and didn't even think of Sam.

The spray of glass covered her hair, her jacket.

"Are you hurt?" The man leaned down to look at her huddled in the Jag's squashed interior and continued to pull away chunks of shattered glass caught behind the wipers.

"No."

"Grab my hand. Try to lie down, stretch out and ease yourself onto the hood. That's right. Come on. I don't want to frighten you, but we might not have too much time."

Fire. He's afraid of fire. Engine smells of oil and gasoline were pungent now. Pauly quickly wiggled free of the Jaguar's seats and, hanging onto her purse, pulled her body across the dash, then out into the open. The snow felt fresh. The big flakes were fast blanketing the scene of destruction. With the help of the man she slipped to the ground, wobbling only a second on unsteady legs.

"Okay, now?"

She nodded. He turned to run his flashlight beam back across the Jag's front seat.

"Jesus. You didn't say there was someone else. How bad's he hurt?"

But Pauly didn't answer. She was already jogging along the perimeter of the pile-up, towards the edge of the highway, the fields beyond. She had to get out of there.

"Hey. Come back here." The man's voice was muted by the soft whiteness that quickly enveloped her, leaving only the crunch of her footfalls in answer.

Chapter Twelve

Pauly was three miles from the B&B. The snow was five inches deep and sticking to her boots and pants legs, making walking laborious. Should she have stayed? Not left the accident and made sure that Sam got help? She shivered and not from the wet and cold. This man could have masterminded everything. He was in a position to set up Randy and her grandmother, but who was in it with him? She was fairly certain that Hofer had a part, and Sosimo. But what about Steve? Or Archer and Tom?

She left the highway and climbed the steep embankment that put her on Rio Grande Boulevard. The snow was letting up and it would be darker now as she got further from the muted halogen glow of the arcing lights that loomed over the highway. Rio Grande was lighted intermittently with older, smaller street lights that cast an eerie shadowless illumination straight down in irregular, round patches along the side of the road. It was like walking from one spotlight to another.

She'd follow the road to where it ended at Alameda, then cut over to the bridge and leave the pavement and lights to follow the path along the river back towards the house. She'd stay off of Paseo de Norte. She hadn't planned on sneaking back to the B&B unnoticed, but maybe this was best. Was her grandmother in danger? She stopped. She hadn't seen her grandmother since yesterday. Grams hadn't been up that morning, and she hadn't been there when Ed had found the things in the motor home.

Pauly started to jog but was just too tired to keep it up in the clinging snow.

Of course, there could be a simple explanation. Grams could have gone shopping. It was possible that she was in town. Hadn't Ed said she'd gone for supplies? But it was also possible that she was being held against her will. Pauly couldn't let herself think that Grams might be injured or worse. She stopped to knock the snow off her boots and take a couple of breaths. This kind of thinking wasn't getting her anywhere. She had to stay calm.

A pickup with chains clinked past, disappearing into the feathery dark. If she'd been noticed, there was no indication. She thought of walking up to one of the houses along Rio Grande Boulevard and calling. But call whom? What did she have to say? There was a lot that she hadn't shared with Tony, but most of her so-called information was supposition. Circumstantial evidence, at best. What did she really have on Sam? Nothing he couldn't worm out of. She was certain of that. For starters, he could just deny ever having said anything about a fire in El Paso. And the pornographic cards? He could always just get rid of them. Had it been stupid not to take them, Pauly wondered?

No, any real answers rested with Grams. Grams could tell her about Sam. Pauly picked up her pace. The bridge was a quarter-mile away. The snow had stopped but not until it had given extra height to the bridge railings in fat white mounds, clinging even to the still cables overhead. Pauly only paused a second before sliding down the embankment to walk along the path by the river.

She hadn't meant to search for it, but her eyes sought the cross at the base of the cottonwood nearest the water. The monument to Randy, to his death just twenty feet from where she was standing. The snow banked against the tree's trunk and covered two-thirds of the marker.

She started out again. The wet had seeped down the tops of her boots and through the eyelets for the laces. Stopping only made her aware of how wooden her toes felt. But she was close now, she'd be able to get out of her sodden clothing soon.

From a distance the house looked abandoned, not a light on. Which didn't make sense. It couldn't be more than seven. Where was her grandmother? Hadn't they served a meal in the dining room? Her eyes swept the studio above the garage. Was Steve back? The apartment was dark.

Suddenly, she felt hesitant. Some sixth sense? She couldn't shake a feeling that something was wrong. That she might be walking into a trap. She slowed, finally stopping in the last stand of fledgling cottonwoods at the right of the drive. The motor home was gone, but someone might have just pulled it around to the garage. What was bothering her?

Then she focused on the field beyond the garage. Of course. The trailers, motor homes, tractor-trailers, everything was gone. The carnival had left. They had just gotten back at noon. How could they be gone? Was there some New Year's show somewhere? But that was almost a week away. She'd swear no one had told her about another show. Of course, that didn't mean there wasn't one. But it gave the scene in front of her a particularly lonely feel. The B&B seemed abandoned. Was there anyone in the house? Like Grams? She had said she wouldn't travel over the holidays.

Pauly couldn't continue to stand out there in the cold. She needed to change clothes, get something to eat. She took the gun out of her purse and slipped it into her jeans pocket. It was almost an automatic reaction and the right one somehow. It gave her the courage to go forward. But could she use it? If she absolutely had no choice? She'd handled guns before. But shooting frogs with a pellet gun was a far cry from aiming at a human being, let alone pulling the trigger.

She stayed hidden by the trees and circled to the right so that she'd be able to approach the house from the back, completely in the shadows, hugging the windowless north side before rounding the corner and going in the back door. Her heart was pounding. She wasn't overreacting. Something was wrong. She stopped twice, peering into the dusky shadows. The two mounted yard lights overlapped territory, concentrating their light in one area with a radius of about fifty feet. Beyond that, it was impossible to distinguish shapes.

The snow had started again, lightly this time, just flecks, mere shadows of their former selves. Pauly paused. She had to step into the light to get to the back door. Was someone watching her? She felt like there were eyes everywhere. She took a deep breath and admonished herself for being frightened. Wasn't finding Grams as important as her own safety?

She stepped forward, rounded the corner, and willed herself to concentrate on getting to the back door by simply walking normally, not slinking along afraid of her shadow. A warm bath, food, dry clothes, she tried to concentrate on the positive. She had no proof that her grandmother was in trouble. Just an overactive imagination.

She reached the back door and felt for her keys in the bottom of her purse, then stopped and put a hand on the gun. That quieted her. It didn't necessarily give her an advantage, but it kept her from totally being the underdog. She put the key in the lock and turned the door handle. Open. She stepped into the hallway and pushed the door closed behind her.

"Nasty out there," Hofer's voice boomed from the kitchen doorway.

Pauly almost screamed, but didn't. She collected herself. Waited for her breathing to return to normal. He was just standing there, a hulking shadow with the hall nightlight illuminating his knees and keeping his face hidden. She'd forgotten how big he was. But he wasn't moving toward her. Wasn't threatening her in any way. She kept her hand on the gun in her pocket.

"Where's Grams?"

"Turned in early. Sicker than a dog all day. Must be a bug."

He was almost loquacious, friendly even. Pauly turned to go up the stairs.

"There's no reason to check on her." He'd taken a step forward. Pauly paused on the bottom step. "She said she'd see you at breakfast. I think she must have taken a little something to get some sleep."

"Okay," Pauly called over her shoulder, then added, "Where'd the carnival go?"

"Pulled out before the storm. They'll be in Bernalillo for the week. Wouldn't have gotten there if they hadn't started early."

"Is Steve back?"

"Haven't seen him. Doubt if he'll get back tonight in all the snow. The six o'clock news said they'd closed the interstate, north and south."

She heard Hofer go back into the kitchen. Chat over. Was she relieved? Yes. But a lot depended on how she found her grandmother. If it was just the flu, then she was being silly. If it wasn't.... She kept her hand on the gun and continued up the stairs.

Her grandmother's room was two down from hers. She had no intention of not looking in on her. She hurried along the hallway and stopped in front of Grams' bedroom. She pressed an ear to the door. There was no sound coming from the other side. Pauly turned the door handle, slowly, quietly. Locked. Her grandmother never locked her room. Well, at least, Pauly didn't think she did. Certainly as a child, she remembered the door was always open. But maybe later, after she'd opened the B&B.

A locked door didn't necessarily mean that there was a problem. Pauly walked past to her own room but couldn't shake the feeling of dread. If she could just talk to her grandmother, just see her. If she'd been sick, maybe she needed her. Pauly flipped on the light and took in the comforting, familiar shapes of her furniture. Then turned and locked her door.

First order of business was peeing. She crossed to the bathroom, pausing to pull a turtleneck sweater from a dresser drawer, along with a pair of heavy wool socks. Dry clothes were important, too. And seemed to make a difference.

She didn't linger in the bathroom. Dressed, she crossed to the light and flipped it off. In case Hofer was watching, flushing the toilet, running water in the sink, and now the lights might make him think she was going to bed.

But she had already formulated a plan. She could not stay in the house with Hofer. Irrational, maybe, but she simply couldn't. And she had to make certain that her grandmother was safe. She added a flashlight to a pocket in her jacket opposite the gun and the keys to the truck. After one last look around, she walked to the French doors that opened onto a cedar deck that faced the mountains, but more importantly curved around in front of her grandmother's bedroom.

She opened the door a crack before stepping out. The night was quiet. Everything might as well be wrapped in cotton; the snow muffled all sound. But that part, at least, was on her side. She padded quietly around the corner, staying close to the side of the house. Her grandmother's room had identical French doors that opened onto the deck. An assortment of patio furniture that hadn't been stored in the fall took on surreal humpbacked shapes. An umbrellaless table flanked by snow-laden plastic chairs was pushed up against the house.

Pauly pulled the table to one side and eased towards the door. Tightly closed blinds kept her from seeing into the room.

She tried the door; it gave under her touch. She pushed inward but didn't step back in time to duck the dislodged rim of snow that plopped onto her shoulders from the casement above, just missing going down her neck. She stepped into the room and aimed her flashlight at the bed.

The sudden glaring stream of light bounced off the crisply made bed. No Grams. And it looked like there hadn't been for awhile. The room looked untouched. No clothes lying around, no open books on the nightstand. It was model-home perfect, with dust ruffles that matched polished cotton chair covers that matched fluffy valances, everything in shades of pink and deep rose...then she froze. The noise put her on guard. Just a tiny click. But her eyes were riveted on the doorknob across the room. The door leading to the hall. She watched as it turned ever so slowly to the right.

Pauly didn't wait to see if it would open. She backed out of the room, pulled the French doors closed, propped a deck chair securely under the knob and fled, around the corner to the stairs that would lead to the yard below. And then what? She didn't know. But when she reached the bottom, she ran away from the house, towards the woods, and didn't take a breath or look back until she had reached the trees.

And when she did, she felt foolish. All was quiet. No one was following her. The doors that opened onto the deck from her grandmother's bedroom were securely shut, chair in place. But Hofer had lied. If there wasn't something very wrong, why had he lied about her grandmother being in bed? And where was her grandmother? Was she being held somewhere? Somehow, she felt that Grams was still here. If she wasn't, why was Hofer there?

To kill her…before or after they killed her grandmother. It no longer mattered as long as both of them were out of the way. The thought came to her in a rush and seemed to sear through her being. And make total sense. They'd run out of options. She was not only expendable; she was a hazard. She shuddered. Was Hofer waiting until Sam brought her home? He must have known that she'd been with Sam. Sam had called someone from the bar. She no longer believed it had been his secretary. Did Hofer know about the accident? Sam could have called again. She'd left the phone in the Jag. She stopped herself from going on. This was crazy.

In all likelihood Sam was on his way to the hospital. He had probably already been there an hour getting stitches, unless his injuries were more serious…. She was pinged by a stab of conscience. Whatever his crime, she hadn't stayed, waited with him until he got help. She had simply run. Left the scene with his gun. Had she been too quick to assign guilt?

The sound of the back door opening snapped her back to the present. Someone was leaving. Coming to find her? She stepped back into the trees and worked her way to the right. The thick brush hid her movement. She pulled the gun out of her pocket and waited. Nothing. If someone left the house, he didn't come in her direction.

What was she going to do? She was standing in ankle-deep snow, the wet cold being pulled up her legs like a sponge. If she could just get to the truck. But would it start? She'd left it beside the garage earlier. Even if it did start, could she get out? It was chancy. The roads were almost impassable. But wasn't it a four-wheel drive? She had to believe that she could get out. And then she'd call Tony. Get to the nearest phone and call Tony and tell him everything. She wasn't putting her grandmother in jeopardy, she now realized; maybe she'd be saving her life.

The plan seemed right, maybe because nothing else came to mind. She could make it to the back of the garage without being seen from the house. Then start the truck, get going before she was noticed. Before Hofer confronted her…or worse. That was the question. What was the "or worse"? She thought she knew.

She inched along, shuffling in the snow instead of taking steps; there was less noise that way, no giveaway crunch. The last layer of powder swirled around her ankles before settling back. The night was beautiful in its crystal whiteness. It was a shame that she couldn't enjoy it.

She could see the truck, now almost buried. Snow had drifted to the fenders and covered the windshield. She felt defeated. How could she sweep the snow off, get in, start it and not run the risk of detection? That would all take too much time. But what else was there? If her grandmother was still here, she'd need help to find her. She had to get out. Get the police to come back with her.

She quickly crossed the thirty feet of open space, then paused before she rounded the corner of the garage and stepped in front of the truck. All was quiet. Gripping the edge of the sleeve of her shearling jacket, she rapidly brushed the snow from the windshield in several stiff-armed movements that cleared a two-foot swath in front of the steering wheel. That would be enough to see, at least until she got to the highway. She knocked snow from the door, opened it, and slipped behind the wheel.

She pulled off her gloves, put the flashlight and gun on the seat beside her, locked both doors, dug in her pocket for her key ring and put the key in the ignition. One turn, a groan, a pump on the gas pedal, another turn and the engine caught. Thank God. She made sure it was in four-wheel drive, slipped the gearshift into reverse; then screamed as a face pressed against the driver's-side window. Hofer, in a rage—yelling obscenities, pulling on the door handle, kicking the door, slamming his fist against the glass.

Pauly gave the truck gas, let out the clutch, revved the engine, but she was only slipping sideways, wheels spinning, then a moment of traction.... She rocked the truck forward, then slammed into reverse, pushed on the gas, then forward again. Now she was moving backwards, tedious, slow-motion inches, but movement. When the butt of his pistol shattered the driver's-side window, she ducked, grabbed her gun, whirled and shot. Two shots, upper chest and forehead, at point-blank range. The truck shuddered silent as her feet slipped off the pedals.

But instead of falling backwards, Hofer reared upright, straightened, wavered towards her, leaned precariously in the window as a look of astonishment broke across his craggy features. Pauly twisted her body to the side, opened the door and pushed with her full weight against the metal. The door caught Hofer in the midsection and pushed him backward and over to fall heavily, his bulk folding in half, a splatter of blood looking black against the white snow.

Pauly gulped air. She'd killed someone. Self-defense. She had just reacted, hadn't really thought. She let the gun clatter to the floorboards as she slipped from behind the wheel to stand over the body. Hofer wasn't moving. She didn't have to feel for a pulse to know that he was dead, but she knelt anyway and pressed two fingers to the side of his neck, then rocked back on her heels, oblivious to the cold, and stared. How could she have done this? Did she really have to? Could there have been another way? But he had smashed the window. He was coming at her. He wasn't just standing there hoping for a friendly chat. Would the cops believe her?

"Looks like I missed the show."

A scream escaped through her chapped lips. Pauly tried to scramble up, only to sit down hard in the snow, her legs refusing to hold her. She was staring at the barrel of a revolver.

Something large and menacing. She didn't have to look up to know the source of the voice, but she forced herself.

The bandage covered the top part of his head and wound into a hump that looked strangely like snow perched on his brow. His cashmere overcoat had a rip in the sleeve, but otherwise he didn't look the worse for having survived an accident some hour and a half earlier, which had given him enough time to get another car and drive all the way back.

"I should have suspected you before." Pauly was amazed at how steady her voice was. Because she really wasn't surprised? Probably. It shouldn't have taken the stack of pictures in the glove compartment to point a finger at Sam. He had been in a perfect position to mastermind everything, set Randy up, falsify the wills, monitor her actions, manipulate her grandmother. Her grandmother...of course, Sam was Grams' sixth husband. Why hadn't she seen it before?

"Sam, where's Grams?" The shiver that skipped up her spine had nothing to do with the cold.

"Can't help you. I just got here." He pushed at Hofer's thigh with the tip of an ostrich leather boot. "Wasn't very smart, was he? But then, we all underestimated you. A little Miss Nancy Drew when you put your mind to it. And the guts to shoot a man...now, who would have thought.... You'll excuse me if I don't take my hat off to you." He nodded slightly.

He didn't seem upset by Hofer's death. But there was no missing the snideness in his voice. He was playing with her. Mocking, deciding what to do? Which was a good question. What was he going to do? There was every indication that this was not how the scenario was supposed to have played out.

"Keep your hands where I can see them. Now get up." He had moved to look inside the truck and, seeing the automatic on the floorboards, scooped it up and put it in his pocket. Then he put his large revolver on the seat. "Turn around." She thought of running but realized that fright or cold, or both, had turned her legs to boards. When she didn't move fast enough, he jerked her arm, twisting it and not letting go. She had no energy left to resist. Zombie-like, she let herself be jerked towards him.

"I think I need to keep you from becoming brave again. My poor Pauly, just too smart for her own good." He grabbed her other arm and quickly laced a length of clothesline around her wrists, taut enough to cut off circulation if she pulled against the knot. Pauly tried to protest, but he only pulled the line tighter. Then picked up the gun.

"Now we'll go see if we can find your grandmother."

"I thought you said—"

"Maybe I lied."

He was pushing her in front of him along the side of the truck, around the corner of the garage. He kicked open a side door and dragged her over the threshold. She stumbled and almost fell, but he didn't turn on any lights. The yard lights filtered through the row of snow-covered windows in the garage doors. When her eyes adjusted, Pauly could make out Grams' Lincoln. A jeep was at the far end, four stalls over. And it was running. Grams. Had they set up something to look like suicide? Carbon monoxide poisoning?

"Sam, what have you done to her?" Her voice was a wail.

He glanced at the jeep and chortled, guessing her fears. "Too easy. Your grandmother would want her death to be a little more adventuresome, don't you think?" He kept the revolver pointed her direction and walked over to press a button on the wall that instantly sent one of the metal garage doors clattering upwards on runners, finally sliding to a rest above the jeep. The cold blast cleared the air of fumes. Pauly took a deep breath.

"Did you kill Randy?" She had to know. Couldn't he tell her now? She wasn't going anywhere, at least, not alive.

"Still the good little wife, eh, Pauly? Trying to solve all the puzzles." He was close to her again and reached out to caress her cheek. There was a twisted tenderness to his touch. Pauly shrank back.

"I want to know."

"I just bet you do. You were right, you know, about one thing. I bought you a husband." He reached out to touch her again. "How does it feel to be an old-fashioned bride in a prearranged marriage? That's what you were. Randy needed the money. I needed a little leverage over your grandmother. You came in handy with a fat dowry. I just had to get rid of the old girlfriend and tell Randy to promise you the vine-covered cottage." Sam stopped to laugh. "What a fool. You remind me of Lulu when it comes to men."

Pauly winced. She was a far cry from her grandmother when it came to men…or, was she? Her recent track record was dismal.

"At least my interests are normal." She spit it out. His hand tightened on her arm. "Is that why my grandmother is having her marriage annulled? Did she find out that you like to molest children? That you married her to have access to the carnival and a steady stream of new victims?"

Sam seemed to think this last was uproariously funny. "Don't confuse sexual preference with my interest in making money. My old pal Hofer introduced me to a lucrative business *and* your grandmother. Marrying her seemed to be the best way to safeguard that investment. It could have worked out. I did care for her."

"I don't believe that," Pauly said.

He jerked her around so that his face was inches from hers. His breath smelled of liquor. "You're as big a fool as she is. There's more to life than having someone in your bed. We could have all been rich. There are thousands of people out there who thrive on what we provide…showing children the wonders of sex…introducing them to the pleasures of their bodies."

"Like Congressman Garcia?"

"Yes. He's a client. Quite a good one, I might add."

"Is that why you had Randy killed? Hired a sniper…. Because he found out about the congressman's interests? Might have used the information as leverage, which might have pointed a finger at you?"

"He wasn't very smart, your husband. Refusing to play ball on that water project to tip his findings in favor of the South Valley. It didn't win him any favors. But, no, my dear Pauly, Randy's death was meant to have been a family affair." Sam slowly smiled, then reached out to squeeze her shoulder.

Pauly sharply inhaled. She had been meant to die. Die with her husband on their honeymoon. Did she feel a tiny bit of pleasure for screwing up everyone's plans?

"My little investment in your marriage came with a money-back guarantee. With Randy out of the way—and you—your will left everything to your grandmother. I couldn't lose. I'd keep the million I had to come up with to get him to marry you, and I'd have both your interests in MDB, Inc. It was my money that started the company. Surely you know that. Randy didn't have the proverbial pot when he came to me with Archer's idea." He paused. "This would have been a lot easier if you'd been in the balloon with him, my dear. Or if you'd just died in the fire. It would have spared both of us this unpleasantness now. But no, our little Pauly is so resourceful. How many more lives does my kitten have?" She stepped back as he caressed her cheek.

"But why smear Randy's name? Set him up to look like a pedophile?"

"Ah, that. You were right. Randy had threatened to expose Sosimo. He said he had evidence of Sosimo's 'hobby,' I think he called it. Said he'd send a copy to Sosimo, show him what he was talking about. Sosimo knew it wasn't an idle threat. Randy obviously had what he said he had."

"But I found the pictures in Randy's office. They were never sent."

"I know. When Sosimo didn't receive the pictures in the mail before the wedding, he was scared shitless that they had been left lying around. It worked out in his favor to have you find the envelope. It certainly raised a few suspicions and kept you from running to the police." Sam paused to smile. "Just to keep you guessing, I slipped a picture and adoption papers into Randy's safe deposit box. And the clipping of hair. That was a nice touch, don't you think?" Sam chuckled softly. "All the children had adoption papers. Made the little operation seem aboveboard in case we were questioned. I should have been more careful to match the correct papers with the photo. Ah well, I guess I can't be perfect. I didn't think it would make any difference. I knew you wouldn't want to point a finger at your poor deceased husband. And then there was the bracelet—that was my idea. Made your dearly departed seem so very much in love with you, didn't it? A little trinket that Randy's dear friend Sosimo picked out just for you." Sam's expression was smug.

Pauly shivered. She was revolted by this man standing beside her. How could she have misread him? She wondered how long it had taken her grandmother to figure out his duplicity. And Randy, had he had second thoughts about blackmailing Sosimo? Or had he really forgotten to drop the pictures in the mail two days before the wedding? Pauly guessed she'd never know.

"How did Randy get the pictures?"

"By accident. Hofer let him use his darkroom. Randy was a little too curious for his own good. Stumbled across some unprocessed film, probably thought he would be doing Hofer a favor by developing it."

Pauly could just see Randy using someone else's equipment, snooping without even realizing that he was doing it—violating someone else's space but trying to be helpful at the same time. Randy would have thought he'd found a gold mine in the pictures. He would have seen them as the one thing that would keep Sosimo off his back. Poor naive Randy. And she meant it. She felt a tear roll down her cheek. He truly had been an innocent.

"So you hired a sharpshooter? How did you just happen to find one of those?" Would he name Steve? Had he hired Steve to slip on a ski mask and wait for them in the cottonwood?

"They're a dime a dozen if you know where to look. Now, my dear, chatting has been lovely, but I've run out of time. You'll excuse me but we need to get on with this."

He suddenly thrust her forward, then held onto her arm as he reached around to open a door that led to a large workroom. But this was where the snakes were kept. Hadn't Grams said that there were snakes? And Steve had even invited her to look at them.

"Oh, my God. No." She tried to resist, wedge her knee against the doorjamb. She wasn't going in there. Not snakes. She screamed and got cuffed sharply on the ear.

"You'll do as you're told. Don't you want to see your grandmother?"

Pauly went limp. Grams? Dread coursed along her veins in waves. Was Grams already inside? Sam flipped on an overhead bank of weak fluorescent lights. It was worse than what she'd imagined. A cage, chest-high with five-foot sides, rested on a metal frame and stretched the full length of the wall, some twenty-five feet. Another one the same size ran along the back wall. Their three sides were metal, the fronts glass and their tops a solid piece with attached lights. But the tops were at an angle, askew, tilted to entice the occupants to escape. Oh, my God. Her stomach churned. Then she saw her grandmother and almost fainted.

Grams was lying on the floor. Dead? There was no movement. But it was Grams' face, her lack of makeup, of hair that made her stare. Instead of the bushels of white-blond tresses that always cascaded over her shoulders, there were just wisps of gray, funny wiry strands twisting upwards at intervals from her scalp with a fringe over her ears. Her grandmother had no hair. She'd never seen her grandmother without a wig. So this was underneath, this balding, slick-pated skull shrunken and tissue-thin across the crown.

Pauly burst into tears. She must be dead. She couldn't stand to think Grams had suffered. The skin on her face looked sallow in the light, completely devoid of color. And something else was wrong. Her grandmother had no eyelashes or eyebrows. The years of constantly painting and pasting everything in place had probably denuded her.

Pauly ran to her and dropped to her knees, cursing her bound hands which kept her from touching, taking her grandmother's hands in hers. She leaned forward and put her cheek in front of Grams' mouth. She was breathing, raggedly expelling soft puffs of air.

Before Pauly could comprehend what was happening, Sam knocked her flat, face down, grabbed her ankles and wound clothesline around them. "We wouldn't want you to try to escape now, would we?" Then he stood up and kicked her grandmother in the hip.

"Come on, Lulu. You have to act lively. Our friend here doesn't like his food dead." But her grandmother didn't move.

"Leave her alone."

"And just what is this little pretend hero going to do about it?" Sam gazed down at her, bemused, fully in control.

Pauly hated his smile. She squirmed onto her back and digging in her heels sat up. Sam was filling a bucket at a sink in the corner. Then he turned off the tap, picked up the bucket and calmly walked back to stand over her grandmother. Pauly suddenly realized what he was going to do.

"Sam, no." She shrieked and scooted towards him.

But it was too late. He tilted the bucket then tossed its contents in her grandmother's face. The gallon of water washed down the front of Grams' blouse, soaking her and plastering the thin material to her chest. The grapefruit-perfect breasts were suddenly displayed in graphic detail, taut nipples pushing through soaked cotton. Grams sputtered, thrashed around, rolled to her side and tried to sit, but her hands were tied the same as Pauly's.

Pauly bent over her, trying to say something soothing. But her grandmother pulled away. She didn't open her eyes, just muttered incoherently.

"What have you done to her?" Pauly was screaming.

But the question was addressed to an empty room. Pauly heard the door close and a key turn in the lock. They were alone. Pauly tried to get her bearings. She was alive. Grams was alive.

Then the horror of the situation flooded her consciousness. They were not alone. The rustling coming from the top of the cage along the north wall forced her to glance up.

She screamed. The head of a python pushed over the rim of its cage. His eyes never left them. They were only fifteen feet away, sitting like stunned prey. And he was hungry. Was there any doubt of that? Someone had kept this reptile lean and mean, prepared for just this kind of feast.

Huge shiny black eyes watched her, nostrils flared. He was pausing, head reared, weaving slightly. He had to be eight to ten inches wide at the midsection. He opened his mouth, a gigantic yawn, then his jaws snapped shut. Did snakes smell their food? Or was it sight? Were they drawn to something that moved? She couldn't remember, but did it matter?

Suddenly, her grandmother struggled to sit up, feet flailing wildly, her head banging against the cement floor. Before Pauly could move, the first snake struck. With a speed that seemed impossible for its length and bulk, it rushed them, ducking its wedge head under her grandmother's waist, pausing to wind itself around her grandmother's torso. Slowly its length turned into coils and her grandmother's body was lifted off the ground, rolling with the movement of her killer.

Pauly was immobile, staring, trying to comprehend. Then she acted. She pushed back out of the snake's way and struggled to her knees, then to her feet, falling heavily against a workbench that kept her upright. Then she hopped towards the cage in front of her, butting her shoulder against the glass. Nothing. It must be some kind of industrial thickness. If she could break the glass, she'd have a weapon—something to cut the ropes at her wrists and ankles—and the snake. She tried again and again, and only managed to make her shoulder go numb.

She frantically looked around. She needed a heavy object—something to shatter the glass. The snake was oblivious to her actions and continued to wind around her grandmother, slowly, a rhythmic, mesmerizingly, deadly advance.

There was no time. She dropped to the floor and wiggled her way towards the tangle of snake and human and tried to lever her feet between a coil and the body of her grandmother. But it was no use. She wasn't strong enough. She couldn't get any leverage. The splintering of the outside door pushed through her concentration. Someone was battering the thing, tearing it off its hinges.

Then Steve was beside her, cutting the bindings at her wrists, her ankles. But what did this mean? Whose side was he on? She started to struggle.

"Pauly, listen to me." He shook her. "You've got to help me. Now. There's no time. Just do what I do. We've got to carry your grandmother outside. The snake will release in the cold and wet. But we've got to hurry."

She didn't ask questions. And she didn't allow herself to think of the snake—nor whose side Steve was on. He was helping, wasn't he? She followed his example and wrapped her arms around Gram's legs and the tail-end of the snake and hoisted the bundle off the floor. It almost staggered her. But she kept her footing, straddling the bodies. Steve had grabbed the front and, with her waddling along behind under the weight, he started towards the door.

"Hang on. Don't let them drop until we're outside. We can save her, Pauly. It's not too late. Just a few more steps. We're going around the corner, now straight ahead."

Pauly kept her head down for balance, but she knew Steve was leading her out of the garage through the open space where the jeep had been. Had Sam gotten away? Did she care? She fell backwards as Steve suddenly dropped his end at the edge of the drive and began to roll the snake and her grandmother in the snow. He was down on all fours tugging and using two hands to push the writhing mass forward and then over, moving them slowly into a four-foot-deep drift along the side of the garage.

"Hurry. Pack snow around him." Steve was pulling the snake's head back away from its prey. "Don't worry about your grandmother. The cold will be better for her than these jaws."

Pauly did as she was told, frantically mounding the wet stuff with bare hands and not feeling a thing. The snake slowed its thrashing. She could feel it relax then slip into a stupor.

"I need your help." Steve was motioning her to move to his side. "I want you to apply steady pressure here along his body by pulling back when I do. Ready?"

She didn't even grimace. She was beyond repulsion. They were winning. She put two hands around the smooth live coil and pulled, once, twice, a third time. Steve was pulling and unwinding, starting with the snake's head, twisting it back, around, back some more.

"Okay. I want you to go to your grandmother's shoulders and pull when I tell you to."

Pauly followed instructions, slipping her arms under her grandmother's shoulders, not thinking about the snake, forcing herself to concentrate on her grandmother and Steve's orders.

"Now. Pull." He twisted, bracing with a knee against the snake's body. "Again." Steve slipped sideways but scrambled back upright to clasp the snake tighter, using raw strength to keep the suffocating coils from winding tighter. Pauly could see his muscles strain the fabric of his jacket. "That's right, get a good grip on her shoulders, ease her straight back."

Pauly strained to drag her grandmother out of the snake's grasp. Her body moved a few inches, then a foot, then stopped. "Just keep going. Don't let up on the pressure."

Pauly wanted desperately to wipe the sweat off her forehead, keep it from stinging her eyes, but she didn't. She tugged again. More movement. She inched backwards.

"You've got it. She's free."

Steve was beside her now, lifting her grandmother, running towards the house. "Put her in the living room. I'll start a fire."

Pauly ran to open the back door, then up the stairs to her bedroom to gather blankets, a heating pad and one of her flannel nightgowns. Feathers and satin just weren't going to cut it this time, and she figured that Grams would understand.

"I'll call 911," Pauly said as she tucked another blanket around her grandmother.

"Already have. I put in a call when I found Hofer. Can you handle the fire? I'm going to go put Herman back in his cage." Then seeing her look, he added, "It's not his fault that he was hungry. Speaking of hungry, there's a couple of kids in the kitchen waiting for hot chocolate. I just happened to find them tied up in Hofer's darkroom. Other than a few scratches, they'll be fine."

Chapter Thirteen

Pauly sat by her grandmother's bed in the hospital. It was a private room, and they had brought a cot in for her. But she wasn't tired. She was past tired, exhausted but just sitting there, warm and safe. Knowing that Grams was going to be all right was bringing her back to life. Grams had broken ribs, a concussion, and had been drugged; but she was going to make it. Pauly couldn't believe how lucky they'd been. Lucky to have had Steve find them in time.

Tony had looked in the door shortly after they got there but had been shooed out by the handful of nurses and a doctor. Finally, the hospital personnel left, leaving in their wake the tubes and beeping monitors that meant intensive care. And she continued to sit there watching her grandmother, holding her hand, whispering that everything was all right. The doctors didn't think she'd wake up for a few more hours, but that didn't dissuade Pauly from being reassuring. She had a feeling that Grams could hear her.

Steve came in a little after midnight with a sack full of Lotaburgers and motioned for her to follow him back to the lounge. She hesitated, but curiosity was beginning to kick in. They hadn't had a chance to talk, and she had about a hundred questions. She ran a comb through her hair, put on lipstick and a touch of mascara. The effect was good, but she wondered at the effort. Who was she trying to impress? She thought she knew. She only hoped she wasn't trying to impress a hired killer.

Steve had arranged burgers, fries, and drinks on a coffee table and hadn't waited on her before digging in. He was obviously famished, but then so was she. She picked up a hamburger and found herself staring at him. Something was different. For one thing, he was wearing an open-collared shirt. She'd never seen him without a turtleneck.

"Most people think I've lost weight or shaved my mustache." He was grinning.

"You never had a mustache," Pauly began, then gasped, "The tattoos. The tattoos are gone."

"One nicely appointed spider's left on my ass." Cheshire-cat smile.

She didn't take the bait, if it was that; she just shook her head. "I don't understand."

"Semi-indelible tracings. These were in pretty good shape for about six weeks. They do this kind of thing for the movies all the time."

"So, your tattoos were just part of the act?"

"Got me in the door but kept me out of your shower." He grinned. "Don't tell me you're going to miss them?"

She made a face. "I might not be able to live without the Rape of Europa inked into a bicep."

"If it means that much to you, I could always get the real thing."

"Let's try it this way for awhile," she kidded back.

"Which sounds like I might have a chance at a friendship."

He was serious now, watching her face, searching for some reassurance.

She took a deep breath. "Is any of what I know about you true?"

"All of it."

"Even the part about being a PI hired by Archer?"

"Especially that part. But someone hired me before Archer did. He came into the picture later."

He put his hamburger on the coffee table and bent forward in earnest. "Pauly, I've got to say this first. I can't stop thinking of you, thinking of you standing naked in front of the shower. Do you know what it took not to join you? Not to just climb in the shower and say to hell with a few fading tattoos? I wanted to tell you then. Who I was, what was going on. But when the two boys disappeared, I couldn't take the chance. Things were too close to winding down. I needed to get to the authorities."

"What was going on?" She wasn't ready to let him see that he'd said about the most wonderful thing that she could think of, that she hadn't been rejected Christmas morning, that he had wanted her as much as she wanted him. "Is there a beginning? Some starting point that would make sense?"

"Yeah." He picked up his soft drink and sat back. "I was in prison for pushing steroids. That part was true. With no prior record, I was subjected to a little white-collar treatment, minimum security facility, access to a few amenities, it wasn't bad." The smile was unconvincing but he continued, "I met a man there. Nice guy, former priest—"

"Sosimo's brother?"

"Yeah. How'd you know?"

"Your turn first. I didn't mean to interrupt."

"Manny was great. Compassionate. Really into revamping the prison system. We worked out in the gym together; I did a little coaching. He swears that he was set up by his brother. That it was Sosimo who anonymously sent information to the bishop, as well as to the newspapers. Can you believe that? His own brother? Sosimo framed him. Even got children to testify. He felt his life was ruined. His family had disowned him. A defrocking is tantamount to murder in the small New Mexico town where he grew up. His mother suffered a stroke, no doubt brought on by the publicity of his case."

"Couldn't he have done anything?"

"Not after the testimony and the pictures."

"Pictures? Sophisticated fakes—I've seen some of Hofer's handiwork."

"Pretty graphic, I guess. The Church didn't waste time. They couldn't be liable.... They cut him off. He had the choice of a retreat or choose to work in the prison."

"What did Sosimo have to gain?"

"Cover his own tracks. Divert attention. It was a great ruse. No doubt, it garnered sympathy. If you prove the firstborn brother is unfit for society, and a priest to boot, who's going to suspect that the other brother, an elected official no less, is out procuring? That he's also a pedophile? Maybe this state puts more faith in their congressmen than in their priests. Anyway, it seemed to work."

"It seems like setting his brother up would be inviting Manny to retaliate."

"Who said he didn't?"

"A priest?"

"Last time I checked they're all human."

"And that's why he talked to you? Hired you?"

"Hired may not be the right term. He begged me to help him. Pauly, this was a man tormented by the fact that his brother had stripped him of everything he'd ever had to live for. When I first met him, he was in the clinic after an attempt on his life. Knowing that I'd try to help seemed to keep him from trying again. I told him I could hold out for two months without having to work. I'd give him that."

"How did you know where to start?"

"Manny had found out about the carnival. That is, I should say he suspected Sosimo had access to a pipeline of young victims and thought the carnival was the source. It seems Hofer had been Sosimo's bodyguard at one time. So when he found out that Hofer was a partner in your grandmother's operation, he put two and two together."

"What were you supposed to do?"

"Gather information, prove that Sosimo was involved, prove that Hofer was procuring."

"And then what?"

"Manny was going to use the information to prove his innocence. At least he'd have concrete ammo to show why Sosimo might have wanted him out of the picture. And I think he wanted to ruin Sosimo. An eye for an eye. Priest or not. Between Paco and the rest of what we know, I'd say Manny's exonerated."

"What did Archer have to do with all this?"

"I questioned him at Randy's funeral. Just a long shot because there was a tie-in to Sosimo. I mentioned the water project and the South Valley, and said that I was working on a case that seemed to overlap and that I thought we should talk. He jumped in to say that he thought his partner had been murdered, said that he thought Randy had foolishly threatened Sosimo with some pictures. He wasn't explicit, but said he'd thought that Randy had dropped them in the mail. Said he'd be in touch, would try to help. Then when Sosimo showed up looking for a package, I got a frantic call from Archer saying that he'd bet anything that you had them or at least copies, and might foolishly try to use them in some way."

"After I gave him the envelope, why didn't he turn them over to you?"

"He had second thoughts. He was scared of how I might handle things. Exposing those pictures could have really been a problem for MDB. They didn't trust me and needed to gag you in the worst way."

"So he hired you to keep an eye on me?"

"Seemed like I was robbing him of a thousand dollars a month just to do something I would have done anyway."

He grinned. She didn't think it was all that funny.

She paused before blurting out, "Did you kill Randy?"

"What?" He seemed truly startled.

"Did you shoot the pilot of the hot-air balloon?"

"Why would I do that?"

"Because Sam Mathers hired you to do it."

"Pauly, that's crazy. It's true I joined the carnival the week of the accident. But what made you think I was involved?"

She took a deep breath and didn't take her eyes off his face. "The killer wore a ski mask. I took pictures from the bridge just before the pilot was shot. There was someone with a ski mask in a cottonwood to my right and you had a ski mask in your closet, in the pocket of a leather jacket."

He burst out laughing. In fact, there was some indication that he was finding it difficult to stop. Suspecting him couldn't be that funny.

"Pauly, you stole my mother's first knitting project. She retired last summer and knitting was supposed to be the new hobby. I thought I'd lost it somewhere. I was *hoping* I'd lost it. Believe me, it isn't a treasured possession. I was relieved that it was gone."

She looked sheepish. "I didn't really steal it. I sort of borrowed it. I've just been keeping it safe for you." She didn't know whether she felt relief or was a little irked at his laughter and decided to change the subject. But she couldn't deny the tingle of excitement. He was innocent.

"Did you know about Sam?"

"I figured it out when I realized he'd married your grandmother."

"Have they caught him?"

"Tony said he rolled the jeep about a mile from the house. The guy has shit for luck, two accidents in one night. They also picked up Sosimo about eight."

"What will happen to Sosimo and Sam?"

"Prison time for Sosimo. And something a little stiffer for Sam—by last count he can be tied to three deaths. I'm sure you won't mind testifying."

Pauly shook her head. No, she wouldn't mind at all.

"What will happen to Paco?"

"Davy's mother came forward—both boys are staying with her until the one can be returned to his mother in Mexico. Then Paco will live with her and Davy. I think he's going to be all right. He wants to stay with the carnival."

"Was it Hofer who brought them to Albuquerque?"

"Yep, and planted evidence that they'd been in the motor home."

Pauly was quiet, then she got up and moved to sit on the couch beside Steve.

"Where exactly is the spider?" She kept a straight face.

He grinned. "Sounds like an invitation to drop my drawers."

"Not here."

For a second she thought he was serious, but he leaned over and whispered, "I haven't had a vasectomy," and solemnly folded thumb over little finger leaving three extended in a scout's honor.

To receive a free catalog of other Poisoned Pen Press titles, please contact us in one of the following ways:

Phone: 1-800-421-3976
Facsimile: 1-480-949-1707
Email: info@poisonedpenpress.com
Website: www.poisonedpenpress.com

Poisoned Pen Press
6962 E. First Ave. Ste 103
Scottsdale, AZ 85251